W9-BQJ-015

"McNamara is an excellent writer of detective fiction, every bit the equal of—and often more in control than—best-selling former L.A. police detective Joseph Wambaugh."

San Francisco Chronicle

"A bloody good book ... it grabs the reader by the throat and won't let go until the final genuinely moving confrontation."

San Jose Mercury News

"The chief demonstrates that he knows the territory and he can portray the exhilirating and the seamy sides of police work. He also can spin a pulse-throbbing tale with accomplished skill."

The Kansas City Star

"McNamara has the magical touch. He knows how to grip his readers with human emotion and raw action. ... *Fatal Command* is filled with the daring bravery of a policeman and the frightening sense of responsibility that forces him to weigh legality against morality. It's a tough book but an honest one."

Ocala Star-Banner

Also by Joseph D. McNamara:

Fiction

THE FIRST DIRECTIVE*

Nonfiction

SAFE & SANE

*Published by Fawcett Books

FATAL COMMAND

Joseph D. McNamara

FAWCETT GOLD MEDAL • NEW YORK

This book is dedicated to Richard White and Henry Bunch and their colleagues in the San Jose Police Department who continue their work; to Tom McEnery, the kind of mayor who makes a good police department possible; and to my wife Rochelle, who makes all the good things possible. My son Donald's advice was helpful, as was my daughter Karen's. Liza Dawson's patience, skill, and encouragement made a real difference.

One

THE SUN GLARED AND SWEAT SOAKED MY SPORTS SHIRT as I watched the white Cadillac pull into the driveway. Crazy Phil Caruso slid out of the car and unhurriedly walked up the path to the front door.

From one hundred and fifty yards away I casually swung my binoculars, pretending to follow the flight of a pure white gull coasting against a sky so blue it was almost painful. My police radio was turned down so it wasn't audible to anyone outside the car. I had logged in with communications. I was available if they needed to get hold of me, but for good reason I hadn't informed them of the stakeout.

I lowered the glasses and tried to look as laid back as the other characters in the beach parking lot. It was probably a wasted effort. The people on either side of me weren't laid back. They were spaced out. On my left, two slender young men in a blue Ferrari-308 held hands and stared from behind dark sunglasses at the golden-reddish sun sinking slowly into the Pacific Ocean. They were sharing a roach and the bittersweet odor of burning cannabis reached my nostrils.

Ten feet to my right a thickset man dozed behind the wheel of a new, bright red Porsche convertible. I could hear him snoring. His resplendent beard and colorful sports shirt didn't obscure the middle-aged paunch and balding forehead. In the passenger seat next to him sat a stereotype of a Valley Girl eating a vanilla ice cream cone. She was about eighteen. Her honey blond hair was arranged in an attractive ponytail, and she had clean, even features. She wasn't wearing a bra and when she turned in my direction I lifted my eyes from her firm breasts, covered by a flimsy white T-shirt. Her eyes were almost as blue as the sky and they locked on mine. Before I could turn away she stuck out a long pink tongue and very slowly licked the ice cream cone from the base to the top, never once shifting her glance from mine.

As her companion continued his blissful snoring she opened her mouth wide and fitted it over the top of the cone. She sucked the ice cream upward, her eyes still on mine. The driver came awake with a snort and reached over to cup her breast. She never broke eye contact with me as he slowly caressed her. Suddenly she smiled, sensing my own sexual stirrings. Annoyed more at myself than her I looked back toward Petrie's house.

Sixty-five minutes later, at 2015 hours, both couples were gone and I trained the binoculars on Caruso as he left the house. He carried a package wrapped in coarse brown paper. It looked about two feet long and less than a foot wide. He stuck it under the front seat on the driver's side.

I gave the Caddy plenty of lead, grateful for the growing dusk. Just before the freeway entrance Crazy Phil pulled into a Gulf station. While the attendant filled his tank he made a phone call. From where I parked I could see him talking animatedly into the receiver. After hanging up, he returned to the car, paid the attendant in cash and pulled out of the station. He and I both took it law-abiding slowly on Highway 17 crossing the mountain back into the Valley. I was sure that the package under the front seat was the reason for his caution. It didn't seem likely that a mob button man who had earned the nickname in Chicago of Crazy Phil would be this respectful of the fifty-five-mile-per-hour speed limit. After all, few other people in California were.

During the half-hour drive over the winding road I smelled the sharp clean aroma of the redwoods. Riding through the mountains, I never failed to wonder about the thousands of hardy individualists living in expensive homes deep in the woods. They had fled from Silicon Valley's entangled government and mass of people. Each year they braved tinder-dry summers and the equally frightening potential for mudslides during the winter rainy season. When calamity struck, however, they were as American as the rest of us and clamored for emergency services and disaster reimbursement.

Caruso continued to look ahead even when we pulled into the turn where the million or so lights of the Santa Clara Valley—Silicon Valley—glowed up at us. A few minutes later we were driving through the level streets of the valley floor.

The once fertile prune orchards had been destroyed by the explosive growth of sprawling electronics companies and tract housing. Tiny chips of silicon had revolutionized the computer industry by reducing the size of the machines and increasing the speed and power of calculations, thus doing wondrous things for all of us—whether we liked it or not. Some ingrates complained that the rapid growth had sent housing prices soaring and created traffic jams that rivaled those of Los Angeles four hundred miles to the south. Smog and crime had soared. But for a decade, progress had been our most important product. The result was that almost two million people were now jammed into the two hundred fifty square miles that had once been known as the Valley of the Heart's Delight.

Caruso drove at a steady thirty-five miles per hour. When we were about five miles from our nifty new police headquarters he abruptly signaled a left turn into a crowded parking lot. I cruised by, noting that the Caddy had slid into an area marked NO PARKING. In my side mirror, I saw Crazy Phil walk through the door of Lefty's Fun Palace nightclub with the package under his arm.

A couple of streets down the road I made a U-turn and slowly approached the parking lot. This part of town wasn't pictured in the convention brochures. There were lots of gas stations, used car lots, and warehouses, all closed now for the evening. But the nightclub parking lot, which had room for around two hundred cars, was almost full. I wondered what everyone was gathering for—it was pretty early for Saturday night partying.

I was dressed in jeans and an open sports shirt. The .357 Magnum I carried would have been conspicuous, so I stuffed it under the spare tire in the trunk. I took a five-shot, snub-nosed Smith & Wesson Chief's Special from inside the uninflated spare and put it into my right pants pocket. The Chief's Special didn't quite fit, so I covered the protruding handle with a handkerchief. After a moment's hesitation I stuck my badge into a back pocket. Girded for whatever, I headed for the entrance. Four young women ahead of me looked back and started to giggle. I resisted the impulse to check to see if my fly was open.

Aside from the garish neon sign, it was an undistinguished place. Faded white paint did a half-assed job of covering a one-story structure that could have been a factory. There were no windows and it was about two hundred and fifty feet long.

We bunched up at the entrance. There were other women in the doorway ahead of us. They chatted and laughed. It must be a singles place, I thought, yet there were several older women. Apparently singles came in all sizes and ages at Lefty's Fun Palace. A large, surly goon with a broken nose and pockmarked face carded the youngest of the women. I squeezed past him.

"Hey, son of a bitch," he yelled at me. I kept going, moving to the right toward the rear of the room, not wanting to stand in the bright light in case Caruso was meeting the city hall character we had seen him with earlier that day. The guy would certainly recognize me. The bouncer started after me, but had to retreat to handle a new wave of femininity descending on the door. I moved farther back into the darkness. I couldn't see anything around me, but the front of the room was well lit and I spotted my subject talking intently to a short man sitting at the fifty-foot bar that hugged the left wall. Directly opposite the bar was a small stage. Tables crowded each other as far as I could see in the dim light.

The thug who had been guarding the door motioned to an even larger and uglier specimen to take over for him. He walked to the bar and spoke with Crazy Phil. The little man sitting next to him turned sharply, looking back toward where I stood in the shadows. Sure enough, it was Thomas Nicastri, Esquire, Mayor Middleston's legal adviser. Our observation of him earlier this morning had been the first indication that this surveillance could lead to big stuff—political dynamite. He wore the same somber pin-striped suit. I sat down at one of the small tables.

"You're not supposed to be here," someone said after several seconds.

For the first time, I realized that a woman was sitting next to me at the tiny table. The room was so dark I hadn't seen her. But now my eyes were slowly adjusting to the lack of light. She seemed young. Maybe twenty-eight, although she could've been a couple of years younger. It was difficult to tell because large tinted glasses partially hid her eyes. I could make out that her short brown hair was curly and that she didn't seem to be wearing makeup. Hardly a crowd stopper. She was dressed in a white blouse with a black oversized bow tie and a pleated, navy blue skirt. The conservative clothes were out of place in this zoo. A stenographer's notebook and a pen were on the table. Amplifiers blared the pulsating beat of hard rock in the crowded, noisy room.

Nicastri held up his hands to Crazy Phil, palms outward in a placating gesture. Both men kept peering back in my direction. They were about one hundred and fifty feet away and the darkness made me reasonably confident that the mayor's aide hadn't recognized me. I glanced at the woman sitting next to me. She didn't look happy about my being there.

"Are you gay?"

"What?"

"You keep looking at those men like they fascinate you."

I stole another glance at the front of the room, then quickly slumped down low in the chair. Another bouncer had joined the men at the bar and all of them were looking in my direction.

"And that makes me gay?" I would have to sit next to a weirdo. I looked around to see if I could move to another table, but the place was jammed. Only then did I realize that they were all women. The huge room was filled with women. The only men were the waiters and they . . . I stared at them. The waiters wore suspenders over bare hairy chests. The suspenders hooked into bulging nylon briefs. These guys were hung. My mouth was gaping open. I shut it.

"It's okay. I don't have anything against homosexuals," she assured me. "But the management keeps the men behind that folding wall over there until the show is over."

"Show?"

"It's starting; you lucked out. They won't be able to throw you out now, but you better disappear fast if they try. They're rough."

The musclemen from the bar moved in our direction as a male stripper pranced onto the stage. The lights grew even dimmer as spotlights closed in on the dancer. A feminine roar filled the room. I kept my eyes on the bouncers. Caruso and Nicastri trailed them, but stayed in the aisle along the wall as the strong-arm boys suddenly rushed into the crowd and seized a guy who had been sitting at a table a few feet in front of us. He resisted, taking a half-hearted swing, but the bouncers knew their business. One of them pinned his arms and the other used a sap. I heard the ugly crack as it met his skull. He sagged and they pulled him away from the table. A sweet-faced, gray-haired woman with metal-rimmed granny spectacles cheered them on.

"Get him out of here. We want to see the show," I heard her say. They were only ten feet in front of us.

"I tell you this ain't him. The guy must be further back and he looked like a cop," the man who had tried to stop me at the door said to his buddy.

My heart began to race and it wasn't from the same emotion that was heating up the women in the room. This crowd clearly didn't offer any cover. I looked around for a way out. They would be back for me as soon as they dumped their first victim.

"My God. Are you really a cop? They'll kill you if they find out," the woman at my table said. She had spoken figuratively, but I had seen Crazy Phil Caruso's rap sheet. The bouncers were thugs, but probably without guns. I had no such illusions about Crazy Phil. I shook off a chill.

"I am a cop. What are you? A reporter?" I asked.

"I . . ." Her eyes widened. "They're coming back."

I pulled the S&W from my pocket, all too aware that I didn't dare fire in this mob of people. Also, I didn't believe that the three fellows, deliberately searching through the crowd for me, were going to be bluffed by my pointing a gun at them.

"Get down on the floor. I'll try to hide you until they pass. I know a side exit. Maybe we can slip out."

I hesitated. She seemed sincere, but I didn't like the idea of waiting helplessly.

"It's all right. I understand. My brother's with the LAPD," she said.

There wasn't much choice. They were almost on top of us. I sat on the floor. She shifted forward to the edge of her seat and covered my head and shoulders with her billowy skirt. I was acutely aware that to cover me she had straddled my shoulders with her legs. My ears rubbed against her thighs as she moved, straightening the material over me. I wondered if she wore panties. . . . She tensed, her thighs tightening on my head like a vise. I guessed the searchers must be getting near. I squeezed the handle of my revolver.

"Will you people please sit down. We can't see." Her voice was cool but annoyed.

"Sit down! Down in front!" A chorus of angry voices joined her protest.

They were so close I could hear one of the goons mumble, "Raunchy bitches."

The pressure of her thighs loosened. I felt her lean forward, her hand patting me on the head through her skirt. "They're moving on. Stay still for a few minutes. I'll watch until it's clear." Covered by the skirt, I felt the warmth of her body and inhaled her sweet, faint fragrance while listening to the room rock with female sex noises and wailing music.

"Are you O.K. down there?" Her voice was throaty. I resisted a momentary impulse to playfully bite her thigh, wondering what it might do to that very feminine voice. I recalled my first vision of her. I had been too hasty. She was attractive and a very sexy lady. Instead of biting I nodded my head up and down in answer to her question.

She took a deep breath. "Don't do that. I mean move your head that way." I thought there was a slight catch to her voice.

"You asked me a question. I tried to answer," I said, pretty sure that she couldn't hear me with the room noise and the muffling effect of her skirt. It was hot under her skirt. I tried to keep my mind from wandering away from the danger, but it was an effort as she shifted uneasily in her seat and her scent wafted past my nose.

"What?" I was right. She couldn't hear me. But she caught on quick. "Oh, I understand. You were nodding your head yes to my question. Uh, they're standing to the side looking in this direction. You had better stay where you are for a while, but I'd just as soon you kept your head still.''

I licked my lips and ran my wet lips and tongue across her thigh, grinning in the darkness. She didn't say anything, but reached forward, firmly grabbing a handful of my hair through her skirt. She yanked my head forward so that our skin was no longer touching and held me steadfastly in that position. A few minutes later she said, ''Give me your hand.'' She removed the skirt from my head. Like a child, I placed my left hand in hers. Like a cop, I kept the Chief's Special ready in my right hand. ''Follow me, and stay low,'' she said.

I looked toward the stage as a loud roar filled the room. The stripper was down to his G-string and several women had rushed forward to stuff folding money into his crotch. A cute young redhead evoked a roar when she jiggled his balls after depositing her money.

We moved through the darkness toward the rear of the nightclub. My companion moved confidently through the crowded darkness. When we reached some heavy velvet draperies that hung from the ceiling, she led me until she found an opening that I hadn't seen. We parted the drapes and five feet from us was a fire exit. This time, I moved ahead and, holding my gun at ready, I cautiously opened the door. I looked out into the darkened parking lot. Fifty feet to my right I could see the entrance. The white Cadillac was still in the no-parking zone.

Arm in arm, in case anyone was watching, we walked the twenty-five yards to where I had parked. I opened the door of my car on the driver's side. Quickly, she slid across the seat. As I closed the door, I found her looking at me. Just the slightest hint of color came to her face before she glanced away. Was she remembering me under her skirt? I was. But I shouldn't be, damn it. This whole thing was moving at a hundred miles an hour and I didn't know what the hell was going on.

"What's your name?"

"Janice Bell."

"Is your brother really an LA cop?"

"Yes. He's a sergeant. What's this?" She held the Hound Dog, which she had almost sat on.

"It's a surveillance tracking device for cars. How come you knew your way around that place in the dark?" She put the Hound Dog between us on the seat.

"I was given a tour yesterday."

"And the notebook?"

She laughed. "It's for my job."

"Which is?"

I could see her deciding whether or not to tell me. Finally she shrugged. "I'm a corporate analyst for an investment firm. This nightclub is one of a number of properties owned by the corporation that we're examining. This is my fourth visit, but the first time that I've actually witnessed that . . . that spectacle inside." She removed her glasses and studied me.

"When you looked the place over you saw that these cats could be rough?"

"Yes."

"And drugs? Do they move a lot of drugs?"

"My brother's a cop. I'm not." Her large, almond-shaped brown eyes were steady.

"Public support is so inspirational to those of us in police work."

It didn't even get a smile.

"Why don't you have a back-up team if you're a narc?" she asked.

I was thinking of a plausible cock-and-bull story to give her. Over her shoulder I saw the front door of the nightclub open. Crazy Phil Caruso and Nicastri came out and walked directly toward us. Caruso ripped the brown paper off the package. My heart skipped a beat. Even at this distance I could see that it was an Uzi. He slipped a fifteen-round magazine into the weapon.

"Well? Aren't you even going to answer—"

I put my arm around her. Pulling her toward me, I

covered her still open mouth with my lips. She pushed furiously against me, reaching for the door handle, but I held her immobile. "You son of a bitch. I'm sorry I helped—"

"Shut up. They're coming and they've got an Uzi. An automatic assault rifle. One of them knows me and we're both dead if he recognizes me."

"Oh . . ." She looked in their direction, then her arms shot outward and pulled me tightly into her. Dimly, I was conscious that in addition to her fine long legs, she possessed a narrow waist and generous breasts under her businesswoman's outfit. She was trembling, and it was not from passion. She had seen the weapon Caruso carried.

They walked in front of the car. "It couldn't of been a cop. And if it was, it was probably some vice squad creep. There's no way it could have anything to do with the deal. I tell you there's nothing to worry about, Phil." Nicastri sounded nervous. There was none of the arrogance his voice usually had when he visited us in the police department carrying "suggestions" from the mayor.

I started to pull away when I was sure they had moved on, but she held me. I looked at her slightly open lips. Her glasses were pushed back on her head and her white teeth were visible in the dark. I wanted to look to our rear to see what was happening, but I stared at her. To my amazement, I kissed her and she responded, holding me tightly. After a time, she sighed and pushed me back slightly without letting go. "I have something to tell you," she said.

Oh, Christ, I thought, she's going to talk about love.

"I was so scared I wet your seat. I'm sorry."

I pushed her out of the way, groping for the Hound Dog.

"I said I was sorry about the seat. You needn't be so rough."

"I don't give a damn about the seat. This surveillance equipment is so sensitive that if it gets wet it won't work. I've got to slip it under that white Cadillac over there before those guys get back." Phil and Nicastri were still walking toward the dark corner of the parking lot. Nicastri gestured rapidly with his hands as he backed away from Caruso. They must have been ninety feet away from us.

"Give it to me," she said.

It did feel a little damp. Reluctantly, I handed her the magnetic transmitter, thinking she was going to dry it on her skirt.

"It wouldn't be good if they saw you out there." She calmly got out of the car and walked toward the big white car.

"Damn it, Janice, don't take a chance." She ignored my urgent whisper.

I looked in the direction Caruso and Nicastri had gone. They were nearing a storage building in the left corner of the lot. I held my breath.

A staccato burst from the Uzi exploded through the night air. I turned to see Nicastri slumping to the ground. Crazy Phil raced toward the Caddy . . . and Janice. The assault rifle he had used to blow away Nicastri was tucked under his right arm. The Uzi weighed less than four pounds. He carried it easily. Jumping out of the car, I yelled "Caruso!" as he passed me, but he never saw or heard me.

Braced into a firing position, I lined up a perfect sight picture on him as he ran steadily toward the Cadillac. I started to squeeze off a round, but Janice was frozen in my line of fire. Caruso saw her. Without breaking stride, he raised the weapon and fired a burst. She toppled to the ground. I let go all five rounds, double action. Caruso staggered, but kept going. I ran after him, using a line of parked cars for cover. Janice was slowly crawling away from the big white car.

From the way Crazy Phil moved I knew that he was hit. Just before getting into his car, he swung the gun with one hand and fired a volley at me. I dove to the pavement. By the time I was on my feet again, he was speeding out of the parking lot. Incredibly, no one seemed to have heard the shots. We were still the only ones outside.

I ran to Janice and knelt next to her. Please, please, I prayed silently—don't let her be dying. She clutched her abdomen. Blood was flowing through her fingers. "It hurts." She was crying.

"Keep your hands pressing right where they are to stop the bleeding. We're only two minutes from the hospital. You'll be OK." I picked her up. She was heavier than I thought. I moved unsteadily back to the car and stretched her out on the back seat the best I could. Her eyes were closed and I wasn't sure she was conscious.

I radioed communications, telling them to notify the emergency room at County Hospital that I would be arriving with a patient shot in the stomach. I also directed the dispatcher to send units and an ambulance Code 3 to the southeast corner of Lefty's parking lot on a probable 187, homicide, and to put out an APB on Caruso and his white Cadillac, warning that he was armed with an Uzi. I managed all this driving one-armed through stop signs and red lights.

There were two uniformed orderlies waiting with a gurney outside the emergency room entrance. We had her in the treatment room within five minutes after being shot. She was unconscious. Her color was close to the pallor that I had seen too often. The question was whether or not five minutes had been too long.

That morning I had supervised a quiet stakeout. Now the mayor's aide had been gunned down and an innocent young woman was near death.

TWO

BACK IN FEBRUARY, WHEN WE DECIDED TO GO WITH Louis Robinson to Silicon City, I thought the change of scene had ominous similarities to an article appearing in *National Geographic*. It was on El Nino—an alteration in the jet stream that had caused a warm stream of water to displace the arctic current flowing along the California shoreline. Sea life moved out of its natural habitat with catastrophic results. Giant sharks entered coastal waters previously foreign to them and preyed upon species weakened by an unfamiliar environment. I wondered what kind of sharks inhabited the new waters we were popping into.

The day of decision started harmlessly enough. It was one of those magnificent Northern California days. Sunny, temperature in the mid-sixties and the air crystal clear. I had the morning off and used it for a brisk workout in Manny's downtown gym, enjoying the smell of sweat and rubbing lotion that never left the place no matter how long they left the windows and doors open.

Fat Charley came over and touched the light bag I had been tapping bare-knuckled. "Hey, Fraleigh, I got a new kid from Guadalajara. He's way too good for you, but no one else is around. Wanna go about three or four quick ones with him?"

Charley let go of the punching bag and stood next to it. I hit the bag with my left hand, slamming it into his face to let him know that he had violated protocol by stopping my rhythm drill.

"You used to be all right when you was boxing, but now you're just another prick cop," he said and started walking away.

I should have let him go, but I got into the ring with a kid they had dubbed Lightning Pedro. He was twenty-two. He had me by about thirteen years and it made a difference. He boxed my head off until I got lucky late in the second round with a left hook to his jaw. I followed with a good combination and Fat Charley and one of his flunkies jumped into the ring and separated us just as Lightning, glassy-eyed, was sagging toward the canvas.

"Jesus C . . . Christ, Fraleigh, did . . . didn't you hear the bell?" Fat Charley whined. "You could of hurt the kid. In another year we think he can be a contender."

The euphoria of tagging Lightning Pedro wore off during the day. I had set up a dinner meeting that night with Captain Louis Robinson, who surprised me by saying the treat was on him; he had been about to ask me and my partners out. My partners, Paul English and the Block, were in big trouble. I wondered why Louis was inviting us to dinner. On the all-too-frequent occasions when I had asked Louis to help us out of bureaucratic problems, refreshments had always been on my tab.

"Fraleigh! Where have you been keeping yourself?" Louis grinned when I appeared in his grimy basement office. He had been transferred out of the detective bureau into administration for intervening in our behalf too many times in the past. "It must be at least two months since you came to me so I could get you guys out of another jam."

His homely mug turned handsome for a minute when he smiled at me. A big man, he dwarfed my five ten, one hundred ninety pounds. Looking at his middle-aged bulk it was hard to remember that he had been a track star in his East Palo Alto high school days.

"Your face is all red," he said, releasing me from a bear hug.

"Too much sun, maybe."

"Sun, my ass. You've been sparring again." He shook his head. "You're too old, Fraleigh. Let it go. Some kid is going to rattle your brains once too often and I'm not sure it hasn't already happened."

"My god! A black, two-hundred-forty-pound Jewish momma to worry about me. Ain't I lucky? Hey, Louis, you better tell Sarah to take it easy on the grits. You must have put on ten pounds since I saw you. I'll buy dinner but only if you promise to keep the bill under my weekly take-home pay."

"Very funny. But I said I would buy." He stretched and I saw his four-inch-barrel Smith & Wesson Magnum underneath the blue sports jacket. They hadn't allowed him to do any real police work in almost a year, but Louis still packed his piece.

On the way out we passed one of the police chief's pet rats, a useless sergeant on desk duty who ran to the chief with all the inside gossip. He watched Louis and me walk down the corridor together, but averted his eyes as we passed. He would have another little nugget of information for his patron.

We drove in my homicide squad car, a creaking, four-year-old unmarked Chevrolet. I pulled into the Pacific Pub parking lot, a headquarters' watering hole. It was a cop's bar—California style. The parking lot had the usual mix of small sports cars and four-wheel-drive Broncos with oversized tires. The cops driving the sports cars with ski racks on them would have blow-dried hair or curls from permanents. They hadn't yet been stung by alimony or child-support payments.

The guys belonging to the Broncos would be the hunters and campers, older men hoping to latch onto some young chick who would go for the economical weekend with nature and not dent their finances, already reduced by unwise marriages and/or breeding.

Louis and I stood in the doorway trying to spot an open table through the thick smoke. Cops were too brave or too stressed out to be influenced by the health scares over smoking. Noise battered against us. It was payday and quite a few of the uniform and dick day shift had come in to cash their checks. The pub was always happy to oblige. Few people left without buying a round or two of drinks and a certain number could always be counted on to close the joint.

At one end of the bar a group was loudly playing liars dice for dollar bills—a blatant penal code violation that a hundred or so cops were ignoring, along with a fire department sign that said that occupancy by more than seventy people was unlawful. There was a giant TV screen at the far end of the bar where another noisy group was cheering the replay of the 1985 Super Bowl like it was live. Louis smiled at the screen. He had taken a hundred bucks from me on that game.

Tit Hansen, a patrolman grunt for one of our enemies, Captain Foley, was drunkenly trying to get a pack of cigarettes out of the machine. He had gotten his nickname because he had tagged along with Foley for five years, getting one tit job after another, avoiding the street in return for kissing Foley's ass and doing his dirty work. He turned to me. "Hey Fraleigh, did you guys solve the great Gallo wine caper yet?"

It was close. Foley had been sticking us with wino stabbings for more than a year. The blood rushed to my head and I shuffled into position to hit Hansen with a left hook as a couple of dicks at the bar laughed at his comment. Louis moved between us, taking Hansen by the shoulders. "You've had enough, Hansen. You better go on home. You almost got cold-cocked just now."

"Yeah, OK, Cap," he said, nervously moving out the door, never taking his eyes off me.

"Cleaning his clock won't stop Foley from harassing you guys, Fraleigh," Louis said.

"I know, but it would make me feel better. How do nothings like him get on the Department?"

Above the beer taps, Teddy Roosevelt in a western outfit glared out at the noisy drinkers crowding the long bar. To Teddy's right was an even larger picture of John Wayne wearing army combat fatigues and a helmet. It was a cop's bar, all right. I told Louis that the Block and English, now forty minutes late, would be joining us when the whim moved them. They were out looking for a witness to a fatal stabbing.

We sat in a booth being ignored by the hired help, but turned to look when there was a loud noise at the door. We watched the entrance of my partners. Arnold Schulster, aka the Block, had slammed open the swinging doors and was advancing like a Mack truck. A busboy carrying an overloaded tray of dishes moved hastily out of his path, as did a couple of alert burglary dicks on their way out of the joint. The Block was five-eight and two hundred eighty pounds. His bullet-shaped head sat atop a size nineteen stubby neck. He was balding and his beady eyes had made many a suspect weak in the knees.

Red-faced, he bellowed at me, "You gotta stop them from assigning us these bullshit wino killings, Fraleigh. I'm sick and tired of trying to get statements from bums who puke all over themselves and piss in their pants when we're talking to them. Some of them even shit themselves. And if we bust them I got to search the fuckers and worry about getting AIDS or hepatitis or some other fucking disease." He was a Civil Liberties Union lawyer's dream. A caricature of police brutality. No matter that he was relatively law-abiding in that regard. His appearance and speech even gave some of the cops pause.

Paul English, who was four inches taller and weighed in at around one seventy, said, "Don't be so uncharitable about the homeless, Block. Besides, I noticed that your unpleasant duties never seem to affect your gluttony. Somehow you always manage to devour the Pub's biggest steak and drink more beer than anyone else.''

Marge, the waitress, came over as he spoke. Paul always had that impact on waitresses. "Don't he look just like Robert Redford, Fraleigh?'' she said. "I just want to hug the dear thing whenever I see him.'' She put her arms around Paul and did just that.

He obliged with a good-natured squeeze, although Marge wasn't up to his usual standards. She wasn't bad, but Paul traveled only with beautiful women.

"Marge, pull yourself together, you're letting this sex criminal distract you from your duties.'' The Block gave a rare smile. Marge was one of the few women he was comfortable with, and besides, he had just gotten in a dig about the charges against Paul.

"My God, a sex criminal too. He's got it all.'' She embraced Paul again.

I noticed Louis's eyes following her blond ponytail and swinging rump as she retreated to get our drinks. Me, I didn't think she was in Sarah's class. When I was without relatives or friends in California, Louis and Sarah had almost made me a member of the family by frequently inviting me to dinner. Sarah was a lovely woman whose easy laugh and personality warmed those evenings.

"You better hope the judge looks at it the same way as Marge does, English, or it's the joint for you. No more muff diving. You'll be getting cornholed instead,'' the Block said.

"I have confidence that justice will favor me, but in your case, Block, I'm afraid your appearance and crudeness may be more than even your great protector, Fraleigh, can overcome.''

Louis chuckled, but I had been hearing it all week. Both of them treated it as a lark that they were under felony investigations. After a little research I had found that the statutory rape charge against Paul was a phony. The girl's mother had been shacking up with Paul. When he ended it she accused him of diddling her fifteen-year-old daughter. However, she had made similar complaints against her former husband and she was a basket case—in and out of Camarillo mental hospital four times in five years. Paul had met her during one of her relatively brief sane periods. The Department hadn't discovered her questionable credibility because certain high-ranking people didn't want to see Paul cleared.

The Block's case was similar. One night when he was off duty and visiting his mother he had arrested a Peeping Tom, who complained that the Block had beaten and falsely arrested him. Witnesses supported the Block and the suspect turned out to have a long record of child molesting. Fortunately for all concerned, when the Block visited his mother he was careful not to drink. The old tyrant wouldn't even let him in with the odor of booze on him. So he was clean.

Nevertheless, it was unwise to take such things lightly. "Listen, you two. You may think it's a joke, but the Department is probably going to fire you and charge me with failure to supervise. Right, Louis?"

Louis nodded agreement.

"So what? You and Captain Robinson can get us out of this bullshit. It ain't the first time the brass tried to do us," the Block said before Louis had a chance to speak.

I sighed. "What do you think, Louis? Are they serious about going after us?"

"I think you know the answer to that. You guys exposed a lot of political corruption during the Stone case."

A year earlier we had investigated the disappearance of millionaire Adolph Stone's teenage daughter. Paul, the Block, and I had almost been killed in an ambush. We had been badly wounded but healed quickly enough to nail some political big shots. During my convalescence I had fallen in love with a beautiful, but dangerous, psychologist by the name of Sandra Fortune. She turned out to be deeply involved in the case and the wounds she left me hadn't quite healed. Nor had the top brass's animosity toward us diminished. Louis was right. We had pissed off some powerful people.

"I don't think they can make the charges stick, but you never can tell. And it will cost a fortune in lawyers' fees," I said, referring to our current problems.

As far as I could tell Paul hadn't heard a word. He was smiling and blowing kisses at an off-duty police-woman at the bar. She had been a moderately success-ful fashion model before joining the force a couple of years ago. Now she was overtly destroying her reputa-tion as an iceberg by flirting with Paul in a saloon crowded with cops. But I had seen Paul thaw a number of icebergs. "Paul, if I can interrupt your carnal mes-sage exchange with the gal at the bar, maybe we can discuss how to keep you from getting fired and going bankrupt at the same time."

"Lighten up, Fraleigh. Remember Plato's words, no evil can happen to a good man, either in life or after death. And we know Louis will intervene if he has to."

Part of Paul's M.O. was to drop little tidbits from his Stanford education into our conversations. The Block and I had an unspoken agreement to ignore them. If we responded there was a danger that he would deliver a whole lecture from his cursed memory.

Louis enjoyed himself during dinner. For reasons I didn't understand he often found the Block and En-glish's antics humorous. "Well, Louis," I said after we finished eating, "are you going to be able to intervene in behalf of these two misunderstood policemen?"

"Not this time, I'm afraid. In one month I'm being sworn in as police chief of Silicon City."

I had a cold feeling deep in the pit of my stomach. I remembered waking up in the hospital after the Block, Paul, and I had almost been wiped out in the Stone case ambush. Louis had been there.

"Silicon City? Where the hell is that? I never heard of Silicon City!"

"That's because it's a newly incorporated city. Can

you imagine the chance to set up your own department from scratch? To do it professionally, the way it should be done, instead of always compromising and adjusting the way we do here.''

I *did* recall reading about the formation of a new city. Right in the middle of Silicon Valley was an area of one hundred square miles made up of eleven small towns and some unincorporated county land. Electronics companies making computers, disk drives, microchips, software, terminals, and other components had proliferated in the area while the residential population had jumped to more than half a million. Dynamic growth wasn't all that unusual in California and, like other cities, Silicon City was born out of a need for order, efficiency, coordination, and the good old-fashioned desire of taxpayers to save bucks on the costs of public service. The issue had been placed on the ballot in the last general election and more than two thirds of the suckers voting had bought the idea of forming a charter city. Six months later they had elected a mayor to set it all up for them. Now the new mayor was hiring Louis to put together and run a brand new police department.

"You're crazy, Louis. It won't be any different. There's still going to be politicians inside and outside the department. You'll have the same do-gooder citizen groups that think dialogue and officer-friendly programs stop muggers, dope dealers, and killers, and that a cop is brutal when he uses force to keep himself from getting maimed or killed. That is, until something happens in *their* neighborhood. Then they want you to set up a little fascist state to keep them and their brats safe. And . . . hey. Wait a minute. I also read that the new city is going to have a pilot project for casino gambling if the statewide referendum on legalized gambling passes. You'll have mob action all over the place.''

"But it doesn't have to be that way, Fraleigh.'' Louis's eyes were shining. "We can do it better. If you run a good clean police operation, you can get public support. We could pull it off. And the mayor is a terrific guy. His father started Middleston Electronics; they were the first in the industry to have a minority employment and training program. They even provided college scholarships to poor kids with promise.''

''That's the second time you used the word we, Louis.''

''I want you to come with me. You'll be chief of detectives.''

''Just because you're out of your mind doesn't mean I'm crazy. Chief of fucking detectives! Listen, Louis, I don't want to be chief of anything. Being a sergeant is bad enough. But at least now I can get out and nail some animal that needs to be locked up. Do you think I want to sit behind a desk covered with work orders and go out at night to make speeches to the ladies auxiliary of the Rotary? You can stick that.''

''Chief of detectives! Fraleigh!'' The Block's raucaus laugh responded through the room. Several people turned uneasily, thinking the fire alarm had sounded. Was it an earthquake? The Block continued his brilliant observations at a slightly lower decibel level, sort of like the wave at the Super Bowl. ''Fraleigh's the most antibrass guy in the Department, Louis, er, Captain. I mean he can't even supervise English. How's he gonna do a whole bureau?''

''On the contrary, Block. Fraleigh's an authoritarian type. Once given authority he'll crush dissent.'' Paul added his profound opinion.

''Seriously, Fraleigh.'' Louis used his napkin to wipe away some saliva on his lips. He had choked with laughter as they commented on my supervisory ability. ''If you come with me you can run your own show. English and the Block can be your aides as senior detectives.''

''Louis, I can't believe this. You're not even chief yet and you're wheeling and dealing. Trying to suck us in. What about these charges against the Block and English? Are they going to mysteriously disappear?''

''I think I can assure you of that. The power clique

here wants us out. We stepped on too many influential toes through the years. I'm probably crazy for taking you characters with me, but remember how we solved the Stone case? You guys did an outstanding investigation despite headquarters opposition. The charges against the Block and Paul will vanish along with us. What do you say?''

Instead of answering I asked Louis, ''What about Sarah and the twins? Are they agreeable to this?'' I was almost part of his family and I didn't for one minute think moving to a new location and a high-risk job would appeal to Louis's wife.

''Sarah and I have split. I've had my own place for a month.''

For the first time during the evening he looked depressed. ''Come on, Louis, that's got to be something temporary. Was it over this move?''

''No. And it's not temporary and I don't want to talk about it. Got it?''

At that moment Captain Foley came over. I had noticed him trying to meld into different groups in the bar without any success. My team may not have been universally popular, but we were accepted as bona fide cops. Foley was known as a brownnosing pencil pusher.

''Louis.''

He nodded, then turned to us. ''After you men finish your dinner, make sure you return to complete your reports on that homicide.''

''Yeah. I bet the grand jury just can't wait to get the evidence on who killed that juice-head,'' the Block said. I noticed that he had consumed a lot of beer and the way that he was looking at Foley . . .

''Take it easy, Block,'' I cautioned.

''I've warned you before about being disrespectful toward victims,'' Foley said. He was slurring his words slightly and his face was flushed. He jabbed his finger into the Block's chest. ''Furthermore . . .''

''Keep your paws off me, asshole.'' The Block stood up.

We had an audience now. "Don't let him talk to you like that, Captain." Several cops at the bar who were feeling no pain yelled to Foley, hoping that he would aggravate the Block into belting him.

I felt the situation getting out of control. I tried to slide out of the booth to get between Foley and the Block, but like Louis I was pinned in.

Incredibly, Foley grabbed the Block by the arm. "You're coming back to headquarters with me."

The Block shook his arm free and his hands closed over Foley's throat. Even Foley knew how easy a choke hold was to break. He clasped his hands together and brought them sharply down on the Block's forearms. But the hold didn't break. The Block simply lifted Foley off his feet and continued to choke him. Foley's face turned red and he pounded his fists ineffectively against the Block's arms. The bar crowd was screaming encouragement.

Louis and I shoved and the whole table went over. We tried to pull the Block away from Foley. Other people joined us and I went down on the wet, slippery floor. I heard a fight break out at the bar when someone tried to grab the pool of money in the liars dice game. Regaining my feet, I saw the Block smash his fist into the face of the dick who had managed to pull him off Foley. Foley grabbed a beer bottle and swung it at the Block's head. A fist came out of the crowd and caught me on the side of my jaw. I slipped to the ground again. Getting up, I was caught in a mass of swinging, fighting bodies. Foley passed in front of me, trying for the front door. I hit him with a right he never saw and smiled as he sagged to the floor. I took a couple more blows to the face trying to get to the Block. Then a gunshot exploded in the room. The pub would have more slugs added to its wooden ceiling timbers tonight.

The shot did it for me. I made for the door along with a good part of the crowd. The Block was already outside. I joined him and a moment later Louis and Paul came out. Louis laughed, holding up a swollen right hand. The Block was bleeding. He took out a handkerchief and wiped blood from a cut on his forehead. Paul had picked up a chunk of ice someplace which he was applying to his swollen mouth. He broke it and gave me half for my right eye, which was going to be closed by morning.

"Louis, it will be a privilege to be part of your administration," Paul said, never quite taking his eye off the policewoman from the bar, who had appeared to minister to his wounds.

"Me too, Cap." The Block grinned. "I'm ready to go."

"Fraleigh?" Louis raised his eyebrows.

I shrugged. "As if we had a choice now."

"Don't be a spoilsport, Fraleigh. You guys are a team. I need you three with me," Louis said, taking my ice and applying it to his hand.

Three

BROODING ABOUT OUR PENDING MOVE, I DIDN'T GET much work done the next day. It was 2100 hours and dark when I called it a day. I tossed the three case files I had been working on into the drawer and routinely locked the desk. I had worked with some terrific cops and had been here thirteen years. Not that my seniority or civil service status would be that much protection from the brass with Louis gone. And who knew what they would do about the bar brawl last night.

Funny, I never fully appreciated how important Louis's support was until I found out he was leaving. He had shielded a lot of other good dicks in the bureau too. But we weren't going to just a new location. Both Louis and I would be top management. Out of our normal depth. Who the hell knew what kinds of political intrigue and backstabbing were routine at those levels?

I was the last one out of the squadroom and, dedicated to the taxpayers as I was, I turned off the lights. I took the back staircase down one flight and left the building from the rear entrance. I headed toward my car, which was parked, against regulations, in the far corner of the almost deserted public parking lot for the police building. It was a street closer than the employees' lot I was supposed to park in. Absentmindedly, I noticed that the area was dark. The street light in this corner of the lot was out. Getting into my car, I saw a cigarette glow from within a late-model white Plymouth parked about twenty yards to my left.

I turned the ignition on and put the car in reverse. Shit! That familiar wobbling of the vehicle told me I had trouble. Getting out, I saw that the rear tire on my side was as flat as a soggy taco. I glanced at my watch. 2115 hours. My hopes of getting a shower before picking up Stacy weren't going to work out thanks to the damn flat.

Leaning into the trunk to pull out the spare, I noticed that the Plymouth had turned and caught me in its headlights. That was strange, because the car should have been going on in the opposite direction toward the exit. I pulled the spare out quickly and moved around out of the light to where the flat was, but I didn't start changing the tire. Something was funny. I looked at the Plymouth and was temporarily blinded. After a moment it turned and pulled out of the lot. Shrugging, I squatted and started changing the tire. When I had the flat off I turned it in my hands, looking for a nail or something else on the bottom surface that would explain why a fairly new tire had lost its air. I couldn't find anything, but turning it sideways I knew immediately what had happened.

The whitewall side of the tire had two neat puncture holes. The kind made by an icepick. Earlier in the day I had received a call from Tony White, one of the state probation officers. "Fraleigh, I got some news for you. Your old buddy Icepick, Ned Dorn, has been put into a work furlough program."

"God damn. I thought he got twenty years."

"Well, you know how the flim flam works. He got ten as an accomplice in the first robbery-homicide and ten more for the extortion stabbing. But the judge made them concurrent, not consecutive. Your testimony in the homicide helped nail him and the information you gave us in the probation report that he threatened to ice-pick you when he was released got him some extra time in San Quentin.''

''Extra time? Tony, the son of a bitch is out in three years.''

''It's really been slightly more than four. He got credit for time served while awaiting trial. But you know the old con game. He's been born again. Got great witnesses saying he's made his peace with Jesus. The Alternatives to Incarceration Program got him a job. He's seen the light. The state's cost-effective early release program is the greatest thing to ever hit the system. Officially, he's still listed as being incarcerated. Of course, the judges and politicians ain't telling the public that they got to let people out so they can make room for the new arrivals.''

''For God's sake, Tony, the guy's a psycho. He's iced at least ten people.''

''Yeah, but we only proved the one. His juvenile stuff didn't count. I just wanted to make sure you knew he was back because of that threat he made.''

''Yeah. Thanks Tony.'' There was no use giving Tony a hard time. He was as disgusted as I was with fictional sentences.

I shook off a chill, remembering looking into Dorn's icy gray eyes. He was a twisted psycho who'd been in and out of jails all his life. As a twelve-year-old elementary school student he had slashed the face of the girl at the next desk. It had been downhill after that. I had finally been able to put him away when he killed an elderly bodega owner during a robbery. Personally, I believed he was good for another ten killings, but the bodega owner was the only one we ever made him on. The newspaper had done a lengthy piece on him as the prototypical disturbed child, but his eyes had convinced me. Dorn would kill until killed.

Prowling under the unlit street lamp, I wasn't surprised to find broken pieces of the glass globe. It had been taken out. But with what? It made a difference. A pellet gun was one thing. A firearm another. Looking up at the light, it was too dark to tell what had been used to shoot it out. I glanced at my watch again. An investigation and crime report were required. On the other hand, something as petty as this would get Icepick a big six-month parole revocation, if that. And it would take damn near as long a hearing as his murder trial. The hell with it.

Pulling out of the parking lot, I was surprised to see the Plymouth, making no attempt to hide, boldly pull behind me. I was going to be late picking up Stacy. I decided I needed to have a little chat with Icepick Ned.

The idea of where best to do that came to me when I spotted the Macy's parking garage on my right. The store was closed and the parking area just about empty. I accelerated, leaving the Plymouth some distance behind me. I sped along the entrance road, then hung a sharp left, shooting up the ramp to the second-floor parking section. Right where the ramp leveled onto the floor I jammed on the brakes and threw the gear into park, stopping the car in the middle of the lanes so that there was no room to pull around it.

Slamming the door, I ran back five feet to hide behind the supporting pillar at the top of the ramp. The Plymouth, not wanting to lose me, took the ramp a little too fast. By the time Icepick realized he couldn't pull around my car he was stopped at an awkward angle of incline. I jumped from behind the column and shoved my Magnum into his face through the open window of his car.

"Welcome home, asshole. Just keep your hands on the wheel where I can see them." He blinked into the barrel of my gun, then glared at me. "All right. Nice and easy, use your right hand to put the car in parking gear. Keep your left on the wheel. You don't want to give me an opportunity to pull the trigger, Ned."

When the car was in park I yanked the door open, pulled him out, and roughly slammed him down on the hood. "You can't do this. I know my rights," he said.

"Assume the position or I'll break your skull open and you'll be back in Quentin trying to defend yourself from charges of assaulting an officer." Grudgingly, he moved his hands and feet into a spread position while I gave him a thorough frisk with my left hand, never failing to keep him covered with the Magnum. I respected fast hands. Especially if they might be holding an icepick. After I was sure he was clean I slapped on handcuffs and positioned him in front of the headlights. I searched under his seat, under the cushions, in the glove compartment, the back seats, and even the trunk. The Supreme Court wouldn't have liked the trunk bit, but they didn't have to deal with quick-handed icepick killers in dark parking lots. I found nothing. He and the car were clean.

He was between my car and his, close enough to the rear of mine so that the exhaust fumes made him cough. I left him there, still covering his chest with the Magnum. "So what gives, Icepick? Why did you flatten my tire? And how come you're following me?"

"I know my rights. I don't have to say anything. I did my time. I paid my debt to society. I own this car and I'm just out for a ride. I can't help it if you're nervous."

I stared at his sallow face illuminated by the headlights. A bony skull with dark greasy hair lying listless across it. The crazy, intense eyes glowed with hatred. I didn't get it. Brazenly following me. He was without a weapon so he hadn't been out to do a hit. He had gotten rid of whatever he had used on the street lamp. I checked his license and registration on the radio. Legit. He owned the car and had a current driver's license.

"You just happened to be in the police parking lot. And now you just happen to be out for a ride in Macy's garage when the store has been closed for half an hour. Stop the crap. No judge or jury is going to believe it."

"There's not going to be any judge or jury. I checked with a lawyer. He said I can drive anywhere I want. It ain't illegal. But you searching my car is. Now I'm going home unless you're going to shoot me.'' He sneered, slowly coming forward.

Reluctantly, I took off the handcuffs. The bastard was crazy, but he knew the law. There was nothing to charge him with. In a way, it was a compliment. I knew a number of guys who under the circumstances would have "discovered" a couple of bags of cocaine in his car, but Icepick hadn't figured me for that kind of a cop.

He got into his car and backed down the ramp. It was incredible. This punk was baiting me and quoting his lawyer. What had he said? He couldn't help it if I was nervous. What a screwball. Or maybe society was crazier than he was.

I was already twenty minutes late. As I left the garage I looked carefully for the Plymouth. I sure didn't want the creep to find out where Stacy lived. I cruised the side streets for a couple of minutes until I was certain there wasn't a tail before driving to her place.

Stacy Holbeck's reaction to my being late was about the same as her reaction to my going to Silicon City. I had met her seven months earlier when I was on a Mom and Pop homicide case. Pop Umberto hadn't been a criminal genius. He had taken a one-hundred-grand insurance policy on his wife three weeks before he slipped a healthy dose of cyanide into her evening hot chocolate. He successfully confused things for a few days by calling the police department and complaining that his wife had been poisoned by the chocolate mix. He had also complained at the hospital emergency room. He got the idea after seeing the television stories about the Chicago Tylenol poisonings a few years earlier.

Cops had rushed around town removing hot chocolate tins from grocery shelves. We had used up almost as much energy as the lawyers who frenziedly tried to sign up Umberto to sue the manufacturers. They disappeared with the first indications that Umberto had stuffed the cyanide in himself.

A few days after the murder I went to the hospital to get a statement. Stacy was the supervising nurse—a pert brunette with an official manner. She had a good memory and I recorded her version of the dialogue between the suspect and the emergency room staff. "He really did do it to that poor woman, huh?" she asked after I had turned the recorder off.

"The path of true love is never smooth," I said.

"Ah, a tough homicide detective, right?" She smiled at me and I realized that without the official manner she was attractive.

She went to the file cabinet and I watched her strain her white, starched nurse's outfit as she bent to put the file away. Feeling my eyes on her, she straightened up, tilted her head slightly, and raised her eyebrows.

"I've always wondered how one gets into a tight, starchy outfit like that." I said.

"Well, Officer, you start off by buying me a drink and talking nice to me."

She was considerably more cautious than her words implied, however. It took a couple of weeks and several dates before I was able to get her to visit my humble pad. After that she spent at least one night a week at my place and we were comfortable with each other right from the start.

We had both been burned by bitter divorces and I had screwed up things even more. In a recent investigation I had broken a detective's first rule by falling in love with a woman in the case. Somehow, I had managed to break with Sandra Fortune when I discovered how deeply she had been involved, but I couldn't forget her. I was determined that this was to be just a fun relationship. Stacy agreed. And we did have fun sharing common interests. On days off we would visit the San Francisco Zoo, stay at the Centrella Hotel in Pacific Grove while touring the Monterey Aquarium, or drive over the Golden Gate Bridge to Sausalito, where we sipped wine and took in the San Francisco skyline across the bay. Once we even toured the Winchester

Mystery House in San Jose, where Stacy challenged me to explain the mystery.

"There's no mystery about it. Mrs. Winchester kept adding staircases and doors that didn't go anywhere and rooms she didn't need because she was eccentric. If she hadn't had all that money she would have been a fucking nut and they would have put her away."

"Always the cynical cop." She took my hand and we left to splurge on a fancy meal in Paolo's east side restaurant.

"Now you're splitting in two weeks—just like that," she said when I told her about our impending move.

"But it's not *just* like that. I tried like hell to talk Louis out of it and if the Block and English weren't so strong about going I don't know what I'd do."

We had driven a couple of miles from her condo to TGI Friday's in the Vallco Shopping Center to have a late-night beer and supper at one of the window tables. As usual the place was crowded and noisy, full of people younger than us shopping for company. She didn't say anything and turned to look out the window. Her eyes were tearing slightly.

"What's wrong? It's only a twenty-minute drive from here. It's not like I'm going to Los Angeles."

"It's that you'd do something like this without talking it over with me." She wouldn't meet my eyes.

"What are we doing now?"

"Now? When you've already decided? You really know how to make a woman feel like a piece of furniture, Fraleigh. I want to go home."

Eighteen celibate days later, I traveled to the newly born Silicon City. It wasn't much of a trip. Twenty minutes north on the 101 Freeway and a left turn led me through much the same landscape I came from.

Mostly, it was a sprawl of condominiums or tract housing selling at double or triple what they cost back east. That was OK though. The Yuppie engineers and middle-level managers who worked in the electronics industries believed that paying too much for housing was a status symbol. If you couldn't hack a Mercedes in the driveway, BMWs were acceptable. Volvos were tolerated, but barely.

Of course, there were neighborhoods of Hispanics, blacks, and the newly arrived Vietnamese who were expected to gratefully hold down the menial jobs and to keep their pickup trucks and brats out of the higher-rent districts unless they had come to put in a lawn or build a patio.

And in the higher elevations the estates of the nouveau riche entrepreneurs could be found. They were far enough away from Yuppies and minorities to feel secure. They were also a sufficient distance from the electronics companies' toxic spills, which slowly seeped into the water supply. The superrich drank Perrier or bottled spring water from Colorado, but after all, one *did* have to be concerned about the dogs and horses and shrubs.

Louis had arranged an appointment for me with a real estate agent. Charles Bently was thin, gray-haired, and eyeglassed, the personification of the middle-aged dry-balled real estate agent. His ten-year-old Mercedes was parked outside the real estate office, which had a phony brick exterior. The bakery and supermarket on either side of the agency hadn't bothered to camouflage their roughened adobe exteriors except for a whitewash finish. Bently had me yawning before we arrived at the first of the three "properties readied for my review." My weak protest that all I wanted was an apartment went unacknowledged.

Bently seemed disappointed when I accepted the first place he showed me. It was a furnished garden apartment. I could move in as soon as the bank financed the mortgage. The agent assured me that it was an appropriate price. It was twice what I thought it was worth, but then again the salary Louis had quoted me was twice what I was making. Who was I to quarrel with the

American dream of a higher salary and less disposable income?

I did pay attention to Bently, however, when he described the security systems, which he thought were important to a man in my "position." I had never thought of it that way before, but the last couple of years had produced very personal close calls. Nor had I forgotten Icepick Ned. So I listened as he told me about the security guards and state-of-the-art burglar alarms. One other advantage for me was that the one-bedroom joint backed on an open county green space containing a jogging track and par course.

The next Thursday I moved in. The Block and English were in the capable hands of Bently, the real estate agent. I did notice that his capable hands trembled somewhat when his first mention of housing prices earned him the Block's baleful stare. Paul's vague smile seemed to make him more nervous. I shuddered at the thought of this odd cop couple living together.

Saturday I ran from 0900 to 1000. It would make the administrative nonsense of the rest of the day more bearable. I would be making vital decisions over office space, who got the larger desks, who got windows, who got walls—the "real drama" of urban police work would fill a long exasperating day.

The jogging course was fairly crowded. A shapely blond with her hair tied back, probably in her late twenties, gave me a smile and a nod as I passed her. I smiled back and slowed up. While she was catching up I contemplated the tight, bright red shorts, remembering how they had caught my eye as I overtook her and how tightly they clung to a nicely curved rear end. I got the dazzling white teeth again as she drew abreast.

"Don't run so fast, I won't be able to keep up with you," she said.

Gentleman me, I stayed at an even pace. "Isn't it a marvelous day." She took a deep breath, which did wonders for her snug blouse. I tried not to gawk, but she did have a magnificent figure and come to think of it, it had been a long time since Stacy and I had cuddled.

"Are you always so garrulous?" Her smile was teasing.

"There are certain things that take my breath away."

"Lecherous, but not so terribly corny a line under the circumstances." She had absorbed my admiring scrutiny without flinching.

"I haven't seen you on the course before."

"Just visiting town for a business survey," I said, noticing that her ring finger was bare.

"Business, how interesting." She laughed. "What sort of business?"

"Just management. Nothing very interesting."

"Oh, but I'm very interested."

I nodded a friendly goodbye and started to pull away. Nosy women, even as delectable as this one, turned me off.

She kept pace with me. "You're right, it's too beautiful a day to talk about business and since I'm just an ignorant female I wouldn't know whether or not you were stringing me a line." Her open grin took the sting out of the words. I eased my stride. "You certainly keep yourself in shape." She was looking me over from head to toe. I could swear she let her eyes linger on the crotch of my nylon running shorts.

We did a leisurely two miles, chatting about nothing in particular. She was Lorraine and I was Fraleigh by the time we had completed the circle and were heading toward my apartment complex. "The most wonderful part of this experience is a relaxing shower and a light breakfast afterward," she said.

"I've got a hot shower, orange juice, coffee, and toast right up ahead."

"Am I being invited?" she challenged.

"Definitely."

I was just a little uneasy when she accepted. It turned out that she declined the shower, but agreed to have coffee on the little patio outside my condo. "You make good coffee," she said, sitting upright so that her blouse was stretched tight. She had deep blue eyes and she looked at me, waiting for conversation.

"Glad you like it. Do you run here often?"

"Once in a while. I thought executives stayed in hotels. How long will your visit be?" she said with no trace of guile.

"I thought perhaps you were a regular when you said you hadn't seen me here before." I ignored her pointed question about the apartment, trying not to notice the film of sweat that covered her. I had offered a towel but she had tossed it unused onto an empty chair. I wondered what she'd do if I reached over and licked the salt from her neck.

"Did I say that? Perhaps I was just flirting. But about the duration of your visit . . . ?" Again she smiled, but. . . . Suddenly I realized that she was playing with me. Sexual teasing? Maybe, yet there was something else.

"Since I'm new in town maybe you'll recommend a good restaurant and have dinner with me tonight?"

"Mm, you do work fast. And actually I know nothing about you."

"Oh come. You've seen almost all of me there is to see." I had tossed my wet jogging shirt on the chair.

"Yes." Again the smile. "You do have awfully hard muscles for a businessman."

She couldn't know any different, I thought. "Come on Lorraine, what do you say? Let's have dinner and do the town."

She glanced at her watch. It was one of those with a stop watch, calendars, and who knows what else. "My God. I'm late. I have to run."

We stood up and she ran her hand along my still sweaty arm. I took a deep breath and felt a tremor run through me. "All right, mysterious businessman. A light dinner and disco. OK?" she said.

"Great. Where and when do I pick you up?"

"Meet me at eight o'clock at Darrel's on Chestnut Street. It's casual dress."

"Don't you want me to pick you up?"

"No. I'll be coming from a meeting and it's more convenient this way." She squeezed my arm and walked toward the nearby parking lot. She turned and waved. "Thanks for the coffee."

I watched her get into a deep green, new-looking Jaguar sedan. I wondered where the dough for the financing came from. Each time I tried to get personal she had parried my question with a general comment. I hadn't particularly wanted to disclose my own job in Silicon City so I hadn't pushed the personal stuff.

I entered Darrel's at ten after eight to find that there was already a line for tables. I threw my name in for one. The place didn't have enough light in it to read a newspaper, but the slim young people crowding the bar seemed more interested in each other than newspapers anyway. I checked the designer jeans, high-heeled boots, and hairdos of the energetic, healthy-looking young women crowding the bar. After all, I was a policeman, my job was to be a trained observer.

"Stop gaping, Fraleigh. A few of those young women are capable of devouring an innocent visitor."

Lorraine had appeared as I was scanning the bar. "I was only looking to see if you were here, Lorraine."

"Of course." Her smile mocked me. "I called in for a table. Why don't we just sit down?" She led me confidently through the mob to a table on a raised walkway that overlooked the disco dance floor. Her white wool slacks were not quite as tight around her ass as her running shorts had been and I didn't discern any signs of panties underneath. I wondered if she would split a seam during spirited dancing.

"Cocktails?" a young, golden-haired college kid who should have been practicing football asked.

I looked inquisitively at Lorraine. "I'd like a dry white wine," she said, her eyes roaming over the waiter, who smiled winningly at her until he saw me looking at him.

"Er, would you like the wine list, sir?"

"Yeah."

He left to fetch it. "God. You are the toughest-looking businessman I've ever seen, Fraleigh. That waiter was positively quaking. It must be your nose. Was it broken?"

I wasn't delighted with this turn of conversation. "If he was trembling it was when he was looking at you, Lorraine."

She reached across the table and squeezed my hand. "How gallant. It almost makes me forgive you for checking out all those women at the bar while you were waiting for me."

Fortunately, the waiter returned at that moment with the wine list. I ordered a moderately priced Napa Valley Sauvignon Blanc. Waiting for him to return, I studied Lorraine. Her hair was still tied back with a bright yellow ribbon. The ribbon had been a different shade in the morning and now she was wearing more makeup. She wore a turquoise blouse that wasn't as tight as the one she had worn on the jogging track. Still, no one was going to wonder whether or not she was flat-chested. I hadn't missed the heads turning to watch her when we had walked to the table.

"Well, what do you see, Fraleigh?"

"A beautiful woman who drives a green Jaguar."

"Thank you," she said, fluttering her eyelashes at the waiter, who handed us menus. He gave her a restrained grimace and turned to me for approval of the wine. We read the menu while he went through the wine-opening ritual. I tasted the sample he presented me and nodded my approval.

"I'll have the quiche," she told the waiter.

The two beers I had before leaving for the restaurant were lying heavily on my stomach. I thought about the dancing we would be doing later and decided to stay light with the food. Besides, with all her suspicious cracks about my being so tough, it wouldn't hurt to go along with the quiche.

"The same," I said.

Her laughter was deep and pleasant to listen to, providing it wasn't at my expense. "What's so funny?" I asked.

"Quiche. I just couldn't help wondering what your colleagues' reaction would be if they heard you ordering quiche."

She was right on target there. I smiled, thinking of the Block's reaction. "Now, now, Lorraine, I thought the woman's movement disapproved of sexual stereotypes."

"Forgive me. You know, for a moment there when you smiled you showed a different person. You play everything very close, but just then you really relaxed and I saw a little boy peeking through. A nicer person."

I was tempted to tell her the truth then. To compliment her on her astuteness and to laugh with her over how right she was about the way cops reacted to a man ordering quiche. It was standard to hear one guy ragging the other about being a quiche eater. But I didn't like to tell women what I did for a living until I got to know them better. It was an old precaution of mine.

The music had started and we watched dancers gyrating under the hallucinogenic floodlights flashing off a large rotating mirrored globe. The beat of the music pounded deep.

"How about a little warm-up before the food arrives?" I asked.

She nodded and we moved out onto the floor. We started slowly. I tried to read her eyes as we moved in rhythm to each other. Within a minute we were moving more quickly without a thought to the others on the dance floor. The beat was rolling over me now and there was an almost feverish excitement in her eyes. But after a few minutes, she banked the fire. "Come." She took my hand. "The food has been served."

We were both overheated. I saw her perspiration again and found it just as exciting. The quiche wasn't bad and the mood of the room was hypnotic. I noticed that the wine was almost gone. "How about another bottle?"

"I don't want you to drink so much that you'll be useless later," she said, gazing at me calmly without a hint of coyness. Her words made me as hard as a rock.

I tried to stall about going back onto the dance floor until the bulge in my pants subsided, but Lorraine just got up and moved to the floor. She was flushed and her blue eyes, which I had thought cool on our first meeting, were anything but. They shifted from my eyes to my swiveling crotch and her breathing grew more rapid. People bumped into her, but she was oblivious. The two of us were the only people in the world. I couldn't take any more. "Let's get the hell out of here." We had spent all of an hour and fifteen minutes in the place.

"Yes. I'll follow you in my car."

I would have preferred that she come with me, but I dropped enough money on the table to cover the check and left without arguing. Outside in the parking lot she pushed up on her toes and softly covered my mouth with hers. Her tongue darted between my lips and touched mine. She pulled way as I started to put my arms around her. "I'll be right behind you," she said. I watched her get into the Jag and then went to my car. My face was flushed and blood was pounding in my ears. I checked the mirror constantly. I didn't want to lose her. At one point I got uneasy. There seemed to be another pair of headlights behind her making all of the same turns we were. But when we pulled into my complex she was alone and I couldn't very well ask her if she had been followed, and there were other things on my mind.

The ten-minute drive to my condo had taken five. Once inside there was no conversation. I took her in my arms and ran my tongue over her still perspiring neck. She leaned her head back with her eyes closed and I kissed her ears, eyelids, nose, and forehead as her fingers deftly shed her blouse and bra. I didn't need her to tell me what she wanted. I cupped her full breasts in my hands and ran my tongue swiftly over them, savoring the slightly salty taste of her sweat. At first I just softly touched her nipples, then tongued them as rapidly as I could. She moaned and reached between my legs, stroking and gently pushing me in the direction of the bedroom.

At the foot of the bed she pulled her slacks off and stood naked. I was a few seconds behind her in getting my own clothes off, staring at her light blond pubic hair. I pushed her down on the bed and thrust hard into her. She was warm and moist. She gasped and I was startled to realize that she had come. My own passion was mounting and I moved back and forth into her with all the power I had. She matched the violence of my own thrusts and again peaked with a cry just as I experienced an incredibly sharp burst of pleasure and exploded into her. She just lay there with her arms around me, taking deep breaths while I slowed my thrusts until the last of the sharp sensations was gone.

"Stay inside me for a while," she said and I did. When finally I did separate from her she smiled at me and I found myself smiling back. I went to the refrigerator and poured two glasses of Chablis and brought them back to the bed. Lorraine sat with a pillow behind her.

"This wine is so nice and cold. You must belong to that One Minute Manager school of business, Fraleigh," she said.

"Complaining?"

"Not if there's an encore."

There were two encores. After the last one I must have dozed. I awoke alone and found myself slightly relieved. I rolled over and before falling into a deep sleep reflected that a sensitive part of me was going to be as sore as hell in the morning. What a woman.

Four

IN THE MORNING I STAGGERED OUT TO MY CAR AND into my first day at work. My concerns about soreness had been justified. I started the car and shifted into reverse before I realized some jerk had stuffed a circular under my windshield wipers. I got out and crumpled whatever advertisement they were peddling and started to toss it to the ground when I spied one of the security guards eyeing me. Littering was probably a major felony on his beat. I didn't want to ruin his day so I tossed the ball of paper into the back seat.

At first glance police headquarters looked like a medium-sized computer company. In fact, it had been. The whole civic center had been a cluster of electronics company buildings. We had inherited the modern new facilities of a company that had failed to anticipate the success of Japanese firms in capturing a major segment of international sales of microchips. The city had gotten a good buy on the two-story redwood structure that spread out over nicely landscaped grounds.

Louis's and my job was to take eleven separate small police departments and organize them into one giant one that could provide patrol and detective services to a population of over a half million people. The top priority was, as Louis kept reminding me, to provide an emergency response to 911 calls in less than five minutes. This sounded easy until we realized how many cops it took to guarantee that response twenty-four hours a day, seven days a week, fifty-two weeks a year. Cops are the only ones still making house calls twenty-four hours a day. At the same time, we had to have a training unit, a SWAT unit, a traffic enforcement unit, a crime prevention unit, school crossing guard units, detective units, internal affairs units, and so on. Most important was a payroll unit. The troops were sticky about getting paid every other Friday.

About ninety percent of the new department's one thousand sworn officers were grandfathered in at existing rank from their previous department. Naturally, they would want to continue the same rules of conduct, radio signals, and other procedures as they had in their old department. One of my unhappy tasks would be to come up with one set of procedures that were workable and made everyone happy. Ha!

I spent the day meeting with a skeleton support staff and looking through office catalogues. My new secretary, Denise, was in place, and so at 1600 hours I said good night.

That night the mayor was throwing a bash reception in Louis's and my honor. I would shower and rest before appearing. Lorraine had taken her toll.

One of my perks as chief of detectives was my very own parking space right outside the building. As I was getting into my car, I spotted yet another flyer under my windshield. I looked at the other cars surrounding mine. None of them had been similarly honored. I pulled the piece of paper from under my windshield wiper and read it.

YOU CAN RUN BUT YOU CAN'T HIDE, it said. Halfway down the page was the graceful drawing of an icepick. Before reaching into the back seat to retrieve the paper that had graced my windshield in the A.M., I looked around carefully. When I was sure there were no would-be assassins present, I retrieved and uncrumpled the piece of paper on the back seat. It was a duplicate of the one I had just removed from my windshield.

This time I handled both pieces by their edges and went back up to my office. The fingerprint unit was unmanned after hours on a Saturday, so I locked the two pointed messages in my desk. I also decided that it was useless to try to reach Tony White. Parole officers weren't known for being available Saturday evenings. Monday would be time enough, but I did take a Chief's Special out of my desk and hook it onto my belt opposite the Magnum.

Driving home, I tried to reconcile myself to the fact that a nut like Dorn not only had my new work address but my home as well.

Nobody followed me to the mayor's humble abode. Louis had briefed me on the family. Mayor Solomon H. Middleston's father had done the garage workshop bit, starting with nothing but some research ideas and ending up with the fourth largest electronics company in the world. Now he was chairman of the board. His son was Yale College, Harvard Business School, for five years chief executive officer of the company and now the hot-shot new mayor of a highly publicized new city. The media had loved it. Not only the glamour of the high-tech world capital, but also the possibility of its becoming the center for legalized gambling in California.

The day before the party Louis said, "I think it would be nice if the Block and English were there also. Let them come in tuxedos. It never hurts to have some extra security. We'll be having some of the wealthiest people in the state here and the women will be loaded with jewelry. We sure don't want something to go wrong."

I winced. "Louis, I don't think that's a good idea. You know how they can be sometimes."

"No. I disagree. I think that's what's wrong with policing. We're too immersed in our own subculture. It's important that the troops associate with the outside world. Just tell them to behave and to pay attention to anyone without a name tag. The guests will be checked at the entrance.''

Behave? That was like telling lions and tigers in the jungle to be well-mannered, I thought, approaching the Middleston mansion. The place went with the glamorous, high-tech image, but was probably just a little too small to house our entire thousand-officer police department. The Tudor-style structure was set well back from the road. A long, circular driveway was chock full of expensive cars, some with uniformed chauffeurs. The gardening expenses alone were probably double my yearly salary.

A five-piece band played music that no one in the ballroom was listening to. I hated to think what it cost to heat the joint. I had ignored Louis's suggestion on the tuxedo, but was glad that I wore a tie with my four-year-old blue blazer and gray slacks. Solly the Mayor, as he had instantly been dubbed by the Block, was splendid in a light blue summer tux. He was tall, had light brown hair, and was handsome if you liked department store mannequins.

''So. You're Fraleigh.'' He greeted me without a smile or any other sign of enthusiasm. His handshake was weak and he pulled his hand back quickly. Gracious to a fault. Louis, standing next to him, shrugged and patted me on the shoulder. This was the terrific mayor he had used as motivation to move to Silicon City.

I was trying to think of something to say when Lorraine walked up to us. Her soft blond hair wasn't tied back now. It was flowing over her shoulders, accentuating the low-cut black gown that she wore as if it had been sculpted onto her.

''This is my wife, Lorraine,'' the mayor said.

''Fraleigh! How good to see you again.'' She once again unleashed the dazzling smile.

The mayor turned, staring hard at me. ''You've met?''

"Oh, yes. We were running the par course yesterday morning. He explained all of his wonderful management theories to me."

The mayor's face tightened, if that was possible. "I see." He kept his voice even.

I wondered what my face looked like. I had a knot in my stomach.

"Enough of your shop talk. I want this rugged-looking devil to dance with me." She took my arm, openly pressing her breasts against me while firmly resisting my effort to pull away. People watched as she twirled about lightly and I followed, lead-footed, on the small dance floor. "I can't believe you would rather talk with that ass than hold me in your arms," she said, affectionately running her hand through my hair. "So, Mr. Businessman, are you really as good a detective as Louis says you are?"

"I can detect that you just caused me a lot of grief with your husband."

"Don't worry about it. In five minutes he'll be snorting white powder up his nose and he won't even remember you . . . or me," she added. "Take a look around at the two bars. One at each end of the room. What do you see?"

One thing I saw that didn't fill me with joy was the Block, bulging out of an ill-fitting black tuxedo. It was the only one in the room. There were other formal outfits, but like the mayor's they reflected the warmer weather. Block was standing near the bar, swilling beer from a bottle and glowering at the people in the cavernous room. The redness of his face led me to believe that his consumption had been considerable. A short distance away, Paul was surrounded by women. He wore a fashionable outfit similar to Solly's, but his good looks and casual cool made him more elegant than the mayor.

I decided not to answer Lorraine's question by commenting on my colleagues. I was pretty sure that one way or another they were going to bring themselves to her attention before the night was over. Instead I said,

"I see a moderate number of well-heeled types. Probably engineers, lawyers, whatever, and some of their women." A goodly number of whom had ticked off their husbands by hanging around Paul. "No young people though," I continued. "They must all be mid-forties or over. Is there an age barrier you have to hurdle to get an invite?"

"I'll have to watch you, Fraleigh. You are observant. What you see is the alcohol generation. The young people are upstairs. In honor of your's and Louis's occupation they have been instructed to do coke only behind locked bedroom and bathroom doors tonight. Before Solomon's entrance into politics he prided himself on providing lines of coke along with hors d'oeuvres." She said it with such a wholesome smile that I thought she was pulling my leg. But sure enough, when I looked at the elaborate curving staircase leading upstairs, I didn't see Scarlett O'Hara bouncing down. I saw two expensively dressed young couples, stoned. They were so high that they almost didn't negotiate the last curve in the staircase.

"I want to meet that incredible man." Lorraine pointed at the Block.

I protested and tried to steer her to the opposite side of the room, but she disengaged her arm from mine and walked right up to him. "Hello," she said. "I'm Lorraine Middleston."

"Hiya, hon," the Block replied. "This stuff is all right." He indicated the Heinekens beer he was drinking. "On my lousy salary I got to drink the cheaper piss. Excuse the French, but you know what I mean."

"Er, Block, don't you think you ought to check outside. You know, security." I motioned frantically with my head.

"Absolutely not," Lorraine said. Her eyes were excited. "What is your name?"

"It's Arnold Schulster, lady, but they call me Block."

"Block. How marvelous. I can see why." She felt

his massive arm. "Yes, it's like a block of steel. You must be very strong."

He flushed with pleasure. I noticed uneasily that people had drifted over. Lorraine was a magnet. "This is Superior Court Judge McArthur." She introduced us to a tall, dignified, gray-haired man in his sixties. He towered over the Block, who was frowning. He hated judges. Several other men were introduced. There was a corporate president, a venture capitalist, an attorney, and the president of Silicon City's largest bank, each of whom was introduced by Lorraine to "this fascinating policeman—the Block."

He was eating it up. It was just what I hoped wouldn't happen. Between swallows from the beer bottle, the Block asked his newly acquired audience. "Hey didya hear the one about the guy with a glass eye?"

"Yes," I said promptly. "No jokes tonight, Block. OK?"

"Oh, don't be such a drag," Lorraine said. "Please tell it just for me, Block."

"Yours to command, ma'am." He bowed clumsily. Some of the Heinekens spilled out of the bottle onto the sleeve of Judge McArthur's white tux. A couple of people chuckled. But not the judge. "Well, you see this guy had a glass eye that he kept at night in a glass of water next to his bed, but one night he gets a load on and he forgets. He slurps down the water and swallows his eye."

The judge had stopped rubbing the beer spot on his jacket to stare at the Block. No judicial temperance was in his expression. He looked like he was smelling something unbelievably foul. The others had similar expressions. Only Lorraine smiled her approval. I saw the mayor and Louis approaching.

I had heard the joke before. "Block, I really don't think . . ."

"Shush. Go on, Block," Lorraine said.

"Well, the guy is too embarrassed to tell his doctor that he swallowed his own eye, see? So he tells the sawbones that he's got a pain in his stomach." He paused to drink some more beer, but the joke's humor overwhelmed him and he choked. Some of his beer-laden spittle dropped down his mouth onto his shirt and some sprayed the judge's frilled shirt and jacket. His Honor looked down at the wet brown spots on what had just a minute ago been a gleaming white outfit. Lorraine was shaking with soundless but hysterical laughter.

I saw that Louis and the mayor had joined the group in time to see the judge's jacket get sprinkled. Louis's hand grabbed my arm. "Fraleigh . . ."

Lorraine pushed his hand away. She held a finger to her lip, indicating silence. The Block went on with his joke. "So the doctor goes over him, but can't find nothin'. Finally, he says, I got to give you a rectal. Bend over. And he does. Lo and behold, staring out of the guy's asshole is his glass eye. The doctor stands up and says to him, real indignant, Look here, Mr. Smith, you have to trust me if I'm going to treat you."

There was dead silence except for the Block's loud laughter. "You get it? The eye was looking right out of his asshole."

Lorraine, weak with laughter, leaned on me. Tears ran down her face. She whispered, "Look at those pompous fools. It's priceless."

The way Louis was looking at me wasn't priceless. I shrugged and put on my I-told-you-so expression. Solly scowled at his wife, occasionally taking time off to glare at me.

"Hey, do you want to hear another?"

The audience drifted elsewhere. Except for Louis. He eased me away from Lorraine, who was telling the Block how much she enjoyed his joke. "Damn it, Fraleigh, why did you let the Block get drunk and tell that stupid joke? And where the devil is Paul? The mayor thinks he disappeared upstairs with Judge McArthur's wife. You better look for him."

"Hell, McArthur's at least sixty. I don't think there's a problem."

"You're wrong. His wife is half his age and a fox."

"You know Louis, leaving those two guys in their own police subculture isn't such a bad thing."

Suddenly, he was laughing as hard as Lorraine had been. "It was pretty goddamned funny watching their faces. But you better round up Paul. The mayor needs the judge's political backing."

I started after Paul, but Lorraine intercepted me and once again we were whirling around the dance floor. Across the ballroom, I saw that Louis was talking with the mayor. They both looked in our direction with very serious expressions. When Lorraine noticed them, she moved closer and put her head against my chest. "What's going on, Lorraine?"

"Now, Fraleigh. You were so delightful yesterday. I hope you're not going to ruin our beautiful relationship by getting sullen."

"You knew who I was all along. You were laughing at me. I don't get the joke."

"I can see that you're in an unpleasant mood this evening. I won't intrude, but perhaps we can jog again in a few days."

With that she walked away and up the stairs. I collected the Block and escaped. He was snoring before I got out of the driveway. I checked the rear-view mirror in case friendly Ned Dorn was around. We weren't followed, which was just as well considering the Block's condition.

The next day Louis told me that Judge McArthur had located his wife upstairs with Paul. They were engaged in activities that convinced the mayor he had lost the judge's political support for the indefinite future. In the days following, the Block and Paul took a number of Lorraine's playful telephone calls to the office asking if I wanted to go jogging. I had successfully avoided seeing or talking to her. My two colleagues found the whole thing immensely amusing, but for me it was painful to know how easily she had set me up on the jogging path. I remained puzzled as to why she had done it and what I had gotten into, no pun intended.

Five

Early Monday morning I gave the two icepick flyers to the fingerprint unit to see if any latents could be lifted. I decided to hold my call to Tony White until I heard the results. I didn't have long to wait. Gail Henderson, the technician, was back in an hour.

"Beautiful, isn't it, Chief?" He pointed to a well-developed thumb print. He was fifty and bald. With his white smock and thick eyeglasses he could have passed as an electrical engineer in one of the nearby computer companies. Actually, he was a damned good fingerprint man. I waited, guessing what was coming next.

"It's yours, of course. But it does show the effectiveness of our techniques."

"What about the other one? The one I rolled into a ball."

"A partial of your right index finger. Other than that, nothing. I'd say someone has been careful. Probably wearing gloves."

"Any hope on making the paper or writing?"

"The paper is common drawing paper. It can be purchased in any store and the printing doesn't help. I'm sorry. Is it important?"

"Not unless someone sticks an icepick in me."

"Well, be careful until we get some more evidence."

He smiled and shuffled back to his lair. There wasn't much use in calling Tony White, but I made a vow to keep my eyes open. In the meantime, I sent him a copy of the flyer and a note that there were no prints.

The days were long the first month, but they flew by. I found that Louis didn't have much time to spend with me. He was at City Hall a lot and on the lunch and dinner rubber chicken circuit. I got a general sense of direction from him, but by and large I was making the decisions and running them by Louis afterward, when I caught up with him. There was no assistant chief and Louis had decided to leave the chief of patrol position unfilled until he had time to make that choice personally. By default I was in charge. I was assigning all personnel and organizing both patrol and detective units.

I suspected that Louis was delegating like crazy to me more because the mayor had him tied up than because of his faith in my managerial abilities. Me, who could I delegate to? The Block or English—the thought was ludicrous. Yet I did have to admit they were a help doing the employment and assignment interviews.

We were limited by the patchwork agreements that had been made with the various local jurisdictions being absorbed. In many cases we were mandated to take sworn personnel and honor their rank and seniority. Fortunately, we did have the power to make assignments and we hadn't inherited too many lieutenants. Often we could appoint people to supervisory positions.

Paul and the Block sat in on the interviews. Although they expressed their views and phrased questions to the candidates quite differently, it was surprising how often their assessment of a candidate agreed with mine.

One stiff-backed candidate for commander of the burglary squad impressed the Block as "an arrogant, pompous asshole," while Paul English saw him "as lacking in interpersonal skills." Mostly I agreed with their analysis if not their terminology. Also, I found that being interviewed by the Block and English was an ordeal that put the candidates through their paces. There was no need for me to plan the interview questions so that we could observe the person under stress.

Paul's questions were contorted, if eloquently phrased. A young sergeant, Phil Short, a contender for the boss of the homicide squad, started out confidently enough. Then Paul asked, "Given the escalation of violence in the United States over the past two decades, how should a homicide squad respond innovatively, remembering Aristotle's advice, 'Well begun is half done.' "

Short's eyes glazed at the mention of Aristotle, but he was game. Neatly dressed in a conservative blue suit, he straightened his tie, which didn't need it, and said, "Well, I guess what Aristotle meant is to plan whatever you're going to do thoroughly so that whatever you implement will work. O. W. Wilson said the same thing in *Municipal Police Administration*. Homicide work has to rely more on physical evidence and personnel have to be flexible in work hours since we're getting more and more homicides and we can't control production, so to speak." He paused hopefully, taking a breath.

"Wilson, Aristotle. What kinda fucking bullshit is that? You wanna be a ding-dong English professor or a cop?" the Block's grating voice challenged him.

Tiny beads of perspiration were on the sergeant's forehead as he turned to me, appeal in his eyes. "I, er, like you know, he mentioned Aristotle, and Wilson, well, we had to study his book for promotion."

I shrugged. Paul said, "Sergeant, you mentioned O. W. Wilson, but his work is dated. Although Shakespeare told us that 'The past is prologue,' surely you must be familiar with more recent texts on the investigative function."

Short glanced uneasily at the Block's scowl and rattled off three more books, one of which was so recent I had never heard of it. "Of course, you can't learn investigation from books. There's no substitute for experience and on the job training. I'd sure emphasize that if I were homicide commander.''

Forty minutes later he left. His parting handshake was a damp one. Paul and the Block had warmed up the questioning. I contributed only one meaningless query, ''Where were you born?'' which seemed to shake him up even more. He had been clinging to the belief that one of us had to be somewhat reasonable. Yet he hadn't done that badly. I marked my notes to indicate he should be strongly considered.

Others had been thrown by English's soft-voiced references to Plato or Socrates or Aristotle or any of the other illustrious folk popping into Paul's foggy head. Some got over that hurdle but foundered on the Block's snarling counterattacks. One candidate actually got up and walked out at that point. ''A wimp,'' the Block concluded.

''Or a wise man unwilling to put up with this tale told by an idiot so full of sound and fury,'' Paul said.

So went our interviews with the cops. Meanwhile the criminals were uncooperative for the first few weeks. They went about their deviant behavior despite the fact we weren't ready. The Department had been declared operational over my objections. We were not fully staffed in the various dick squads. In fact, we hadn't decided finally what squads we should have. Cops all wanted their area of expertise to be recognized. My head was spinning from suggestions that we form credit card fraud units, sting units, accident investigation units, white-collar crime units, computer crime units, career criminal units, juvenile career-criminal units, organized crime units, and even a residential graffiti investigation unit.

The media was already getting on us over the escapades of the Uzi bandits. Three young punks who had committed four armed robberies downtown used assault rifles that could be bought over the counter. They had sprayed multiple rounds to terrorize victims. Predictably, on their third job one of the nine-millimeter projectiles landed on human flesh. A sixteen-year-old girl, a high school honor student and cheerleader, was hit in the spine. It was doubtful that she would ever again lead cheers.

The local newspaper, radio, and television stations were also interested in our efforts to nail the old man— a gray-bearded bank robber who had successfully made unapproved withdrawals at gunpoint from sixteen of our financial institutions over the past four months. Likewise, the gray van rapist was newsworthy. He had struck at least a dozen times during the past six months. His victims were mostly young female students between ten and fourteen years of age. For reasons we couldn't explain he had recently hit on two women in their sixties. In every case he had pulled right up to his victim and forced her into the van at knife- or gunpoint. He tied her up and sodomized her. He wore a ski mask and we were nowhere on the case. No ID. No fingerprints.

Usually he let his victims out of the van a couple of miles from their homes, without inflicting extreme physical injury, but in his last two attacks he had been brutal, choking and punching them. I could hear the clock ticking on him real loud and the television and radio networks located in San Francisco had local reporters in our city who asked questions about the case every day.

At the same time, my desk was buried under a mountain of purchase orders for desks, file cabinets, calendars, recording devices, and God knows what else. Then there were work orders that had to be approved by me before city workers would come to install walls, doors, phones, and cables for the automated systems. Our empty building had to be shaped up. I had delegated it to Paul until Louis called and burned my ear off.

"Fraleigh, are you out of your goddamned mind? Putting in a purchase order for a three-thousand-dollar sculpture for your office. It's a good thing Nicastri, the mayor's aide, spotted that before it got to the mayor.

And the work order for teak bookcases in your office. Only the mayor has that kind of budget.''

''I was just following your suggestion to delegate. You remember when I told you that I was being assistant chief, chief of patrol, chief of administration, and chief of detectives all at the same time?''

''Delegate? Delegate . . .'' Suddenly I heard his deep, booming laugh over the phone. ''It was English, wasn't it?''

''I'm glad you think it's funny, Louis. But you've got to do something. I'm swamped and that worm Nicastri makes it worse. He's over here every day getting in the way. One of these days I'm going to pick him up and throw him out on his ass.''

''Start-up pains, Fraleigh. The mayor was just saying how similar it was to his experiences in the private sector. And don't mess with Nicastri. He's very close to the mayor. He makes both political and administrative decisions. By the way, the mayor would like to take us to a couple of community meetings and to a business luncheon speech he's making. Can you get over here within ten minutes?''

''Louis, the gray van rapist just hit again. I'm on my way to the crime scene. It's time to show the cops that I'm interested in more than just holding meetings. And we have two more interviews for squad commanders this afternoon.''

''You'll have to delegate. The mayor says these meetings are very important.''

''The rapist is getting more and more violent. We're making him top priority now—before he kills someone. I think I better stay with it.''

''You'll just have to delegate that stuff. These are must appearances and the mayor wants both of us present.''

''OK. I just hope the High-Tech Glamour Boy is prepared when the press climbs on his ass about crime waves.''

''Now, Fraleigh—''

''I mean it, Louis. You should be here, in charge. All this political shit is keeping us from doing our jobs.''

I trekked over to City Hall to find Louis waiting beside the mayor's not quite block-long Lincoln. The chauffeur was a cop selected by Nicastri—another battle I had lost. Police Officer Carruthers had been a member of a fifteen-man department. He had taken a leave and worked as an unpaid volunteer on the mayor's campaign. Six months ago, when Middleston was sworn in, he got his reward. The mayor's chauffeur got unlimited overtime, generous expense allowances, and had the potential for doing even better if he kept Nicastri and Middleston happy. Louis had shrugged off my objections that we shouldn't let cops be used as flunkies. And if we were forced to assign someone, it shouldn't be Carruthers. I wanted to pick someone loyal to the Department.

Six

NOW CARRUTHERS SAT BORED BEHIND THE WHEEL, EN-
joying the air-conditioning while Louis and I stood in
the sun waiting for our leader. Carruthers wore a drab
gray suit, white shirt, and an ugly red tie. His shoulder
holster was conspicuous under his left arm. His attire
wasn't going to challenge the mayor's sartorial splen-
dor.

Middleston strode confidently across the pavement.
Nicastri bustled with self-importance ahead of him.
Louis started to remind the mayor that he had met me
at his house party, but the mayor merely nodded in my
direction and got into the car. Now I understand why
Louis had been standing outside the car. We would be
told where to sit. I ended up in front next to Carruthers,
who had yet to acknowledge either Louis or me. Of
course, he knew who his real boss was. Louis and the
mayor occupied the rear seat and Nicastri a fold-out one
facing them. Nicastri opened a briefcase and spoke to
the mayor about the upcoming events.

"Before the luncheon there will be twenty minutes
of cocktails with the Silicon Valley Manufacturing Association Steering Committee. Chiefs Robinson and
Fraleigh will abstain. You'll know most everyone. There
are only a few new members since the time you chaired

the committee as CEO of Middleston Electronics. I don't have to remind you of the political action committees they control. You received their largest contribution ever. But we can't be complacent. I've heard rumors that they aren't happy about you choosing a black for police chief. Middleston Electronics' affirmative action training plan wasn't universally popular with the group, as you recall. And they may also think that you're soft on crime because you picked a black chief.''

''For God's sake, what's wrong with those imbeciles? We hired two percent more minorities and increased bottom-line profits by three and a half percent because of the tax incentives involved. And the following year we broke the union when we laid off fifteen hundred people and went offshore to Taiwan. We pay eighty cents an hour there and they're damned glad to get it.'' The mayor shook his head.

''Still, the concern is there. That's why I wanted Fraleigh present. One look at him and his attitude should reassure them that we have a hard-nosed cop at the helm.''

''Have him turn around,'' the mayor said.

Nicastri didn't have to order me. I had swung around to ask the mayor who the hell he thought he was talking to.

Louis said quickly, ''Fraleigh was a champion amateur boxer at one time. He's really a teddy bear when you get to know him.'' He winked and shook his head from side to side in a silent warning.

The mayor turned to Nicastri and said, ''I suppose you're right, Thomas. He looks mean enough to impress even the law-and-order fanatics on the committee.''

''I assume we will not be taking Fraleigh to the Black Caucus meeting after lunch?'' the mayor said.

''No. Fraleigh will come with us.'' Nicastri spoke with complete assurance. ''We'll highlight that we have a black chief in charge of this tough-looking white cop.

That will help. They eat up that sort of thing. We don't get a nickel out of the Black Caucus and they're not really important in terms of votes because of the low percentage of blacks voting, but they can be important in your senatorial race—both positive and negative. We can selectively highlight their endorsements with photo publicity and by having black leaders appear with you on certain occasions. On the negative side, if we don't keep them happy, demonstrations or protests are something we don't need. You'll be running as the dynamic mayor of a successful new city. A dynamic first year, prosperity, jobs, and Utopia and brotherhood stuff. We don't want anything to flaw that image. And it's not that difficult to keep them happy—meetings with you, Chief Robinson, and a few of those non-civil-service appointments I had you make should do it.''

"How long will we have to stay at this dreadful business lunch?'' the mayor asked.

"Please, your honor, remember this lunch is a hundred and fifty dollars a plate. We expect six hundred people. It will just about pay for the statewide issue survey that will be the base for the Senate campaign. We won't stay that long. I've arranged for us to stop for a head table intro at the annual B'nai B'rith luncheon.''

"Well, at least I don't have to eat matzo ball soup.''

I could well understand Lorraine's lack of affection for the son of a bitch. Deliberately, I brought back recollections of my lustful night with her, only half listening to him and Nicastri.

"There's a lot of money there, Solomon. Soft pedal some of that anti-Israel stuff in your business speech. And for God's sake, avoid discussing the charge that Middleston Electronics doesn't hire Jewish executives.''

We pulled up in front of the hotel. The doorman opened the rear door for the mayor, who slithered out and was greeted by a fat, balding man with a flushed face, wearing a big smile and a large round button identifying him as part of the Silicon Valley Manufacturing

Association. A blue ribbon dangling from the button said "Committee Member."

"S.H. how are you?"

"Fine, Roger," His Honor replied. "I miss our lunches, but you know how it is with politics. There's never enough time for old friends."

We filed into a small conference room next to the large ballroom, where early arrivals were beginning to seat themselves in accordance with the established pecking order. After about fifteen minutes of shaking hands and fawning over the mayor, the group was called to order by Roger the greeter.

"As you know, our good friend and colleague Solomon is here to make a speech to the association. I prevailed upon him to give the Steering Committee a ten-minute private session before lunch, especially to touch on an issue that many of us are real concerned about—crime. So, Your Honor, if you and the two police chiefs could come up to the front here . . ."

To my horror I saw that there was a table with three chairs. Nicastri shepherded Louis and me to the front, where we sat to the mayor's right. Middleston stood and addressed the fat cats, who moved obediently to sit on the folding chairs facing us. "It's great to be back with you. As I've told Roger, I really miss these luncheons, but I'm most happy to see that the association and especially this committee is as dedicated as ever to influencing the vital issues that shape the future of this valley. Like you, I'm appalled with the rising level of crime, which is threatening the quality of life that our companies have helped build in this area.

"It's no secret that my politics are based upon the same philosophy that I had as a business executive. Contrary to the picture painted by leading left-wing members of the news media, our businesses are indeed value oriented. People come first. We achieve excellence because we value our customers, our employees, and our stockholders as people."

A smattering of applause interrupted him. He held

up his hands. "No. I don't take credit. It belongs to you—the leaders of Silicon City. But I can tell you this— my administration will run under *business* standards. Efficiency will be the watchword, not political patronage. We will deliver essential services to the public— our customers—as economically as possible." I noticed Nicastri give a nod to a wealthy housing developer who had been at Middleston's party. The developer stood and began to applaud. The rest of the group joined him and cheers of "bravo" filled the room. I pretended not to hear Louis's chair scraping the floor as he got to his feet. But I couldn't pretend not to feel the hard fist he gave me as I continued to sit. I stood up.

"I want to assure you," the mayor continued after receiving his due recognition, "Police Chief Louis Robinson will get the most out of his police force. And I can tell you personally that Louis Robinson gives no credence to those who complain that prejudice and poverty led them into crime. He holds no truck with welfare programs that pay people not to work. Violent criminals and thugs will get no sympathy from this man—one of the leading police administrators in the country. And if you don't think criminals in my city are in trouble take a look at the man Chief Robinson has chosen as chief of detectives. Chief Fraleigh learned to use his fists in the ring and he and his men won't hesitate to use them against riffraff of any color who threaten our safety."

This time there was no need for prompting. The committee was enthusiastically applauding the slyly suggested picture of racist police brutality.

"I know some of you would like to ask these two policemen questions, but I'm afraid in my interest in seeing all of you again I've kept our friends inside waiting."

One old bozo wasn't to be put off, however. "Just one question of Mister Fraleigh," he said. "I would like to know how you are setting up the detective bureau. Many of us are disturbed that these killers and rapists don't seem to be apprehended here. What principles will you use?"

The room was in total silence as they all looked at me. For once the mayor was speechless, but a frown of concern was on his face. I didn't have the first idea of what to say. I couldn't tell them about the mess of political and civil service accommodations the mayor had saddled us with, but finally I blurted, "Well begun is half done."

I couldn't think of another word to say. The silence grew as I stared back at the questioner. I felt Louis stir uneasily next to me. He was starting to speak when the old bozo said, "I can see that you're a man of few words and I happen to think that's good in a policeman. The answer you gave is a shrewd one. I built my business on careful planning and implementation of new approaches and I'm glad to hear that you're doing the same thing." With that we all marched into the ballroom for lunch.

Louis and I were once again displayed at the head table and the mayor's speech expanded on the themes he had outlined at the reception. Bursts of applause interrupted him eight times and when he concluded the committee leaped to their feet in support of their candidate. Naturally, the rest of the audience took its cue from them and the mayor received a standing ovation.

After the local television crews finished interviewing the mayor, we headed for the B'nai B'rith luncheon. When we got there I was told to sit in the car. Louis and Nicastri were back with the mayor in exactly eight minutes.

"That went well, S.H.," Nicastri pronounced.

"Yes, it did. Jews have a lot of money. Make sure we hit them for heavy contributions. Fraleigh, what security will we have at the Black Caucus?" the mayor asked with his own peculiar people-oriented charm.

"Chief Robinson and I will be your security," I said. I could have included Carruthers, but I didn't want to distract him from his chauffeuring duties.

"These black groups can get out of hand," the mayor said.

"This group isn't radical or dangerous," Louis said.

"Just to be on the safe side, Mayor," Nicastri cut in, "I contacted Captain Petrie and we will have five uniformed officers outside the meeting hall and five detectives inside."

"Tom, I wish you'd go through me or Chief Fraleigh on these assignments. I've told you before that it can cause real trouble if we don't coordinate things."

"He was in a hurry, Louis. It was my fault really. I still remember some of those Black Panther escapades and I wanted to be sure we were protected," Middleston said.

Louis started to tell the mayor that some members of the Black Caucus even thought the NAACP was too strident, but he swallowed it and stayed silent.

The mayor was almost as well received at the Black Caucus meeting as at the business lunch. The only negative note was a complaint about all the policemen present. Middleston brushed it away, saying, "Chief Robinson and Chief Fraleigh are especially cautious men." There was no talk of stopping welfare cheats. Middleston mentioned his appointment of Louis three times and Doctor Martin Luther King four.

The mayor was on a roll. The black group pressed his hand as warmly as the others had.

"The mayor needs to speak with you, Chief," Nicastri said when we got to City Hall. Middleston had ignored us, getting out of the car and walking straight into City Hall.

"He'll have to wait. I need to meet with Fraleigh right now on several of these cases that are getting red hot."

"I'll tell him what you said," the mayor's aide said as ominously as possible for someone five foot four. Louis put his arm around my shoulder and said, "Come on, old buddy, I'll buy you a beer."

But in a nearby cocktail lounge he ordered a double

bourbon. I sipped at a light beer. "You look tired, Louis. Not that I blame you, having to put up with that hypocritical bullshit all day. I'm tired after just a couple of hours of it."

"Ease up, Fraleigh. The mayor has been under some stress lately. Apparently there have been some problems in raising campaign money for his Senate run. He isn't usually so—"

"So much of an asshole," I said.

He frowned. Then laughed. "OK. I won't bother to try to change anything in that thick skull of yours. Tell me about the gray van rapist and the Uzi gang and how your interviewing is going."

We spent the next two hours on police stuff. He had three more doubles. He cracked up when I told him about the Block's and English's interview questions. When we spoke of cases he suggested solutions and techniques I hadn't thought of. He was so good that he usually just asked me a question and so it looked like I came up with the answer myself. Louis had a masters degree in public administration, but he hadn't learned his people skills in school. That was inside him. It must have been especially frustrating for him to watch Middleston cold indifference.

"By the way, you had me a little worried when that old guy asked you about organizing the detective bureau. 'Well begun is half done.' Where the heck did you come up with that one?"

"Aristotle," I said, knocking off the rest of my beer.

Louis just shook his head back and forth. At 1900 hours we broke up the session. He gave me a friendly punch in the shoulder. It was a pleasant Friday. I left Louis, looking forward to a leisurely weekend, feeling better about things than I had for some time. That is, until I got to the office and found the anonymous note on my desk.

Seven

BECAUSE OF THE NOTE I DECIDED TO BORROW A SUR-
veillance van from friends in the federal drug unit in
San Francisco. The Block picked it up the next morning. The Drug Enforcement Administration vehicle was
roomy and new. That was good. What was bad was the
heat. The noisy air-conditioner would have signaled that
the van was occupied. It would have blown the stakeout
so we left it off.

By 1130 hours on Saturday morning, we were in danger of melting. At least, the Block and I were. Paul
English sat with his usual cool detachment, amused at
our discomfort. He had been bugging us with long-
winded descriptions of the history of beach erosion
along the California coast. I had binoculars trained on
Captain Petrie's Santa Cruz beach-front house. Thirty
miles out of our jurisdiction.

"Hey Fraleigh! How come a few months ago when
you was only a sergeant, we didn't get stuck with these
crap surveillances, but now that you're chief of detectives we got to roast out here? And how come we're
working a cop?"

I answered the Block before Paul could encourage his
bitching. "I explained it to you three times already. The
information was very specific and sounded good. If it's

true, it means that Petrie is a heavy dope dealer." I left unsaid my conviction that the note had come from a member of our newly formed police department.

The note, now resting in my office safe, was on police department stationery, for one thing. In addition, it was penned in standard cop bureaucratese. But what made me really believe that a cop had written it was the promise that a suitcase full of cocaine with a "stepped-on" value of three million dollars would be delivered. Only cops and dopers used the term "stepped-on" to describe the process of diluting drugs of high purity so that street profits are greatly multiplied. Somehow, I couldn't picture a doper typing the note on police stationery and depositing it on my desk.

"Yeah, but he's still a detective captain with twenty years in harness."

"Are you suggesting differential treatment for dope dealers who carry badges, Block?" English said.

I cut the conversation off. "Paul, see if you can get some pictures of that white Caddy. That's the second time it's cruised the house."

Grabbing the Nikon with the telephoto lens attached, he moved quickly toward the window. Anyone looking at the van's outside panel window would see only the standard moronic painted landscape. The specially manufactured one-way glass gave us an unobstructed view.

The Caddy pulled smoothly into the curb. I heard the motor in the camera purring as Paul took one shot after another. The Block picked up the other pair of binoculars. I activated the tape recorder.

"Eleven forty-two hours." I spoke into the machine propped conveniently on the foldout writing bench to my left. "A white, late-model Cadillac, license plate 1HMK853, California, has slowly passed the subject's house twice in the last five minutes. It has now stopped. We can't see how many occupants yet."

Someone was getting out of the front passenger seat.

"Holy shit!" the Block said. I frowned at him. Now

I would have to edit the damn tape. I could just see some wimpy judge excluding the tape evidence because cops used foul language.

Oblivious, he continued. "Look who that is!"

Holy shit, I said to myself.

"It's that little scumball, Nicasto."

"Nicastri," English corrected him. "The mayor's lawyer."

"Paul, don't use all the film. I have a feeling we're going to see more and I want pictures of all the players."

"Don't fret. I have the Minolta loaded, ready to go."

"Goody for you, English. Fraleigh will give you a gold star."

Block turned to me and pleaded, "How long do I have to listen to his college bullshit and melt in this Turkish bath?"

"You? I ought to get hazard pay for having to put up with you two. Paul, can you please reload the Nikon?"

"Hazard pay, my ass. You ought to get a pay cut, Fraleigh. If you were a good supervisor you'd straighten him out. I oughta file a grievance."

"Have no fear, big chief, I have extra film. I will reload the Nikon at the opportune moment providing that you can get the Block to stop harassing me," Paul said.

Another figure was emerging from the car and our highly professional discourse was temporarily delayed as we strained to make out who it was. I could see Paul silently laughing now that he had both of us complaining, but he held the camera steady. We would have top quality pictures from him as usual.

Clicking away, he deftly changed cameras in time to record a dark-skinned man of sixty with an impressive nose slowly getting out of the rear seat to join Nicastri on the sidewalk. The little lawyer was elegantly clothed as usual. His expensive dark pinstriped summer suit made the taller, olive-skinned man in the tan sports shirt and slacks look like a street peddler. Except that no peddler moved with such self-importance. Like Nicastri, he glanced around searchingly, squinting into the sun to look directly at our van. I held my breath, but we had been careful.

We were slightly above and to the right of them, a hundred yards away in the public beach parking lot, and had allowed two compact cars between the van and the street. Our one-way glass window looked over the roofs of the cars. Petrie's house commanded a prime location looking out on the Pacific Ocean. The sparkling blue water and pure white sand of the beach only made the heat in the van more painful. I had to admit the view made Petrie's commute worth it. Our unknown informant had indicated that the residence went for a cool four hundred fifty K. It was a lot of house even for the most thrifty policeman.

Like other houses overlooking the ocean it was spacious, modern, and built close to the street. Large picture windows faced the beach and the upper story had oval windows and multiple stained glass portholes. There were two large skylights on the roof. Wooden shakes weathered gray by the salt air covered the roof and walls of the structure. Sliding glass doors opened to a second-floor deck of about four hundred square feet. There were three chaise lounges and a large outdoor table with six chairs. The table came with a sizable bright green and white umbrella.

"Who is that guy? I seen him someplace," the Block said.

The mystery man reached down to assist a young blond woman from the car. I think we made the ID simultaneously. The Block was the first to speak.

"Oh boy! That's Carol Mansell. What a piece. Look at those tits. And her ass! She can sit on my face any time she wants. And besides the body, she can sing. Not that she did though, when those senators were grilling her." He chuckled; his two hundred eighty pounds shook the van on its springs.

Carol Mansell had been a top-of-the-charts pop singer

for the past few years. Her familiar face and figure had immediately clued us as to who the lean tall man was. "Don Alex Fortono has honored us with his presence," Paul said.

Carol wore a light pink summer dress with high-heeled shoes of the same color. Her neckline was plunging and slits in the dress showed off her thighs and bare legs to good advantage. The wholesome girlish face looked just the same as it did on her television specials. Her heels put her an inch taller than her companion.

The front door of the house was opened by a blue-jeaned Captain Richard Petrie. He was of medium height, solidly built, and partially bald. There was nothing about him that would make him stand out in a crowd. He shook as many hands as he could while hustling his guests inside. Before going in, he likewise did the squint bit, looking up and down the street. He ignored us. The van was just one more vehicle for unloading a bunch of brats on their Saturday outing to the beach. I had heard Paul's camera speeding up and was confident that we had some pictures of the whole group before they had gotten inside.

"Did you get all of them?" the Block asked.

"I certainly did, even though Fraleigh's influence with the Feds wasn't strong enough for them to lend the videotaping equipment that comes with this vehicle."

"Yeah. He couldn't even get us a van with a toilet. Didn't you tell them Fed assholes our taxes pay their salary, Fraleigh?"

"Video doesn't have anywhere near the quality of photographs, especially at this distance," I said, but I wasn't really listening to them. From the moment the little weasel, Thomas Nicastri, had stepped out of the Caddy, I knew we were into some deep problems. But what was really mind-boggling was that he had been joined by the two stars of the recently televised United States Senate subcommittee hearings on organized crime: show business celebrity Carol Mansell and her boyfriend, mob boss of the West Alex Fortono. Fortono had come out of Chicago, working his way up the mob ladder by making hits and expanding gambling and loansharking activities. He was especially valued for increasing the mob's corruption of labor unions and public officials. Ten years earlier he had been designated as boss of all mob activities west of Las Vegas.

"Here comes another from the Caddy. I seen a signal. They opened and shut the blinds in the house twice, real quick. It must of let this turkey know to move his rear end," the Block said. Paul took the turkey's picture for our album.

The driver was just under six feet. He removed a brown suitcase about three feet by three feet from the trunk of the car. He was muscular but its weight bent him over to the right. The door to the house opened when he got to the top step and closed almost before he got his carcass inside.

The anonymous note had promised that a brown suitcase full of Colombian cocaine with a stepped-on value of three million bucks would be delivered to Petrie's house at twelve noon. My watch read 1148 hours.

Without being able to prove that the informant was reliable—that his info had provided at least two previous convictions—I knew we couldn't convince a judge to give us a search warrant.

I kept one eye on the house and the other on the Block, who was pissing noisily into a Mason jar. It showed the progress of scientific policing, I guess. We used to piss all over ourselves, using narrow-necked soda bottles while doing surveillance in automobiles. Although this comfortable van came equipped with a toilet, it was padlocked and a crudely printed sign informed us that it was out of order. Wide-necked Mason jars had been provided as an alternative. What made me uneasy was whether even the big jar was adequate for the Block. The size of his cock reminded me of the old thick rubber billy clubs we were issued and he had been venting into the jar with the velocity of a fire hose for what seemed like an awfully long time.

Finally he sighed and capped the almost full jar. He placed it neatly in its slot on the wooden rack containing three Remington automatic shotguns and four flak-repellent vests. The springs groaned as he returned to plop down behind me on the bench stretching along the van's side wall.

We continued to sit on the house. Skaters and cyclists streamed past on the sidewalk. Unwary pedestrians leaving their cars to walk to the cliff edge and gaze down at the ocean risked maiming when they crossed the sidewalk. It got even hotter. I felt sweat drenching through everything I was wearing. Much earlier, we had discarded our guns to keep them dry. My Magnum was on the folding table beside the Block's nine-millimeter automatic. Paul had placed a six-inch razor-sharp commando throwing knife next to our weapons. I was sure he had planned it in advance to tick me off. I didn't give him the satisfaction of asking why he was carrying an unauthorizied weapon or of inquiring if he was packing a handgun as required. He often employed ankle and groin holsters or equally exotic receptacles for his varied collection of firearms. Marge, the waitress, wasn't the only female to mistake him for Robert Redford. His dreamy blue eyes had lulled a number of criminals into talking their way into prison. The same eyes had also brought comely women sighing their way into his bed. He wore brown walking shorts, sandals, and a "Save the Whales" T-shirt, which earned contemptuous looks from the Block.

Finally I gave in to the heat and followed the Block's example. Fifteen minutes after we began the surveillance he had stripped to his shorts, which were a garish violet with a polka-dot pattern. I pulled off my shirt and trousers. Somewhat more comfortable, I looked over at him and felt an unaccustomed sympathy. Seeing him unclothed made me realize, once again, how right his nickname was. He did look like a massive hulk or block of something. His round head had a grizzly fuzz that passed for hair. His brown beady eyes stared from under dark, bushy eyebrows. He had no visible neck and his huge body was covered with dark hair so thick it looked like fur and nearly covered the bullet wound on his chest. It had only been a year since the Stone case ambush, but his hair grew so quickly that the scar was barely visible. Water ran off him like he was caught in a rainstorm.

Paul held up a hand, warning us to silence. He pointed to the van's rear door. I hadn't heard anything, but now I saw that someone was working the handle back and forth. I silently picked up my Magnum as Paul tiptoed to the rear one-way window. He returned noiselessly to where we sat frozen. Grinning, he whispered, "It's a kid trying a car clout."

I nodded to the Block to scare him off. He yanked the rear door open. I caught a glimpse of two boys around eleven or twelve. They couldn't see into the van's dark interior but I saw that they were both blue-eyed, blond, and golden tan. They could have served as models for some television show about California's beautiful life-style. That is, until they spotted the Block and heard his hoarse command: "Get lost, ya little shits!" Their mouths dropped open in terror and they set a speed record beating it across the parking lot. A vision of them back on Momma's beach blanket babbling about seeing a furry monster in a dark van made me laugh.

The Block had relocked the door. "If you can see anything fucking funny, Fraleigh, I'd like to know what it is. Ever since you talked us into coming up here with you and Louis, its been crap piled on shit. I don't know what the hell I was thinking of when I said I'd come."

"You were probably thinking of the assault charges that would have been prosecuted against you if Fraleigh hadn't negotiated your departure," Paul answered for me.

"You . . . you. . . . " The Block was ready to explode in the heat. "What about the morals rap they had on you? When that broad found out you wasn't just banging her, but her fourteen-year-old daughter, too, she blew the whistle on you.''

I silenced their jabbering with a wave of the binoculars. Paul grabbed the camera and churned out some more pictures of Petrie's guests unhurriedly walking to the car. There was no sign of the suitcase. Its carrier slipped behind the wheel and had his passengers gliding down the street before I had even finished telling the tape recorder that the white Cadillac was rolling south.

There was no possibility of catching them with the van. Their hawk-eyed driver would have spotted it within thirty seconds anyway. I pulled on my trousers.

Sliding in front of the curtain that hid us from anyone peering in the front windshield, I started the motor, turned the air-conditioner on full blast, and drove to the far, shady end of the parking lot, which was relatively empty because of its distance from the beach. Turning the motor off, I switched on the generator so that the air-conditioner would run.

My mind tried to cope with what we had just seen. Four months ago our boss, Louis Robinson, had been appointed police chief by Solly the Mayor and served at his pleasure. We had just observed the mayor's right-hand man in what looked like a big dope deal. We couldn't actually prove that right now, but there was no doubt at all about his visiting a captain of detectives in the company of one of the biggest mobsters in the United States. All of which provided a fascinating question for us law enforcement professionals. What the hell did we do next?

Eight

WE SAT IN THE REAR OF THE VAN. THE BLOCK TOOK three cans from the little refrigerator that also ran off the generator. I had called him that morning at 0600 hours to let him know where to pick up the vehicle. I told him firmly not to stock any beer, anticipating his reaction when he spied the refrigerator. Now, without comment, he handed me a can of Bud Light. He took a Coors regular for himself. Paul was drinking a can of liquid wheat germ.

The beer felt good going down my hot throat. I decided to forgo my stern reprimand of the Block for disobeying orders. From time to time, either he or English came up with some useful suggestions. Today, however, Paul had steered the Block toward an analysis of the situation that wasn't going to help a bit.

"What the hell can you expect from these wops?" the Block asked. "They're always into dope, gambling, pimping, and anything else they can think of. This legalized casino gambling pilot project stuff probably drew them like a bitch in heat."

"Solly the Mayor isn't Italian," Paul said.

"No. He's a fine WASP, just like you. All that means is that you bastards got here first and stole more than everyone else, so now you think you're all hot shit and look down your noses at other people."

"Don't forget Carol Mansell. I think she's Jewish," Paul encouraged him.

"Sure. The wops aren't smart enough to handle money by themselves so they have to have a Jew around. 'Course they ain't dumb enough to trust a WASP like the mayor. But you can't go wrong getting a Jew to handle your dough providing you watch him close and let 'im know he's dead if you catch 'im cheating."

I began to drift out of the conversation as Paul skillfully headed the Block into commenting on blacks, Orientals, Mexicans, Indians, and others.

"Men willingly believe what they wish," Paul said.

"Yeah. Ain't that hot shit? What do you think, Fraleigh?"

The Block brought me back from unpleasant wonderings about Petrie, Nicastri, and the mayor. "The Stanford genius here ain't into talking sense today, but I say Petrie is guilty as hell." I noticed that he had knocked off another Coors while I had been daydreaming. His meathook hands had crushed the can flat, faithfully following examples set by the football players in television commercials.

"It's almost too pat. We get an anonymous note that a cop is doing dope. But when we stake him out, we get DeLorean-caliber celebs. It almost feels like we were set up for something," I said.

"Things either are what they appear to be; or they neither are, nor appear to be; or they are, and do not appear to be; or they are not, and yet appear to be. It is up to the wise to distinguish."

The Block and I were careful to give no sign that we heard what Paul had said. Yet somewhere in that gobbledygook he was probably right.

"Petrie's dirty. I'd bet anything. Our asshole mayor and his so-called assistant are so dumb that nothing they'd do would surprise me. Fortinis is the one I can't figure. He wouldn't get within ten miles of any dope."

"Fortono," Paul corrected him, although he knew it was hopeless.

I didn't agree with the Block. Solly and Nicastri were anything but dumb. But his instincts were correct. The mayor was enormously wealthy and hoods of Fortono's stature financed dope deals, but they never got close to the stuff personally. They had too much to lose.

"You better call Louis, Fraleigh, so he can tell us what the fuck we do next," the Block said.

"Obsequiousness begets friends, truth hatred."

Despite my better judgment, I asked Paul, "Is that supposed to mean anything besides telling us that you went to college?"

"Yeah. It means that you should have got rid of him years ago."

Paul ignored the Block. "Terence advised a century and a half before Christ that it is sometimes wise to protect your friends from truth. Since we really know nothing specific at the moment, it might be better not to burden Louis. After all, he's with the mayor on a daily basis. The knowledge would affect their relationship."

"That's exactly why I want to tell him as soon as possible," I said.

"You forget my earlier comment."

"You better believe we forgot it. But remember this, English." The Block, his good humor restored by the air-conditioner and beer, was in danger of choking with laughter. "Bullshit begets bullshit."

Louis refused to carry a pager, which meant I had to call communications when he didn't answer his home phone. I used the administrative number. After the eleventh ring I hung up and dialed the emergency number. It rang and rang. Saturday afternoon was one of the slowest times for incoming calls for service, and I wondered what the hell they were doing. I also had time to wonder how much more beer the Block was consuming while I sweated in the phone booth.

"Police emergency, Operator Turk." The male voice was high pitched.

"This is Chief Fraleigh. Do you have a number where I can reach Chief Robinson?"

"Yes sir. He called about an hour ago and left one."

I hunched the phone into my neck, holding a piece of paper firmly on the phone booth counter while I got out my pen. Perspiration rolled off my hand onto the paper. "OK, go ahead," I told the communications clerk.

"I'm sorry, sir, I'm not authorized to release this number. In fact, Chief, this is the emergency line and we're not even supposed to take these administrative calls."

"That's all right, Turk. I'll take full responsibility. This is an emergency." I watched a pool of sweat forming beneath my hand where it rested on the counter.

"I'm afraid that doesn't make any difference, Chief. Our written directives say we can't release the number."

"Just a minute." I stepped out of the booth and took a deep breath of hot humid air, pulling a sopping wet shirt away from my skin. A few months ago I would have snarled at Turk, "Listen you mealy-mouthed squirt, give me the number before I come down there and wring your neck." I would have gotten the number instantly. Now I was of too lofty a rank to offend anyone without risking bringing a strike or job action. I stepped back into the phone booth.

"By the way, Turd, I called the administrative number and it rang eleven times. And the emergency number took eight rings. Is is that busy down there?"

"It's Turk, sir, but, er, well, no. I mean I've been busy, but . . ."

"I see. Put your supervisor on, will you."

"Er, she's not at her desk just now, Chief . . ."

"OK, son. I want you to get the dispatcher to call the watch commander to—"

"Er, Chief Fraleigh, sir. If you could give me your

radio number for verification I'll give you the number Chief Robinson left. I'm sure it will be OK.''

"Thank you, Turd," I said, after we exchanged numbers.

"It's Turk, sir. T-U-R . . ."

I hung up, understanding a little bit more about how dictatorships got started. Someone with enough machine guns simply lost patience and started putting people like Turk up against the wall.

I dropped another twenty cents into the phone and dialed the number he had given me. The phone rang four times before it was answered. I could hear a good deal of conversation and some laughter in the background. "Mayor Middleston's residence." Jesus! I held the phone without speaking. The sweat continued to run down my arm. A couple of drops splashed on the floor of the booth.

"Hello, is anybody there?"

The thin male voice was almost a parody of Middleston's Ivy League tones. I swallowed. "Yes. I'd like to speak to Louis Robinson." What the hell was Louis doing with Middleston on a Saturday afternoon?

"Oh, Chief Robinson. Whom may I say is calling?"

"You may say Fraleigh, Chief Fraleigh."

"Yes. Do hang on. I know he's here someplace. I'll locate him directly."

"Delightful," I said, but he had already departed to do his locating. I listened to the crowd noise coming over the phone, wondering how many people were there.

"Fraleigh! You should be here, old buddy. The mayor is throwing a great party. A big new electronics corporation is locating its headquarters here. We're celebrating." Louis's voice had a bourbon blur to it, something that I had heard more frequently of late. "You can't believe who's on my arm. But I'll give you a hint. She's gorgeous and she's giving me singing lessons."

I listened to a sexy feminine laugh and a deep-throated "Oh, Louis." For a moment I toyed with the idea of telling Louis that my guess was Carol Mansell. Instead I said, "Louis, I need to see you someplace private as soon as possible."

"Damn it, Fraleigh, you're not even going to guess, are you? I know you wouldn't believe it, but Carol Mansell and I are harmonizing together."

"Yeah. That's great, Louis, but I still need to see you pronto."

"What? Just when I'm learning to carry a tune after all these years? I really mean it, Fraleigh. Wait a minute. Here, Carol, say hello to Fraleigh."

"Hello, Fraleigh. This is Carol Mansell. We're having a great party. Come on over."

"Yeah, come on over, Fraleigh." Louis had gotten back on.

"I'll call you later, Louis." I realized my little tale of intrigue would have to wait until Louis's blood alcohol count subsided by a few digits.

"You know what, Fraleigh, you got to learn to relax on weekends."

"I'm working on it. Hey, Louis, do me a favor and go home alone, OK?"

"Not if I can help it. This is the chance of a lifetime. Carol swears she can even teach a dummy like me to sing. Call me tomorrow." He hung up.

I returned to the van and told them about warning Louis against singing lessons. Paul raised his eyebrows. "Carol was actually with Louis?"

"That don't sound good," the Block said. "You want I should take her into protective custody?"

The Feds had insisted that the vehicle be returned to their garage by 1800 hours, so Paul drove us a mile inland to the shopping center parking lot where we had met that morning. I told him to keep his distance, to use his car to sit on Captain Petrie's house, and to follow Petrie or anyone else leaving who looked interesting. Under the Block's disapproving, envious eyes, he got into his maroon Porsche and gunned off into the evening traffic. Only in California was a maroon Porsche inconspicuous enough for a stakeout.

"How come I have to drive this heap all the way back to San Francisco?"

"I'm sure Paul would have been glad to do it. Why didn't you ask before he took off?" I said, watching his face turn that peculiar red color it took on when anger and beer combined.

"You're pissing into the wind, Fraleigh. You know damn well he wouldn't of done it."

"Yeah, maybe you're right, but your car's in the city so you might as well do it. We'll make it up to you. I'll buy you dinner before we go back to Petrie's."

"Go back to Petrie's? You're a great boss, Fraleigh. You mean after I busted my balls for you all week, I got to spend three hours driving to San Francisco and back and then work Saturday night, too?"

I hopped out of the van without answering. It wasn't my fault that he got so touchy over the demands of police work. I slid behind the wheel of the new police department Chevrolet Caprice provided for me by grateful taxpayers. Watching the van pull wildly out of the parking lot, I closed my eyes as two oncoming cars banged fenders to avoid hitting the Block.

It took me twenty-five minutes to drive back over the mountain to headquarters. All the traffic was going the other way to the beach. I wondered what it would be like to have weekends off. I pulled into my spot in the police parking lot. Using my key, I opened the back door and went up a rear staircase.

The place was deserted on a Saturday afternoon. A gray-haired detective wearing eyeglasses entered a door at the far end of the room. He sat at a desk and picked up the telephone. If it hadn't been for the Colt .45 automatic in his shoulder holster and the handcuffs draped through his belt he could have been mistaken for a travel agent. The room itself might have been a travel agency office except for the pictures of our clientele posted on the walls. They were as exotic as travel posters, but somehow not as appealing.

There was a note on my desk that Tony White had called that morning. Apparently he had received my note. He called me on a Saturday morning. Impressed, I dialed his number. His recorded voice told me that I should try again on Monday morning, but if it was an emergency I should call the parole agency's central number. I did just that and talked to some jerk in Sacramento who refused to give me Tony's home number even after I explained the whole scenario with Ned Dorn. Hanging up, I got to work.

I ran the Caddy registration on the computer terminal. The Department of Motor Vehicle files in Sacramento showed that a white male named Phillip Caruso was the vehicle owner. He resided at 3240 Thornton Drive in our fair city. His height, weight, hair coloring, and DOB (Date of Birth) indicated that he was probably the Caddy driver. Then I queried the California Department of Justice criminal history file. It showed an arrest two years ago in Los Angeles for assault with a deadly weapon. The charge was still pending.

I also accessed the FBI's NCIC (National Criminal Information Center) in Washington, D.C. Five years ago, Phillip, aka Crazy Phil, had been charged with two felony counts for conspiracy to sell narcotics in Chicago. Charges dismissed. The following year he had been busted on suspicion of murder. A few months later another arrest was listed—again conspiracy to sell narcotics. These charges had also been dismissed. Not too surprising to anyone who followed the FBI ''Greylord'' sting, which had nailed a dozen or so crooked lawyers and judges in Chicago courts.

The mayor's lawyer was keeping strange company, even for California. I dictated the case report on what we had so far and locked the cassette in my desk drawer. We sure didn't want the typing pool to do this transcript.

At 1915 hours, I relieved Paul in the beach parking

lot. No visitors, no action, he reported. I asked him to tell the Block, who hadn't returned from San Francisco, that I expected to be relieved at midnight. Casually, he tossed our three-thousand-dollar Hound Dog apparatus onto the front seat of my car. I missed a swallow as the sensitive electronic device teetered on the edge of the seat, almost crashing to the floor. Unconcerned, Paul gave his dreamy smile and was off.

In two hours my car would be conspicuous as the only one in the lot. However, my immediate problem was to avoid chitchat with the stream of visitors pulling in and out and to watch Petrie's place at least as much as I did the bikini-clad women still on the beach and some of the more spectacular skaters in short shorts. I checked the Hound Dog to make sure the magnet was clean and the transmitter switch on. If you got a chance to stick it under someone's bumper or fender, there usually wasn't much time to fuss. I remember the Block's embarrassment two years earlier, when we lost a tail waiting in vain for the beeper signals to tell us where the other vehicle was going. The next day, he recovered the equipment and found that it hadn't been turned on. He had hurriedly stuck it under the bumper without pushing the "on" switch. Our receiver had been useless. Of course, Paul still reminded him of it occasionally.

I brought Petrie's personnel file with me to go over it once again. As the Block had said, Petrie had entered law enforcement almost twenty years ago. Yet it was a strange career. He had actually only served on active police duty for eleven of those years. He had been with four different police agencies and although he had attained the rank of detective captain he had never passed a civil service promotion exam. Each of the four law enforcement agencies granted him mandatory military leave. He was an officer in the Army Reserve and had held the rank of major since last year. Unlike other cops in the reserves, who did two weeks or thirty days a year, Petrie for some reason had once been extended for a two-year tour, and at other times for periods of six months, fourteen months, and so on. It wasn't clear to me whether the agencies were legally required to grant all of this leave, but they had, and it counted toward seniority.

Two years earlier the politically ambitious county district attorney had appointed Petrie as captain of detectives. It was a political appointment with no experience or testing requirements.

I had argued with Louis. "The DA has twelve investigators. Everybody knows they're gofers. DA investigators are OK for serving process and other minor-league stuff, but when the DA needs investigation he wants real dicks. He comes to us. I'm only going to have three detective captains under me. I don't want one of them to be Petrie, Louis. He doesn't have the investigatory or supervisory background. His title of detective captain is a joke and you know it. What little time he did in policing was on patrol."

"Fraleigh," Louis told me, "to get along in this world you have to go along. I don't have autonomy, and the mayor has taken a personal interest in this one."

"When you were convincing me to come with you, I seem to remember you telling me that we could do it the right way, not compromising anymore."

He sighed. "You're unreasonable. They've pretty much given us a free hand, haven't they?"

"Are you kidding? That little weasel Nicastri is in my office every day putting a plug in for this guy or that guy to be hired."

"Yes, and you routinely turn down anyone that he recommends."

"Right. And you routinely overrule me in half those cases."

"Not routinely." He smiled. "Lighten up. You know the decision has been made. Come on, I'll buy dinner tonight. Come on." He put his arm around my shoulder and pulled me along with him to the door.

Now, scanning the files, I remembered being puzzled

that Petrie's required letters requesting leave extensions had come from some exotic places. Hong Kong, Saigon, Beirut, Tokyo, and other locations. Yet his assignment was always listed as to G-2 (Intelligence) at the Pentagon. I had asked about it when I interviewed him.

"Just routine, Chief," he said. He wasn't insubordinate, but his easy answer, his cockiness were evident. He knew his hiring had been wired. Inwardly he was laughing at me, knowing that the interview wasn't going to change anything.

"Did your military service give you any experience in supervising investigations?"

"I'm afraid it's all classified, Chief. I'm not allowed to discuss it."

I had stared hard at the balding, nondescript forty-three-year-old. His return gaze was steady, unperturbed, with just a shadow of amusement in his eyes. A federal spook buried in local policing. I didn't like it.

I went back to Louis, knowing that I was going to lose, to plead once more not to hire Petrie. I lost. Petrie came on board the next day and was quiet and competent. I forgot about him until the anonymous note. Now I was sitting on his house wondering if a mobster called Crazy Phil would reappear in a white Cadillac.

Nine

STANDING IN THE HOSPITAL EMERGENCY ROOM, I closed out all those memories of how we had catapulted into the intrigues of Silicon City just four months ago. I stood near Janice as the medical team fluttered around. They pulled her skirt off. She did wear panties. They were bikini, but so soaked in blood that it was impossible to identify the color. A tall, thin, sandy-haired doctor peered at me from behind spectacles.

"Out!" He pointed at the door.

"I'm a police officer."

"Did you shoot her?"

"No."

"Is she under arrest?"

"No." I wanted to belt him for not working on her.

"Then please wait outside."

I started for the door. "No. I want him near me." Janice had come to. I walked over and took her hand.

The doctor looked disgusted, then shrugged. The nurse had cut her panties away. There was an ugly wound about two inches below her navel. It was oozing dark red blood.

"We'll need plasma," the doctor said.

"No. I'm not taking a chance on AIDS." Amazingly, her voice, although very low, was firm.

"There's almost no risk and it's imperative that we replenish you. You've lost a lot of blood," the doctor said.

"He can donate." She nodded toward me.

His white-jacketed shoulders stiffened. "Damn it. This isn't a game. You're in critical condition."

"What type blood are you?" I asked her.

"O positive."

I turned to the doctor. "I have the same type. What do you say?"

"Well, if you will then agree that I can begin treating the patient . . ."

He must have learned his bedside manner in a concentration camp. A nurse pushed me onto a table next to Janice. They didn't take our word on the blood types. The nurse took samples from both of us, messed with a quick analysis, and then efficiently set up the apparatus. Within five minutes I watched red drops of my blood slowly flowing from the glass jar above her through a transparent tube into her vein.

The medical team was somehow busy and hovering at the same time. I didn't dare ask anyone how long this was going to take. I knew that I belonged at the crime scene, and should be taking charge of the operation to nail Crazy Phil Caruso for the murder of Thomas Nicastri. I saw Janice's labored breathing and daydreamed about turning the Uzi on Crazy Phil.

The doctor gave an order muffled by his gauze mask. They disconnected me from Janice and wheeled her out, the partially filled transfusion jar with her. The nurse deftly plugged me into another jar, explaining that Janice was going to the X-ray unit.

"And then?" I asked.

"Surgery, I assume."

Twenty-five minutes later they unplugged me and slapped a Band-Aid over the needle hole in my arm. It must have been a half-hour before the doctor returned.

He motioned me over to the X-ray illuminator. He

pushed a switch and light came on behind the black negatives.

"The bullet has lodged in the left lumbar region." He pointed to a small, round, black spot on the picture. "Was she hit more than once?"

"I don't know. He fired a burst of shots. She went down immediately."

"And where were you? Never mind. The point is that the bullet entered here and slashed through her abdomen. I can't tell how much damage has been done, but it is clear that internal bleeding is heavy. It appears that the duodenum, transverse colon, and large intestine have been injured. Surgery is required. You have already given a pint of blood, I can't ask you for more, but it is probable that she will require more blood. I want your agreement that we can use plasma if required."

"I can give another pint safely, can't I?"

"I don't recommend it."

"I'm not asking for a recommendation. Let's not give her plasma until I run out, OK?"

"Why are you so concerned?"

"She was trying to help me. I should have kept her out of it."

"Humph." He turned to leave.

"Doctor?"

"Very well, just stand by."

"Is she going to be all right?"

"I don't know. Severe injury, shock, loss of blood. Still, you got her here quickly enough and she's young and healthy." He turned and left.

They steered me into a side room. One of the emergency room nurses brought me orange juice, coffee, and a doughnut from their lounge. "It will help replenish the blood." She was a small middle-aged woman without makeup. She marched briskly away, but stopped and turned at the door. A surprisingly bright smile lit her face. "Officer, it was awfully nice the way you rushed her in here and gave blood. Don't pay any attention to Jangles."

I frowned.

"The doctor. We call him Doctor Jangles. You know, jangled nerves. He's really a pleasant man outside the emergency room. A good surgeon. Your friend is going to be all right."

I called Louis, waiting for ten rings before hanging up. He lived by himself. Louis never had told me any more about why he and Sarah had broken up.

I wondered where the hell he was. It was near midnight. The mayor's aide had been wasted two hours ago and the police chief was nowhere to be found. The merry mood of Louis and Carol Mansell had come through over the phone when I spoke to them at the mayor's party. I had an uneasy feeling that she was the reason for Louis being incommunicado.

Early on, I had called communications, telling them that I would be at the hospital indefinitely. Louis still had not called in to leave a phone number. I gave them Paul English's and the Block's radio call numbers, requesting that they be directed to contact me as soon as possible. Nicastri had been pronounced DOA at the scene from multiple gunshot wounds. I and the communications clerk who gave me the news managed to control our grief over the loss of such a dedicated public servant. Caruso had been sighted in the area by a patrol officer, but was still at large.

A command post had been established and a massive search was under way. I called the command post. The lieutenant in charge confirmed that there were no new developments. The Block and English had arrived a few minutes earlier. Paul was handling the media. Silicon City's local newspaper and its two television and radio stations were there, as well as the networks from San Francisco who covered all big stories in the Bay area.

I sat for the next hour waiting for the doctor, resisting the urge to contact the command post. I tried Louis twice more. No answer. Time flashed by while my mind rehashed the events of the last four months in Silicon City. Standing in the corridor, I saw the doctor get off the elevator at the far end of the building. I tried to read his face. He just looked tired.

"She should survive. It's too early to tell about permanent damage. The round," he dropped it into my palm, "was apparently a ricochet. A nine-millimeter would have torn a hole through her like a tank. As it is, she's been nicked here and there. We stitched her up and with luck she may turn out fine."

"When can I see her?"

"She'll be out of it until late tomorrow morning."

Looking through her purse for the health insurance information, I had come across her brother's number in LA. When I called, a woman's voice informed me that Ken was working. As gently as possible I broke the news that Janice had been injured. The voice on the other end didn't seem very interested. Then again, it was nearly two o'clock in the morning. I left the hospital phone number.

Walking out the emergency doors I saw the Block, Raoul Chavez, and Paul English get out of an unmarked police car.

Ten

"Do you want the good news first or the bad?" the Block asked.

I motioned them back into the nearly deserted public waiting section of the emergency room. A gray, shriveled old man sat in the corner, ignoring us. I wondered if he had just come in to rest. The nurse who had supplied me with juice and coffee sat behind the intake window. She looked up, staring for a moment at the Block. Her eyes shifted and made contact with mine. The same warm smile appeared. I was going to be man of the year with the emergency room nurses' association.

Paul spoke. "A patrol unit picked up Caruso almost immediately after you put out the alarm. However, a slight problem arose when Captain Petrie, the detective captain on standby, arrived." He paused momentarily to look at the old man, who had yelled, "Bastards!" at top volume. His voice had surprising power. He then continued to stare fixedly ahead.

"Right on, Pop," the Block said.

Paul continued in his dry voice. "Although no one called the Captain, he was there almost instantly."

"How does he account for it?"

"Oh, he was on standby, just riding, and picked it up on his scrambler." Paul raised his eyebrows.

A detective lieutenant or captain was assigned to standby duty after five P.M. weekdays and all day Saturday, Sunday, and holidays. They weren't actually on duty, but they had to be available to respond. It enabled the city to save bucks. They were paid a token amount unless they were actually called in.

"Well, at least Caruso's in custody," I said.

"Not for long, amigo," Detective Raoul Chavez cut in.

"What?"

"It seems that Captain Petrie was so outraged by Caruso's criminal acts that he brutally beat a confession out of him. In front of four witnesses. Caruso even told him where he had dumped the Uzi. We recovered it."

"Yeah. Petrie knocked his teeth out without even giving him his Miranda warnings," the Block added.

"That means the gun is inadmissible," I thought out loud.

"Worse than that," Paul went on. "Caruso spilled so many details that it will be difficult to bring any evidence into court."

"And how does veteran Captain Petrie explain forgetting that illegal force and no Miranda warnings mean that everything will be inadmissible?"

"We figured that you, being chief of detectives, might want to ask him that yourself," the Block said. "As for Crazy Phil, you're slipping, Fraleigh. You only hit him once. In the right shoulder. He's in Valley Hospital. The Doc says it ricocheted off the bone and nicked his right lung. It collapsed, but they blew it up again. They say the asshole will even be able to make the prelim in court tomorrow." He shook his head sadly.

Predictably, statements from the help at Lefty's added up to zilch. No one saw or heard anything and no one knew a Mr. Caruso. Mr. Nicastri, the mayor's aide had been there, yes. It seems there was a pending strike by the bartenders' union. The mayor, naturally, was anxious to intervene to prevent it so that Silicon City didn't lose its valuable convention and visitor business. Nicastri had been there on his behalf. He left after a brief meeting with the manager and union delegate. No one was aware of any shooting until the police had rudely interrupted the strip show.

Crazy Phil said he was meeting Nicastri to demand that he take back the white Cadillac the little so and so had sold to him along with a pack of lies about what fine condition it was in. He just happened to have an Uzi along because he thought Nicastri carried a gun and feared his vicious temper. When Nicastri made a motion toward his hip, Phil fired. The script he had come up with wasn't a threat to Neil Simon. Of course, he made no mention of cold-bloodedly gunning down an innocent woman. He probably thought that no witnesses were still alive to contradict his story.

I brought them up to speed on what I'd seen at Lefty's and on Janice's condition.

"One thing Captain Petrie and his buddy Crazy Phil didn't think of when they set up a Supreme Court-protected alibi is that I was a witness, not only to the murder, but also to Janice's shooting. I'm sure that she can identify Caruso. Block, I want you to take the first watch guarding her. Raoul can relieve you in a few hours. Once they begin to put it together, Janice will be a target."

"So will you," Paul said.

"I know. But it will be worth it when I show up at the preliminary hearing tomorrow and see their faces when the motion to suppress the evidence succeeds, but the judge refuses to cut Caruso loose because of my testimony."

"Are you gonna bust Petrie?" the Block asked.

"I don't know." I hesitated. The hell with it. If I couldn't trust these three I couldn't trust anyone. "I need to know how Louis wants this handled, but I haven't been able to get hold of him."

"That's bad. The goddamn media is all over us.

They're already bitching that they can't get a statement from you or Louis,'' the Block said.

''By the way, this is a copy of a note found on the body.'' Paul handed me a five-by-eight-inch piece of memo paper. I read what I recognized as Nicastri's writing: ''Prototype for molecular solitons, protein molecular side chains and gene bacterial inserts re: Yoshomo Tanaka.''

''Got any idea what this means?'' I asked.

''The little prick was probably running around working for Middleston's corporation,'' the Block said. ''You look like shit Fraleigh. You gave blood, got shot at, didn't get no sleep, and let your new lady get hurt. You better get some shut-eye before court so that you can give your name right when you testify.''

''Block, you . . .'' My new lady! What the hell was wrong with these guys? I wanted a key witness protected and right away she was my lady.

Paul stayed with me while the Block went up to the recovery room to guard Janice. Raoul left to get some sleep. ''Do you think Raoul is up to this kind of assignment, Fraleigh?'' Paul asked.

That question had already been in my mind. Two years ago, Raoul and his partner, members of my old department, had been serving a felony arrest warrant for armed robbery. The suspect opened up on them with a nine-millimeter automatic. Raoul's partner had been badly wounded. Raoul had fired a string of three rounds, more to pull the fire away from the other officer than anything else. One of those rounds had killed a four-year-old boy playing outside an adjoining apartment. The robber had escaped and during the next six months Raoul cracked.

He came from a close-knit Chicano family. Their initial resistance to his becoming a cop had changed through the years to a fierce pride in him. But they didn't support him when he was attacked for killing a child. He hit the bottle, closed everyone out, including his wife. His marriage broke up. Eventually he was relieved of duty and finally resigned from the Department.

He phoned me a month after I arrived in Silicon City and asked if he could interview. He was cleaned up and confident. He had been a hell of a cop and a friend. "Raoul, you look good," I greeted him.

"I feel good, Fraleigh. I went through a bad period, but I'm ready to go back to work. More than ready. I'm broke and I ran up some bills."

"What about the old job?"

"They turned me down flat. Can you imagine? Eleven years. All those commendations. Everywhere else I went they don't know me. Don't want to take a chance. But I figured all the years we worked together would count with you. I heard advertising on the radio that Silicon City P.D. was looking for experienced officers. I know that you and Louis Robinson are stand-up guys."

"I only recommend, Raoul. I don't have the final word on hiring."

"Hell, I'm not worried about that. I know Louis listens to you and I worked for him in General Crimes when he was a lieutenant. He knows what kind of work I can do. You don't have any problem recommending me, do you?" His brown eyes fixed on mine.

"No, Raoul. No problem. I'll speak to Louis."

"You are still hiring, aren't you?"

"Yes. We still have a ways to go."

Raoul Chavez was another issue on which Louis and I argued. He had been adamant. The boy killed by Raoul's stray bullet had been black. The mayor would never stand for it. Community relations would be harmed. I pleaded, "He needs this job, Louis. As a man."

"I don't give a damn what he needs. We're not running a convalescent home. Suppose he shoots someone else? The answer is no."

When Raoul came back to see me several weeks later, it was clear that he thought he had been hired. "By the way, Fraleigh," he said, "I forgot to give you this last time I was here."

I took the paper, only half reading it, trying to think how I could tell him that we weren't going to take him. It was a psychiatrist's report on Raoul. I looked at it more closely. It gave him a clean bill of health. Since we were hiring dozens of cops right then, I was pretty sure that Louis wouldn't pick up his name. Later on, I could explain that the psychiatrist's material was new evidence. Raoul had started Friday. Was it only yesterday? Louis didn't know about him yet.

"I think he'll be fine," I told Paul, hoping to God that I was right, for Raoul's sake as well as Janice's.

I drove to my apartment complex. I was so tired that I started walking away from the Caprice with the empty Chief's Special in my pocket. Remembering Ned Dorn, I went back. Opening the car trunk, I exchanged the small pistol for the Magnum. A sense of apprehension came over me. I looked around the dark parking lot, hefting the magnum in my hand for comfort. I still had it in my hand when I let myself in. My digital clock told me it was 0330 hours. I set the alarm for 0800 and collapsed.

The alarm awoke me from a deep sleep. I was stiff and sluggish, but before hitting the shower I called Louis. There was no answer.

Eleven

I WAS DUE IN COURT AT 0930 FOR CARUSO'S ARRAIGN-
ment and the preliminary hearing. I stopped at the hospital at 0900. The Block came to meet me outside the
recovery room. I didn't like the look on his face.

"I tried to call you. I guess you already left. She's
got complications. The doctor's with her now. He's
some kind of prick, ain't he?"

"Block, what did they tell you?"

I was saved the effort of pulling a diagnosis out of
him. Doctor Jangles strode briskly through the swinging
doors of the recovery room and said, "I'm afraid your
witness's condition has worsened. I sewed her internal
wounds, but there's been a good deal of seepage during
the night. I've reserved the operating room. If the
bleeding doesn't slow, if we can't drain accumulated
blood from the abdominal cavities faster than it's seep-
ing in, I'm going to have to open her up again. If she
has any immediate relatives I suggest that you notify
them. Her condition is critical."

"You told me last night that it looked good."

"Look officer . . ." He took a breath. "I don't have
time to waste arguing with you. Also, she'll need at
least another pint of blood."

I looked at my watch. It was 0910. "I'm due in court at nine thirty."

He opened his hands toward me, gesturing impatiently. "I told you there is relatively little risk of contracting AIDS—"

"I already volunteered, but I ain't got the right kind," the Block said.

I took off my jacket, telling the Block to notify the court that I would be late. "Make sure the DA knows how important it is that they hold Caruso until I get there."

This time it took them almost an hour to suck out my blood. They rushed the jar into the operating room, where they had started working on Janice. A nurse I hadn't seen before provided juice and coffee. I asked her how long it would be before we got some news from the operating room.

"The doctor should send word out in about five minutes."

The Block glanced at his watch. It was now 1015 hours. I was really late for court. I decided to wait ten more minutes.

It was twenty-five minutes before an even younger doctor came out. "It looks like it's working out. She won't need additional surgery. The seepage has slowed perceptibly and the drainage technique was successful. It will probably be another hour or so before she's back in the recovery room."

I thanked him and started for the door.

"Take it slow, Fraleigh," the Block warned.

It was unnecessary. I was moving slow and not by choice. Was it two pints of blood in two days or the pressure? Sandra had been a practicing psychologist when we were together. What was the psychological jargon she used to dump on me. Stress? Combat psychosis? Anomie? Whatever it was, I didn't have time to waste on it.

Nevertheless, the early lunch-hour traffic of Silicon Valley was not to be denied. It was 1135 hours when I hit court, just in time to be handed a note by the bailiff. It was from Paul. ''Fraleigh, the judge granted one thirty-minute recess, but refused the second. He suppressed all evidence, castigated the police department, and freed Caruso. The Hound Dog is still on the Cadillac. I'll follow and call from a pay phone, just in case you-know-who is scanning the radio.''

Shit! I couldn't believe it. The judge had cut him loose. I found the deputy district attorney.

''What the hell is going on, Harvey? We nailed the guy cold and the judge cut him loose.''

''Don't blame me, Chief. The police department hasn't been very impressive on this case. First, there's a clear violation of Miranda, probably some excessive force as well. The judge had to act. I've never seen such clear grounds for suppression.''

''Of course you haven't. It was set up that way. Couldn't the judge have waited a few more minutes for my testimony?''

''A few minutes? You were supposed to be here at nine thirty. It's now almost noon.''

''But we sent you a message why I was delayed . . .'' I gave up.

When I got back to the hospital, Janice's brother was there. He had the familiar strut of an LA cop. He was about thirty, six feet tall, broad-shouldered and lean. I could see a family resemblance. His hair was dark brown like hers. They shared the same even features. His eyes burned into me.

''You let my sister get shot.''

I sat down.

''Is that the way you guys work, you hide behind civilians?''

''Do you want to know what happened or make speeches?''

Grudgingly he sat opposite me. ''The whole thing went down so quick that there was no way to anticipate. I made a mistake. I thought I wouldn't be spotted inside the nightclub. Unfortunately it was one of those women-only nights with a male stripper.''

"Janice was never into that stuff," he said.

"She was doing some research for her job. But when she realized I was a cop and in a tough spot she helped me. She got me out to my car in the parking lot. But it was a whole other scene. No one could have known that the guy would open up with the Uzi.''

"How did it happen?'' he asked.

"The suspect I followed gunned down the mayor's aide without any warning. As he ran toward his car, your sister, unrequested by me, was putting a tracking device under his bumper. He squeezed off a blast and hit her. I emptied my weapon at him, apparently hitting him once in the chest. I'm sorry, Ken. Janice just grabbed the Hound Dog before I could stop her.''

"It's unusual to see a chief of detectives on a tail.''

"A cop may be involved.''

"The son of a bitch.'' His features hardened. I found myself liking him. "I understand that you have the guy who shot Janice in custody.''

"We just got a bad break. The judge suppressed some of the evidence and cut him loose. We'll pick him up at the right time. We have a tail on him.''

"But you were a witness. How could a judge let him go?'' His fists were clenched.

"It was a screw-up. I was here giving a transfusion to your sister. She's afraid of AIDS. We told them I'd be late, but the damn judge wouldn't wait.''

He nodded. "It's the same down south. God forbid that the defendant or his attorney should be inconvenienced.''

The sandy-haired doctor came out and was halfway civil after being introduced to Ken. "I feel much better. We cleaned up the complications. She's weak at the moment. We'll keep her in the recovery room overnight as a precaution, but she should be coming out of it tomorrow.''

Ken and I walked to Janice's bed in the crowded recovery room. She was still very pale and looked thinner, fragile. Her breathing was regular. They had a rubber hose down her nose and intravenous solutions dripping into a vein in her arm.

Ken's eyes were a little watery. "She was always a gutsy kid. I could see it happening just the way you told me. Looking at that hulk," he hooked a thumb in the Block's direction, "I don't think I need to tell you to protect her. I have to go back to LA this afternoon. Keep me informed, will you?"

"You bet."

"You know, she could always outrun me even though I'm almost two years older. In school there was no contest. I was average. She was practically a genius. Maybe that's her problem. She was always getting involved in causes." He paused and turned to face me. "One other thing," he said, looking me straight in the eye. "I expect you to do justice to the people responsible. And I'm not talking about the courtroom."

Twelve

THERE WAS STILL NO ANSWER AT LOUIS'S NUMBER. I slammed the phone down. English was sitting in a chair tilted back against the wall, conspicuously reading a book entitled *The Shame of the Cities*. I made an effort to ignore him. He looked up. "Still unable to reach him?"

"You know, Paul, we have enough to do around here without you reading some dirty novel."

"Beware of stress, Fraleigh. You're getting frazzled. This book isn't fiction. In fact, it's all too similar to the present situation. You know what Shakespeare said, 'The past is prologue.' "

"Your brain is eggnog, English." The Block had come in. "How come I've doing twelve hours on and twelve hours off guarding your sweetheart and this guy is sitting around reading books and quoting prologues?" he asked me. It was Paul's favorite quote and I was tired of it.

"Paul, if it won't interfere too much with your post-graduate reading program, could you let us in on what happened when you followed Caruso."

"I've been waiting to report. My subject was driven forthwith by his lawyer to the Mill Road headquarters of Middleston Electronics Limited. He seems to be in remarkable condition considering his gunshot wound.''

"Fraleigh always was a lousy shot," the Block said.

Paul refused to pick up the offer of banter. "They parked in an executive area. I drove to the visitor's lot. There are security people, so I couldn't stay in my car. I went to the reception desk. An amazingly lovely, cultured young woman greeted me. Are you aware that they require a college degree—"

"Paul, about Caruso . . ."

"Now, Chief, you often lectured us to be patient listeners when witnesses were being relevant.''

"You ain't been relevant in twenty fucking years."

"Speak for yourself, Block." Paul knew he had the floor. We were a captive audience. "As I was saying, Joan and I are having dinner tonight. I think the Lion and the Compass is a good choice, don't you, Fraleigh?''

"Yeah, but we know what you'll be eating after dinner."

Paul frowned at the Block's comment as he continued. "She knows Crazy Phil as Mr. Caruso, a consultant. He enters through the executive entrance. I was unable to loiter, but I did retrieve the Hound Dog. After we recharge the battery I'll visit Joan again. You've been there haven't you, Fraleigh?''

"Yes."

Louis and I had had the grand tour. Middleston Electronics was one of the older Silicon Valley companies, which meant that it had been in business fifteen years—since 1971. The reception area and executive offices were plush. Other buildings, where the manufacturing took place, ranged from barren to sparse. In the clean rooms, silicon was melted into two-foot-long sausage-like tubes, heat-purified, and sliced into wafers. Then impurities were inserted onto the wafers, which made them superb conductors of electricity. Ultimately, the wafers were subdivided into microchips so sophisticated that they told Pac Man, pacemakers, home computers, and missile systems when and how to jump. Louis and I had to don the white gowns, slippers, head gear, and goggles that the workers wore to make and inspect the chips. Even a tiny particle of dust landing on a chip could wreck the elaborate network that told electrons which way to race. I felt like I was in a hospital emergency room.

In other buildings hundreds of engineers worked in small cubicles with tiny bookshelves full of technical manuals. Some of the men (I didn't observe one woman) were ingenious enough to pin pictures of families on the manuals. There wasn't room anywhere else. Each had his own computer terminal. I noticed that the work spaces with portable walls were numbered. I wondered if the inhabitants met for a beer after work. "Say, Harry, how long you been in cubicle 237?"

"I guess it might be eight years now, Bill. How long have you been in good old 343? I started there, you know." Putting up with the Block and English wasn't so bad after all. At least I wasn't confined to a cubicle every day.

Most of the newer companies specialized in one or two activities, but Middleston was big. They made everything from terminals to disks to laser products and were noted for their research.

The mayor had called twice asking for Louis, then for me. I couldn't stall any longer. I dialed the mayor's home.

English was instructing the Block on the pragmatic value of literature to modern policing. "You see, Block, once you really understand Balzac's *Pere Goriót*, you'll understand the distinction between Napoleon's secret police and our common law precursors—the London bobbies."

"Mayor Middleston's residence."

"Chief Fraleigh calling for the mayor."

"Oh, yes! Just a moment."

"You're out of your head, English," I heard the Block inform Paul emphatically.

"To the contrary, Block, our police system imitates Sir Robert Peel's new police experiment in 1829 in London. The difference, so vividly pointed out by Lincoln Steffens in 1904 in this book, was that corrupt municipal political machines controlled our cities . . ."

"Fraleigh, Mayor Middleston. What in the world is going on? My aide is brutally murdered. The killer apparently is free because a policeman beat him up. And neither you nor the police chief answer my calls!"

"Mayor Middleston, I think you can understand how hectic it's been—"

"Fraleigh, I want an immediate report from you. Why hasn't the chief called me? And what is the status of the investigation?"

"Er, Mayor, Chief Robinson is out of town. Naturally, I'm keeping him informed and he's on his way back."

"But what about this newspaper report that Captain Petrie assaulted the murderer and that the judge freed him?"

"We're investigating that right now, Mayor. Chief Robinson instructed me to place Captain Petrie on administrative leave."

"Administrative leave? The prick ought to be in the slammer," the Block said, laughing loudly despite my motions to keep quiet.

"Are you going to let this man get away with murder?" the mayor asked.

I chose my words carefully. It looked like good old Solly could be in this up to his eyeballs. If he was involved I didn't want to let him know that we could bag Crazy Phil anytime we wanted on Janice's and my testimony. On the other hand, he would be suspicious if I gave in too easily to the civil liberties angle by agreeing that the evidence was justifiably suppressed and that there was nothing we could do about it.

"I'm going to talk to the district attorney personally,

Mayor. I think we may be able to appeal that ruling. You know, Captain Petrie was under a strain. He was off duty. His actions were unofficial and shouldn't be an excuse to let a killer go free.''

"Well, the whole thing is outrageous. I'm demanding a complete report from Chief Robinson. You have him call me. When is he getting back?''

I wiped perspiration from my forehead. "He should be here within hours, Mayor.''

"You let him know that I'm unhappy about this.''

"Yes, sir,'' I said as the mayor hung up.

"You got some balls, Fraleigh. You don't even know where Louis is and you're bullshitting the mayor that Louis put Petrie on leave and is running the whole investigation, when you're the one fumbling around.''

"Fumbling? I fumbled all right when I was dumb enough to get you two out of a jam, so that I'm still stuck with you.''

"Horseshit. You know me, Paul, and Raoul are the only ones you can trust. You don't know how many of these other guys are in with Petrie or Solly. Right, Paul?''

"Your analysis, albeit crude, is reasonably on target. As Plato said . . .''

My head was splitting. I needed time to think. "Paul, I want you to do an in-depth research job on the mayor, his business, family, politics, the whole bag.''

He got up, giving me a deep bow. "And Paul''—he stopped in the doorway—"keep your hands off Mrs. Middleston.''

The Block and Paul exchanged glances. Paul came back into the office and sat down. They were about to expand their analysis of my behavior.

"Ha. I thought so. Her too! Christ, Fraleigh, you're turning into as big a stud as Paul.'' The Block's booming laugh spilled out of the office, undoubtedly terrifying Denise, my secretary. She thought of the Block as a modern-day Attila the Hun.

"Out. Both of you. I've got work to do. Wait a minute, as long as I told the mayor that Petrie is on administrative leave, you two go over to his house. Tell him officially that he's on administration leave. Be apologetic. You know. Take his weapons, but let him keep his badge. We'll give him some more rope to play with. Stay awake to anything he says or anything you spot.''

"We'll be alert for any signs of foul play, Chief,'' Paul said. They left smiling. Damn it. As wild as they were, they were sharp. I should have been more careful of what I said about Lorraine.

Thirteen

LOUIS HAD A FAT WITCH GUARDING HIS OFFICE. HE didn't like her and she didn't like him. He was trying to get rid of her, but she was covered by civil service regulations and the process was tedious. I was there at 0800 hours Monday to joust with her. "I'm certainly not going to allow you to see Chief Robinson's schedule," she said, her jowls bouncing with indignation.

"Ms. Phillips," I said, knowing that she hated the term "Ms." almost as much as she hated me, "this is an emergency. I must contact Chief Robinson."

"I have written guidelines and I'm certainly not going to violate them for you." I wondered if she was related to Turk, the emergency services operator.

"Very well, I'm sorry, Margaret."

She stared at me, thrown off balance by my using her first name.

I went over to an empty desk in the office and typed out a short note to Louis. Out of the corner of my eye, I saw her pretending not to be interested. The note read:

> Louis,
> I tried to get your schedule this morning, telling Margaret that it was an *extreme* emergency, but she refused to give it to me even after a direct

order. I know your policy in regard to terminating employees for disobedience, but I have to say in her behalf that she thought she was being loyal to you. Of course, the mayor didn't see it that way.

I signed it and folded the paper, stapling it once. I wrote confidential across the face. "Please give this to the chief as soon as you see him." She ignored me. I placed it gently on her desk.

Five minutes later I got the call. "Chief Fraleigh, this is Karen. I'm filling in for Margaret. She had to go to a staff meeting. She found Chief Robinson's schedule. It's here any time you'd like to look at it."

Immediately, I went to look at Louis's schedule. His first appointment was a meeting in his office with the downtown merchants at 1000 hours. At 1100 the county school superintendent was coming in. At noon, he was speaking to the Rotary. At 1330, he was pinch-hitting for the mayor, welcoming the Western Regional Society of Certified Public Accountants at their annual convention. From 1400 to 1700 hours he was to be at the staff meeting for city department heads. At 1730, he was to attend a cocktail reception prior to a dinner sponsored by Gays for Civil Rights. Louis was to be the guest speaker. Nowhere in the schedule was there a mention of meetings with police personnel.

"Please let me know when the chief arrives. It's very important that I see him right away."

"Yes, sir," Karen assured me.

We began the Monday morning dick bureau staff meeting. The setting always made me feel strange. Silicon City had outdone itself in image. Not only did we have a brand-new building, we met in a conference room that rivaled the one in the downtown Bank of America building. The cops perched uneasily on nicely upholstered wheeled chairs, rubbing their hands over the polished walnut table seating twenty. Others were seated along the walls behind them. After four months, spots already stained the walls where heads rested during our sometimes lengthy meetings. Sergeants' heads, that is. Squad lieutenants sat around the table. I tried to concentrate on the meeting, but my mind was buzzing over Nicastri's killing and Louis's whereabouts. Everybody was so new that I had to be careful not to ask the vice commander about robberies and the homicide commander about frauds. One mistake finishes you for life.

Lieutenant Cathy Stevens sat on my immediate left. She headed the sexual assault unit. Since she was the only woman in the group it was easy to keep track of her cases. Hiring her had been one of my coups. The male herd hadn't even grumbled.

Six years ago she was a sergeant in the Alameda County Sheriff's Department. One afternoon she and her male partner responded to a bank alarm. Her partner, who was driving, had answered thousands of alarms and he knew that ninety-seven percent of all alarms were false, so he pulled in front of the bank. The robbers ran right into them. Her partner took a full blast from a shotgun. He died without getting out of the car. Cathy had been hit in the neck and face with pellets and broken glass. With blood streaming down her face she got out of the cruiser and killed the murderer with three rounds from her Smith and Wesson. The other guy managed to put a slug from his .38-caliber revolver through her shoulder, but she emptied the remaining three rounds from her weapon into his chest. He died forty-eight hours later.

She spent the next five years heading the sheriff's sexual assault squad, earning a reputation throughout the state for professional thoroughness. We were able to recruit her by bringing her in as a lieutenant. The squad dicks called her Lieutenant Stevens.

Understandably, the ten squad commanders and their assistants wanted to discuss the hit on the mayor's aide. I suggested leaving it until last, knowing that I would have to excuse myself to meet with Louis.

I had been in at 0700 to review the watch commander's and night detective's reports. The half million people inhabiting our jurisdiction had engaged in the usual amount of carnage over the weekend.

We went through the new major cases one by one. An eighty-year-old woman living alone in a mobile park had been raped and murdered sometime Saturday morning. Body discovered by her girlfriend, seventy-eight, who was coming over to have breakfast. I pushed the thought of her reaction out of my mind. It sounded like the mobile park rapist again. Four attacks. The youngest victim, sixty-eight. He had beaten all of them. This time a fragile skull had cracked. Newly promoted homicide lieutenant Phil Short headed the task force. He was optimistic that the crime scene might yield latent prints. I wasn't. Did I or the chief want to handle media? No.

There had been fourteen armed robberies. Two victims had been stabbed. They would survive. Another had been shot. He didn't. At 2330 hours Saturday night, a young female Caucasian had walked into Nick's Bar on First Street. Without a word she had fired five shots into the bartender, a twenty-one-year-old college student working part time. The cash register contained all of seventy-two dollars. She emptied it and fled.

We spent a few minutes on that one. No one could remember a female doing anything similar. There weren't any firm ideas on motivation, but a few people around the table speculated that she must have been stoned on PCP. The sergeants sitting in the outer circle dutifully wrote that down. Phil Short announced that his people would confer with the narco and robbery squads as well as uniformed cops working the area. I announced that we would spring for up to a grand through the crime stoppers' program. If the killer was known, someone would pop her. A thousand dollars bought plenty in those circles.

Saturday afternoon, two girls, fourteen and fifteen,

decided to hitchhike home from a shopping center. They had been reported missing that evening by worried families. Early Sunday morning, a jogger in Cloe Park heard a call for help. Both victims had been raped and repeatedly stabbed. The fourteen-year-old was in critical condition. The fifteen-year-old had bled to death. "Goddamn it! What do we have to do to get them to stop hitchhiking? We tell them at every school and neighborhood meeting and they still—"

Eyebrows were raised. They stared at me. I bit off the rest of my words and said, "Any leads?" There was an audible sigh of relief in the room. We were back to routine. Evidence, perpetrators, witnesses.

By 0930, we were discussing a Mom-and-Pop homicide. Mom was sixty-four years old, Pop considerably older at seventy-four. Married thirty-five years. Mom discovered Pop had been diddling a divorcee in her fifties. In the middle of carving Sunday's roast lamb she stuck the twelve-inch carving knife into Pop's stomach. All the way to the hilt. Cherchéz la femme.

I got nervous about the time and excused myself. Louis should have arrived if he was going to make a ten o'clock meeting. From my desk I dialed his office.

"Chief Robinson's office." Margaret had returned from what must have been a short meeting.

"Chief Fraleigh here. Has Chief Robinson arrived yet?"

"No. He won't be in today, Chief. He called in and delegated others to take his appointments."

"What? Why didn't you connect him with me?"

"But you told Karen that you wanted to see him when he came in, not talk to him on the phone," she said sweetly.

I thought about my hands closing over her throat. "Did he leave a phone number?"

"No. However, I did tell him that you had come in to see him. Perhaps he'll call. Oh, the mayor called. He wants to see you in his office at ten-thirty."

"Did you tell Chief Robinson about that?" I asked, knowing what the answer was.

"No. Mayor Middleston didn't ask for Chief Robinson. He asked for you."

I hung up and dialed Louis's home number. No answer.

I cursed her and the civil service system. She had neatly skewered Louis and me without disobeying instructions in a way that opened her to discipline. Of course, we could try, but I pictured her sweetly testifying in front of the civil service commissioners who were appointed by the city council after careful consultations with municipal labor organizations. We would appear to be blundering all over while trying to pick on a lowly secretary. The worst part of it was that the blundering description was accurate.

Paul and the Block came in smiling. Paul was carrying a brown suitcase and the Block a brown paper bag. Block took Petrie's two service revolvers from the bag and placed them on my desk.

"Put them in the safe," I told him, looking at Paul and the suitcase.

"It does look like the same one, doesn't it?" he said.

"All right, Paul, you've aroused my curiosity. Would you like to tell me about it, or shall we play jolly guessing games?"

"He's really getting to be a grouch. Do you think it's age or too much sex with all these women he's got on the line? Hey! Maybe it's a combination. You know, he can't get it up the way he used to and—"

"Block, shut up will you? Well, Paul?"

But Paul was not to be hurried. He had to answer the Block's question, since my psychoanalysis was their favorite topic. "More likely it's related to the dynamics of bureaucracy, although your point is well taken. Fraleigh does seem to be overextended of late."

"Paul . . ."

"Yes, sir. We have plied our sleuthing trade with stealth and cunning in your behalf."

"I wish you'd ply it with some goddamned common sense and straight answers."

"You'd better tell him, Paul, before he busts a gut and we got to fill out all that workmen's compensation crap."

"While the Block was using his charm to distract Captain Petrie, I wandered into his garage. This was one of five suitcases stored there. I believe I slipped it into our car without Petrie being aware."

I opened the suitcase, careful not to damage any latent prints that might be on it. We peered into it. It was empty. "If this thing was once loaded with dope, the lab ought to find traces," I said.

"Not necessarily. The evidence packages and steam-sealing processes we use in the Department are airtight," Paul said.

"True, but not many dope dealers are as scrupulous. And usually they open some of the packages for on-the-spot testing. Anyway, ask them to do a thorough test for trace evidence and prints. I'm not sure we could get any of it into court. It wasn't a consent search and we don't have a warrant."

"Yeah, it was just some of English's stealing."

"Gentlemen of the jury, don't be so quick to convict a conscientious officer of the law," Paul argued. "As you know, a seizure of evidence is not a search. When contraband is in plain view it may be seized. Given the totality of the circumstances, the surveillance, the shootings, Petrie's actions, I believe my actions in securing this evidence were warranted."

"Brilliant, Paul. I wish I could stay to hear more of your legal reasoning, but I've got to go over to the mayor's office and get my ass chewed again."

"Maybe Lorraine will be there, Fraleigh. You two can go jogging together after her old man finishes cutting you up," the Block said.

"Do you think it wise to continue deceiving the mayor about Louis?" Paul asked.

"If you have any better idea than telling him that the

police chief has disappeared and may be shacked up with some organized crime bimbo, I'm open to suggestion.''

I left amid one of their rare silences.

Fourteen

I WALKED THROUGH THE CIVIC CENTER TO CITY HALL. The weather had cooled. The clear dry air and blue skies fitted well with the imposing new, incredibly expensive buildings in which government of, for, and by the people was housed. I found the few bums lying in the grass or scrounging in trash baskets reassuring. Technology hadn't reached them yet. City Hall was even more imposing than the courthouse, public works building, and the main library. The fourteen-story pile of glass and steel looked more like the glitzy modern headquarters of a major corporation than a public building.

In fact, the building was owned by Middleston Electronics, Limited. Just a year before the mayor ran for office, the company made the magnanimous gesture of leasing it to the city for one dollar a year. The mayor's opponent was a black insurance salesman. He didn't even offer a free policy. Solly won an easy victory. The public thought he symbolized their glistening new city. They weren't upset when, after the election, several news stories disclosed that the tax deductions the company received were double the value of the building. Everyone knew how nasty the press was. Mayor Middlestonn't even needed to remind them.

He reminded me of who I was, though. I sat for fifteen minutes in his outer office. His executive secretary, a no-nonsense woman in her mid-forties, offered me coffee. I accepted. She had a younger subordinate who reminded me of Margaret. They wore about the same size tents. Sitting in the far corner, taking one call after another, she still found time to frown suspiciously at me. I gave her my professional Clint Eastwood smile. She turned red and the frowns grew fiercer. No one appeared to get through to His Honor.

The executive secretary handed me a cup of coffee in a china cup. It was real cream, not the powdered junk we used at headquarters. "Tough day?" I asked, smiling.

"Sometimes it gets very busy. The mayor is in such demand. The news media, the public, corporations, and Washington."

It was true. Solly was no slouch when it came to publicity. The new capital of electronic America and its suave, millionaire entrepreneur mayor were hot. He had even taken Louis with him to appear on *Meet the Press* and *The Today Show*. English, the Block, and I had watched a new Louis with admiration. He had been poised and confident.

"The mayor gives so much of his time," she said. "Yet the White House took three days to return his call. Can you imagine?"

I tried my best to be as indignant as she was. A phone buzzed on her desk. She smiled, hanging up. The mayor would see me now. I skipped telling her to feel free to buzz through if the White House should call.

As befitted the king of the heap, the mayor occupied a corner office on the top floor. His office was the same as the one he had occupied as CEO for the company. Thick carpeting, expensively bound books on mahogany shelves, a beautiful antique desk without a single paper on it, and, of course, in the corner away from the windows, a computer work station.

His view of Silicon Valley was superb. Looking north, the bright blue of San Francisco Bay was dazzling. Airplanes were visible buzzing in and out of San Francisco Airport and the day was so clear that to the south I could see the dirigible hangar at the navy's Moffett Field—a familiar, ugly landmark. And to the far south, the smog drifting from the north cozily embraced the east foothills of sprawling San Jose.

"What do you have to report?" Solly had all the warmth of a Gestapo interrogator.

I stared for a few more moments at the view, establishing the kinship between us that only big executives share—life at the top stuff.

"I'm afraid I don't have anything new. But there are some questions I'd like to ask you, Mayor."

He reddened. "Ask me? I want a report on what's going on!"

"Of course. I was just wondering if you could shed any light on why Caruso killed your assistant."

"When will the chief be back?"

"Soon. You see, Mayor, when we have a murder, it's necessary to establish a motive and we just can't imagine why a hoodlum like Caruso would want to kill Nicastri."

"You told me yesterday that Chief Robinson would be back any minute." I had said within hours, but, courteously, I didn't correct him. When I remained silent he said, "I thought one of your men beat that information out of him?"

I refrained from reminding him that the "one of my men" he was referring to had been hired at his insistence. "Caruso gave a preposterous reason. Said he was furious that Nicastri had sold him a bad car."

"Why is that preposterous?"

I felt a new sympathy for Louis. Anyone who had to deal with this man on a daily basis . . . I wondered how long we were going to play charades. "An Uzi is an assault rifle. The same kind carried by the Secret Service when they guard the president. Disgruntled car buyers don't normally obtain them for vengeance. Then too, Your Honor, it's hard to believe that your aide was the kind of man that one wouldn't buy a used car from.''

"You know, Fraleigh, I'm not at all impressed by your performance. If I thought there was any sarcasm over Thomas's unfortunate tragedy . . . or implication about his associating with hoodlums . . .''

I felt the pictures in my pocket. Paul English had reproduced razor-sharp photographs of the players at Petrie's house. What would the mayor do if I pulled them out, saying, "Well, as long as you mentioned associating with hoodlums. . . .'' Instead, I said, "We're just trying to do our job, Your Honor.''

"It seems to me that you at least ought to be able to find the police chief. I'd feel more comfortable with him in charge.''

"I'm sure he'll be here any minute.''

"This Captain Petrie, shouldn't he be fired for what he did?''

I caught a slight note of uncertainty in his voice. The mayor was fishing again. "Your Honor, it's a cumbersome process with administrative review, civil service hearings, and appeals. On the other hand, there is a strict rule that an officer on administrative leave must report every forty-eight hours to his commanding officer. If he's not in my office by five o'clock tomorrow evening, we'll be able to get rid of him for you, quick and easy.'' There was no such rule. It had slid deviously into my head. I was doing a little fishing of my own. I didn't catch much.

"I see.'' He nodded.

"One other thing, Mayor.'' His ice-cold eyes bored into me. I was clearly insubordinate for daring to ask him questions. "I know you're the best there is when it comes to computers. We found this in Nicastri's pocket.'' I handed him a copy of the note. It read, "Prototype for molecular solitons, protein molecular side chains and gene bacterial inserts re: Yoshomo Tanaka.'' As he read it, I said, "We'd appreciate it if you could help us on the meaning."

I had done this just to sting the mayor a bit. Technically, it was against the law to do private business while on the city payroll, but clearly Nicastri had run around doing a lot of business stuff for the mayor. We figured the note was some flunky messenger work he was doing for Middleston Electronics.

"I have no idea what this is." He pushed the note back to me like it burned his hands. His face was pale and I noticed a pulse beating just under his left eye. He stood. "I have another appointment. You'll have to leave."

He didn't know how he was breaking my heart. He was such fun to chat with. I felt pretty good about the interview. I had held my own with Middleston. Even unnerved him a bit over the note. He was probably afraid that I was going to leak to the press that Nicastri had been on Middleston Electronics business when he got knocked off. The mayor had claimed that the guy had died in the line of duty, valiantly serving the public. As soon as Louis got back, we'd figure out how to go about getting the answers to why Crazy Phil was so cozy with the executives at Middleston Electronics.

Fifteen

I checked Louis's apartment. It was locked and silent. He was still away.

I went to the hospital to see Janice. They had put her in a private room on the fourth floor east. The elevator deposited me noiselessly. As soon as I got off I sensed that something was wrong. The nurses' station fifty feet to my left was quiet. Too quiet. A tall blond nurse was standing behind the counter facing two men whose backs were to me. One was squat and heavy with dark oily hair. He wore a cheap blue suit. His companion was a contrast. He was slender, and his colorful sports shirt was not tucked into his designer jeans. Cops dressed that way in warm weather to cover their guns. But neither of these guys were cops. The taller one had long, not-too-clean-looking brown hair that reached almost to his shoulders.

On an impulse, I lifted a stethoscope from a nurse's cart standing in the hallway and slipped it around my neck. A gray-haired woman in a bathrobe stood in the doorway of her room watching me. "You're not a doctor," she whispered.

I was afraid that she might make noise that would attract attention before I got a feel for what was going on. "You're right. I'm a volunteer. We visit patients, play chess, bridge, you know."

"I'm not a fool. Step in here."

I followed the old girl's orders. Whatever was wrong with her didn't affect her judgment. When I was inside I saw that she had been watching the nurse's station from behind her partially closed door. "There's something wrong there. If you're not a policeman as I think you are, I'm going to call the police. There have been policemen guarding the patient in Room 417, but that man in the blue suit—he pointed something at the nurse. A policeman wouldn't do that, would he?"

"Ma'am" I touched her arm. "You're very observant. My name is Fraleigh and I am a police officer. Please dial 911 and tell them I need help on this floor immediately—that a man may have a gun. And stay back out of the line of fire."

Walking past the nurses' station with the stethoscope around my neck, I glanced casually at the two men. Behind the desk two other women were sitting on the floor, terrified. One wore the pink dress of a volunteer. The other appeared to be a nurse. I turned away as if I hadn't noticed. I was four doors from Janice's room— 417. It was on my right. The door was closed and there was no sign of a guard.

"Hey, Doctor, just a minute." I glanced over my shoulder to see the squat man in his cheap blue suit coming after me. His right hand was straight down at his side. His right leg moved and I got a glimpse of a blued automatic hidden behind his trousers. I didn't dare try for the room. If the door was locked . . .

I went right past 417. The end of the corridor was only two rooms away, a distance of about ten feet. It dead-ended into a left-hand L. I kept walking, head turned, my eyes on the gun. "Hey." He yelled again and started to bring the weapon up. I broke into a run. The gunshot thundered and echoed through the hallway. A window at the end of the corridor shattered. I did a head-first dive around the corner to the left past an old man who was serenely walking along pushing an intravenous feeder hooked into his arm. The second shot shattered the man's feeder. He calmly moved himself to the other side of the hallway opposite me. I rolled over on the floor, pulling my Magnum out and shifting it to my left hand. Still in a prone position, I peeked around the corner.

I saw the door to Janice's room slide open a crack. So did the gunman. He had moved cautiously after firing and was hugging the wall opposite 417. It opened away from me so I couldn't see what he saw, but he was still ten feet shy of the room entrance. He switched his aim to cover the door.

We practiced weak-hand shooting each year on the range. I shot expert right-handed. Left-handed, I always felt guilty about wasting ammunition. I fired left-handed. The bullet raised plaster above his head. He turned the .45 toward me. I ducked back around the corner. Six shots boomed out. Three of them sent bullets crashing into the floor where I had leaned out to shoot. Then silence. It wasn't really silence. People were screaming all over the joint. But from a shooter's viewpoint it was silent.

My prone position hadn't fooled him at all. So I cautiously peeked from a kneeling position. He was face down. I looked toward the nurses' station. The slender guy broke rapidly and ran to a staircase exit. The door to 417 opened slowly. I saw Raoul Chavez take a careful look. He acknowledged me with a left-handed wave. It was his call. I stayed put. Slowly, in a two-handed gun stance, he moved toward the downed gunman. I stayed prone, but crawled into the corridor so that I could cover him. This time I held the magnum in my right hand and steadied it with my left so the sights were pointed at the guy in the blue suit just in case he was playing games with us. He wasn't. His games were all over. Raoul kicked the .45 away from him and motioned to me. We both approached the nurses' station with caution, although we were pretty sure that it was all over.

"They were killers. They wanted to know which room Miss Bell was in." The tall blond nurse was speaking. Her long narrow face hadn't regained its color, but she spoke steadily. "He pointed that gun at me." She paused. "God, the hole in the barrel was so big. I worked emergency room for two years. All I could think of was what it would do to my body if he pulled the trigger."

Raoul was on the phone calling in the description of the dead man's partner. "I knew they'd kill that policeman." She pointed toward Raoul. "I told them we had no one by that name. He didn't believe me. He said they were going to start shooting us. Then you walked by. One of them said, 'That's Fraleigh.' I said, 'No, it's Doctor Greene.' " She made an unsuccessful effort to smile at me. "You were clever to pick up the stethoscope."

"You're the clever one. And gutsy. You saved my life." Raoul got off the phone and I went to Janice's room to explain what happened. It was empty. I raced back to the desk. "Where is she?"

"She's been in X-ray for a half hour," the nurse said, looking at me as if I was crazy.

I ran to the stairway, almost bumping into the Block, who was walking from the elevator. "Christ. Looks like you guys had some action." He had come to relieve Raoul.

"Block, take charge of the crime scene. I'm going up to X-ray to make sure Janice is OK."

The X-ray unit was on the sixth floor. I ran the two flights. "You're not allowed in here," the technician told me when I burst through the door.

"Fraleigh. What's wrong?" Janice asked. She was on a gurney, her stomach pressed against the X-ray slide.

"This is the last picture. If you'll just let me take it, you can have all the conversation you want." The technician was a soft, chubby young man who spoke with a slight lisp. Janice smiled and winked at me. I waited outside while he finished his work. Then he brought her out in a wheelchair.

"What's that smell?" she asked. We sat in a small lounge outside the X-ray unit.

She looked much better and I wondered why I smiled so broadly. I realized it was more than gratitude. Despite the danger in Lefty's parking lot she had fit nicely in my arms. And she was intriguing, assertive yet very feminine and she seemed to like me.

A blue-haired woman with an enormously swollen stomach was being wheeled into the unit. I averted my eyes. "Did you hear the shots? The cops shot up the whole fourth floor. No one knows what happened," she said. Her eyes were feverish, excited.

A faded woman who had been holding her hand sat next to us as the attendant wheeled the patient into the unit. "She doesn't have much longer." She wiped her eyes with a wet tissue. "Why don't they leave her in peace? X-rays. Operations. It just prolongs it."

Janice was in a wheelchair. "That's what I smelled. Gunpowder." Her eyes roamed over my jacket, looking for the telltale bulge. "Is Raoul all right? The technician asked him to get the charts from my room. Raoul just left a few minutes ago."

"Raoul's fine." I got up and wheeled her to the elevator. "Two hit men came. One of them started shooting. He was killed. The other is gone."

"I smelled your gun. Did you . . . ?"

"I missed. I was covering for Raoul. He shot the guy."

"How is Raoul?"

"He's OK. Fortunately, no one except the hood got hurt."

"That's not what I meant. I've gotten to know him. He told me about the child. He cried. He still cries. And now this."

"This is different. He didn't miss."

When we got to her floor I wheeled her through the back corridor so she wouldn't have to view the body. A member of the tech crew was digging slugs out of the floor and wall next to where I had taken cover. "You were lucky, Chief. They just didn't have your name on them." He held up two of the .45-caliber rounds dug out of the floor and wall. Janice shivered. I tried unsuccessfully not to. The hiss of the flying lead came back to me. I wheeled her into her room and just about made the bathroom in time to urinate.

When I came back into the room she was lying on the bed with her eyes closed. I could hear a lot of noise coming from the nurses' station. "I'll be right back, Janice." It seemed to me that she was paler than she had been in X-ray.

The hospital was chaotic. Medical personnel rushed all over the crime scene, much to the cops' and coroners' unhappiness. The gunman had been so obviously DOA that they hadn't even tried to revive him. He had no identification on him. Surprise, surprise. The Block was grasping a young doctor by the front of his white coat. "Listen, you wimp. I'm an officer of the law and I don't give a shit if you are a fucking physician. I'll tell you when this area can be opened up."

"Block," I intervened.

The doctor was shaking and pasty. He eased away from the Block toward me. "Who are you?"

"Chief of detectives."

"This man ought to be removed from duty—he's barbaric."

"These assholes better understand that when I tell them to stay out of the crime scene, I mean it. The tech crew ain't even finished."

"It's OK, Block," I soothed him. "I'll explain it to them. Why don't you go in and tell Janice I'll be with her in a few minutes."

Suddenly he was beaming his phony smile. It was grotesque. "Yes, Chief, can I quote her a love poem for you or sing to her?"

The doctor stared at him. "The man is unbalanced. Why do you allow him to be a policeman?"

"He's related to the mayor. Actually, Doctor, we'll be done in a few minutes, but it's very important for legal purposes that we process the scene. You know it's not unlike malpractice suits in court. You need all the evidence you can get."

Malpractice was a magic word. He was walking away before I closed my mouth. I went into a small office where Raoul was writing his report. "How are you, Raoul?"

"Fine, Fraleigh. It was a little closer than I wanted it to be, but had a happy ending. Thanks for that cover shot. It took fire away from me. It made the difference."

I studied him. He was calm and confident. "You did well, Raoul." I patted him on the shoulder. He smiled back at me.

When I got back to her room, Janice was sitting up. She had put on lipstick. "I'll leave you two alone," the Block leered. She colored slightly.

"Don't pay any attention to him."

"He's really sweet," she said.

Sweet? I wondered if she had fallen on her head when she had been shot. "How are you, Janice?" We hadn't really had time to talk on the way down from the sixth floor. I took her hand.

"I'm feeling much better. They think I can leave in a couple of days. It seems that I was very lucky. The bullet didn't touch anything vital and the scare after the bleeding was a false alarm."

I sat down, keeping her hand in mine. "Don't hold it in." Her smile was too bright. I could see that she was scared stiff about the shooting.

Her left hand was at her mouth. "Oh my," she whispered. "Why are they trying to hurt me? It's because I saw the man who shot me, isn't it?" She answered her own question. "Oh, God. When is this going to end?"

I put my arms around her. She was trembling violently and held on to me for a couple of minutes until she calmed herself. For the next hour we talked. I knew the tech crew was impatient to examine my weapon and get a statement, but they would have to wait. I kept my hands in my pockets, because they were shaking. Fortunately, the sharp pain in my stomach wasn't visible. It had been very close. The reaction was setting in, but oddly enough my desire to calm her helped subdue my own agitation. I gave her a rough outline of what was going on, omitting the surveillance stuff.

To get her mind off the hallway shooting we talked more about each other. From time to time, she obviously experienced pain, but made no mention of it. Underneath her chatter, I could tell that she was still frightened. Yet she was a trooper. She picked up on things quickly. A couple of times she showed a sense of humor. Under the circumstances she got high marks for that. I hadn't intended to stay, but found myself reluctant to leave. The orderly stuck his head in. "I have two lunch orders for this room."

"That's for the other officer," I said.

"I don't think the Block will be back for a while. Can you join me? I know you must be busy . . ."

"Sure."

I wasn't crazy about hospital food, but found myself chuckling over her vivid comparisons to jail food. She had worked as a researcher for two months in the Sybil Brand Institute, the womens' correctional facility in Los Angeles. "What did you discover?" I asked.

"That the next time I get shot, I want to be fed in a correctional institution, not a hospital."

"Well, I'll see what I can do. Maybe I can get you sentenced to a couple of years for harassing Crazy Phil by getting in the way of his machine gun."

"Whoever said cops were mean? You're all heart. But why was he freed? I don't understand."

"He didn't get the Miranda warnings, so any statements he made are inadmissible. Not only what he said, but evidence, like the Uzi, can't be used if he told the cops where it was in an illegal confession. The court says it's Fruit of the Poisoned Tree."

"Miranda warnings. Illegal confessions. I've heard that so often, but I don't really understand what it means. What exactly is a Miranda warning?"

"Back in 1966, a guy named Danny Miranda was arrested in Arizona on a rape charge. The cops questioned him in the station house and he confessed to the crime. The U.S. Supreme Court overturned the conviction because the cops hadn't told him he had the right to a lawyer and the right to remain silent. They made it a national rule. That's why we carry those little cards to read to suspects."

"But was he guilty?"

"Oh, yeah. But that wasn't relevant, as they say."

"Did they, you know, beat a confession out of him? Or scare him into confession?"

"No."

"And the confession, I mean, was it correct, truthful?"

"True as true can be."

"I wonder if the woman who was the victim felt as vulnerable as I do." She shook her head. "To think that someone as vicious as Caruso could be set free after everyone knows what he did."

I squeezed her hand. "We'll pick up Caruso soon."

"Will he plead guilty or will I have to testify?"

"Who knows? Don't worry about it, Janice. There's nothing we can do about it."

"I could go away. I could hide. I've read that these trials can take as long as five years with all the delays. I couldn't live with this fear all that time."

I didn't want to tell her that we had trials that took up to twelve years after appeals were granted and new trials orders. "That's not going to happen this time."

"But you don't know. The lawyers can do what they want. You have no say in the process."

"You're right. But we think whoever is behind Caruso will decide that he's a liability pretty soon. He's the weak link. We saw him, so even though Petrie set up a Miranda defense for him, we have a good case for murder. They won't take a chance on him talking to save himself from the gas chamber."

"You're consoling me by telling me he'll be murdered. A sort of justice will be achieved only outside the courts. If not, if it goes to court you and I will have to look over our shoulders for years."

I couldn't get her out of the somber mood. I left with the promise that I would return in the evening. The Block was engrossed in a copy of *Playboy*. The hospital had calmed down.

I kept trying Louis all afternoon without any luck. I nagged Paul into pressuring the county lab on the analysis of the suitcase. They would try to have something by next week. With all these homicides, they were giving dope a low priority.

It took a couple of hours to prepare and sign my statement on the hospital shooting. After that I had at least fourteen briefings about ongoing investigations. We had tried to assign strong lieutenants to squads where some of the dicks needed a kick in the ass to get their work done. We put those lieutenants who needed a kick in the ass with squads where the dicks were self-motivated. Like all theories it worked on paper more than in reality. At 1800 hours I refrained from cold-cocking a lieutenant who was asking me how he could get his secretary to answer the phone when he was away from the desk. I hated to think what a whiz he'd be on a case of serial murders. I told him to get out, with a degree of politeness that amazed Paul, who had returned with a long yellow pad of notes.

"I believe that the aborted attempt on Janice's life has significance for future developments."

I indicated my awestruck reaction to his analysis. "That so?"

"Quite. Although we are ignorant of the criminal motivations driving this case, it does seem clear that the attempt on her life is related to her ability to identify Caruso. I suspect that it was the penultimate attempt.

Had it succeeded, you would undoubtedly have been next.''

"Yeah? No shit?''

"Your newly achieved rank has done little to improve your humor, Fraleigh. However, I suggest that either more attempts will immediately be made on you and Janice, or else Caruso will be eliminated.''

"Well, as Aristotle said, it's time to call it a day.''

"Familiarity with danger makes a brave man braver, but less daring. Take care, Fraleigh.''

I just looked at him.

"Melville,'' he said.

"Oh.''

Driving back to the hospital, I could see Paul's car hovering a discreet distance behind me. Fatigue was flowing through every pore. Yet I was disappointed when I found Janice was sleeping.

"You look beat. Why don't you go home? Get some shut-eye.'' Raoul was back on duty. He should have been placed automatically on administrative leave after the shooting. I had talked to him about it. He opted to stay with Janice. "They aren't going to win this one,'' he said.

"Buenos nochés, Raoul.'' I went out into the mild summer night. In the far corner of the hospital parking lot I spotted Paul's Porsche. It kept me company on the way home.

Sixteen

LOUIS WAS STILL INCOMMUNICADO TUESDAY. AT 0830 hours Captain Petrie walked into my office. I looked at him with raised eyebrows.

"Just reporting in as required, Chief," he said, sliding into a chair.

I debated whether to ask him where he got the idea that he was required to report in. Instead, I nodded hello. The man was still cocky and conveyed the same confidence he had shown when I interviewed him. He'd been wired enough through City Hall to get this job, and he clearly thought he had the clout to smooth over murder, dope deals, and mob ties. I was pretty sure he wasn't acting. He did feel secure.

"Isn't this administrative leave thing getting a little ridiculous? I can't believe the chief is that upset at me for teaching a punk like Caruso a lesson."

Possibly a lesson in constitutional law on Miranda rulings? I wondered. "Well, Petrie, there is the little problem of the judge excluding the evidence and Caruso walking."

"A gutless DA and a liberal judge. That isn't my fault, is it?" He didn't even bother to hide the amusement in his eyes. I knew he hoped that his chatter might lead me to give away some information on where the investigation was.

I smiled my own confident smile. "That's not for me to say, Captain."

"I guess you're right. Can I have a word with the chief?"

"He's not here."

"Out of town?" Again, the taunting smile. I felt a twinge in my stomach. Did this arrogant bastard know that Louis was holed up somewhere with Carol Mansell? I didn't answer, just shrugged, keeping the easy smile on my face. Or trying to. I doubted my success. Petrie didn't miss much.

"Well, I'll stroll along. Be back to see you in forty-eight hours, unless you call."

He walked through the squad room, good-naturedly stopping to have his hand pumped by dicks who congratulated him for taking down an asshole like Caruso. It was too bad that the chief and the courts didn't have balls anymore, they consoled him.

I had asked Paul to work quietly behind the scenes to see if we couldn't find Louis. There was one thing I could do. It was a long shot, but he might have gone back to Sarah. I had put off calling. Sarah was a friend. Louis hadn't told me anything about their breakup, but he had given me the impression that the divorce had been bitter. I figured it had probably gone through by now. I hadn't talked to Sarah in the months prior to our leaving for Silicon City.

"Sarah? Fraleigh. How are you?"

"Fraleigh, you dog. I haven't heard from you in ages. Why the call now?"

Her voice was happy, unaffected, glad to hear from me. "I was just wondering how the twins were." I was a great guy.

"They're wonderful and they miss you."

I had taken them on a week-long camping and fishing trip around three years back to give Sarah and Louis a chance for a second honeymoon. I remembered Sarah fussing over them in the driveway. "Do you have the insect repellent? I packed extra underwear and clothes. If you get wet, you change your clothes. And be good. Do what Fraleigh tells you. Momma loves you." The boys squeezed out of her embrace, rolling their eyes at me. They were anxious to get going.

"They'll be OK, Sarah. You and Louis have a good time."

"I'm terrible, aren't I? I just feel guilty sending them off even though I know they'll be fine with you." She smiled. "You're a real friend to do this, Fraleigh."

"Hey. It will be fun. These guys are my buddies," I said for their benefit. They were about to start yelling any minute for us to leave. We pulled out of the driveway in the front-wheel-drive jeep I had borrowed from the Block for the occasion. I saw a big tear roll down Sarah's cheek at the last moment. The boys missed it. They were already asking me if we could stop at McDonald's for lunch.

Late that afternoon we caught two small-mouth black bass in the river and I scaled and cleaned them for dinner. I tossed them in the pan with some butter and took two containers of milk for the boys and a Coors beer for myself. I cooked the fish in a heavy skillet over an open fire and served them along with a can of green beans mandated by Sarah.

"Even the beans taste good," John said. He was an inch smaller and of slighter build than Albert. I always found it strange that although the boys reminded me so much of Louis, their features were strictly from Momma.

"How did you hurt your hand, Albert?" I asked after dinner as we sat enjoying the fire. I noticed that he was favoring it.

"The same way he hurt his eye," John said. "He's been fighting at school."

I had done plenty of that myself, but as a temporary

guardian I asked righteously, "What was that all about?"

Albert put his head down and sullenly refused to look at me. I shrugged and was about to pass on it. After all, we were going to be here for a few days and I didn't need any cranky kids.

"Bobby Jones called Daddy an Uncle Tom nigger pig. Albert punched him, but he's bigger and he hit back."

"Shut up, Johnny. Big-mouth," Albert said.

"Sometimes it's better to talk about these things, Albert." I noticed that he had a bruise over his right eye.

"Nothing to talk about. He said it and I hit him."

"Why would he say something dumb like that?" I asked.

Albert was a little choked up. "He said Daddy didn't like black people. And that he wasn't even a cop. He just sat behind a desk and did paperwork." They both looked at me.

"Your dad does paperwork now, but you know, before you guys were even born he saved my life. I was a young patrolman. Your dad was my sergeant. I went on a call by myself. It came over the radio as a family fight. I was supposed to wait for another officer, but I was impatient. When I got to the apartment, a little boy about six years old let me in." Both of them were fixed on the story. It was beginning to get dark. I threw some more wood on the fire.

"He told me his mommy was hurt. I went into the other room and saw that his mother had been shot dead. Her husband suddenly came into the room pointing a shotgun at me. I was lucky. Your father was a good sergeant. He knew rookies make mistakes. He followed me on the call."

I got up to stir the fire, but the real reason I moved was that even after all these years it disturbed me how close I had come to getting killed that evening. "Your dad came to the door. I yelled for him not to come in, that the guy had a shotgun. He knew the man. And he knew I was in trouble. He just talked real calm. Called him Mr. Edwards. Your dad knew him from when he had the beat. He told him he was coming in just to talk. No guns. And he did. Edwards was ready to pull the trigger again, but your father talked to him for half an hour, calming him down. Finally, he gave your dad the shotgun.''

"Was that a long time ago?" Albert asked.

"It sure was, but just a year ago your father came with me to arrest a bank robber. The guy had killed a teller in San Diego. I got a tip that he was holed up in a downtown hotel. We didn't have time to round up a lot of people and it was only a tip. We had a picture of the suspect and the desk clerk confirmed that he was in his room. We got a key and quietly unlocked the door, but the guy had wedged a chair against it. Your father got a running start and crashed the door in with his shoulder. When the robber reached under his pillow for his gun your dad yanked him up and punched him out.'' The boys' eyes were wide.

"He's not an Uncle Tom either, is he, Fraleigh," John asked.

"Well, you make up your own minds. Ten years ago he spoke up for the rights of black officers to get promoted and assigned to specialized police units. And he was president of the local NAACP for three years. None of that was too popular.''

Albert's eyes were watering. "He never said any of that.''

Now Sarah said, "They'd love to see you, Fraleigh. Do you ever get back this way?''

"I have to give depositions a week from Thursday.''

"Great, a week from Thursday night. Seven o'clock. I'll make veal parmigiana.''

"You know the way to a man's soul. I'll see you then, Sarah.''

Louis hadn't gone home.

* * *

I had made arrangements to have dinner with Janice in her room at the hospital. She didn't know it, but I had also set up a meeting with her doctor before dinner. "She's doing remarkably well. She needs bed rest, but not special attention. I'll discharge her Wednesday provided she had someone to stay with and take care of her," he said.

I wondered if they were a little anxious to get us out of here. Gunplay in the corridor tended to throw the personnel off schedule. "Wednesday? That's tomorrow. You don't think it's too soon?"

"Chief, your concern over the patient refutes all those hard-boiled cop stories we hear." He continued without even the hint of a smile. "The bullet didn't do much damage. She's healthy and making a fine recovery. You are well aware that in most gunshot wounds, it's the long-term prognosis that is problematic."

"And in this case?"

"That is precisely what I have been trying to tell you. This is a robust young woman. She's ready to leave the hospital. She'll need to take it easy at first. No sex for four weeks. Moderate walking for two weeks, then light exercise for a while, and she should be fine. It's possible that adhesions will form and some day cause internal problems, but no one can predict that."

"Children?" I surprised myself with the question.

"There should be no problem," he said, staring at me.

"Hello there," she said, taking my offered hand. She pulled me closer and puckered her lips for a kiss.

"How are you?"

"I feel like Cinderella. You gave me a little peck as if I was going to fall apart."

"Want me to try again?" I put on my best leer.

"Yes," she said promptly. She patted the side of the bed. "Sit."

I did and she pulled me forward. I carefully put my arms around her and we kissed.

"Hey, bud. This is visiting hours. Not sex hours."
The Block stuck his head in the door.

Janice laughed. Then grimaced, holding her stomach. "He's the funniest man. And not at all so tough when you get to know him. Like you. And Raoul is just wonderful. Both he and the Block spend hours talking with me. Did you know Raoul is going back to his wife and children?" She was talking a mile a minute. "My brother never told me about the feeling that cops have for each other. It's wonderful."

"You ought to write Irish ballads."

"Oh. I'm chattering away with abandon, not giving the chief a chance to pontificate." She pouted in such mock sorrow that I laughed.

"You should smile more often, it does things for you," she said. "And for me. I guess I'm getting better. There's not much to do and I kept waiting for you to get here. Isn't it terrible for me to admit that to you?"

"Not at all. You're hungry and you know that soon after I arrive they'll bring dinner. I read about it in college. Pavlov and all that stuff."

Right then, the orderly opened the door and brought dinner in. He wondered why we were both laughing. In between bites I studied Janice. Her color had returned. She didn't have much makeup on, just a touch of blush and light red lipstick. But she had a glow. Her curly brown hair was shining and framed a pretty face.

"Stop gawking at me. You'll give me indigestion. The food is bad enough."

After dinner, she excused herself to use the bathroom. She walked slowly, but brushed me away when I offered my arm. I sat down and picked up the morning newspaper, which I hadn't had a chance to read. The phone rang, I answered.

"This is Mrs. Winston from the second floor. Is either Officer Block or Officer English there?"

"Neither, right now."

"Well, could you tell them we'll be using Room 213 this evening, please? Oh, never mind. Here he comes now. Thank you.'' And she hung up. What the hell were those two up to now? I tried unsuccessfully to guess what was going on in 213.

"I hate to be a party pooper, but that medicine they gave me is putting me to sleep.'' Janice had returned and was getting into bed.

"Er, Janice. I talked to the doctor.'' She frowned. I cussed myself for floundering. "No. It's nothing bad.'' Her apprehension remained. "Well, he thinks you can leave tomorrow.'' I took the plunge. "I'd like you to stay at my place. We have it alarmed. You'll have your own bedroom. The security will be a lot easier.''

"Why, Fraleigh.'' The concern had left her face. "Do you really think I'll fall for this elaborate shooting scenario you arranged just to get me to your place?''

I pressed two on the elevator button. It seemed to be just another floor of the hospital. Arrows on the wall pointed me in the right direction. It said THERAPY SEC-TION above closed double doors. I went through and headed left toward 213.

"May I help you?'' A hard-faced, middle-aged woman with gray hair looked at me from behind a desk facing the double doors. A name plate in front of her said Mrs. Winston. Her bearing reminded me somewhat of an experienced jail matron.

I walked back to her. "My name is Fraleigh. The Block and English work for me.'' The woman's face softened at the mention of their names. She looked as she must have ten years ago—an attractive, pleasant woman. "I was just going to stop in 213 for a minute.''

"Go right ahead.'' She beamed at me.

The door to the room was partially open. I could hear the Block's grating voice. "And so the space prince aimed his sun beam at the invaders' space ship and dispatched a laser, which cut its magnetic field. In-stantly, the ship began to fade into the past time dimen-sion and inside the capsule the dragon chief pounded the instrument panel in frustration. 'In another minute

I would have destroyed them.' Princess Laura wrapped her arms around the Prince. 'Now you and I and our Cosmos Kingdom people will live in peace during the Century of Light,' she said.''

I moved closer. I saw the Block surrounded by a dozen kids ranging in age from about five to eleven. It looked like a commercial from UNESCO. The kids were all different races and ethnic backgrounds. A little black girl about six pleaded, "Read us another, please." She rubbed his cheek and he smiled at her.

"Sure, Lisa. What do ya wanta hear next?"

I shook my head and closed my eyes. But when I opened them the Block was still surrounded by kids. A brown-skinned boy hit the Block in the arm, punching with all of his ten-year-old's strength. "Hurt?" he asked.

"Hey, Juan, you got some punch there," the Block said, his face full of make-believe pain. The kids giggled and suddenly they were climbing all over him as he roared in mock anger.

Mrs. Winston had been watching me. I went back to her desk. "Isn't he wonderful with them?"

I nodded. "Who are those youngsters, Mrs. Winston?"

"Abused children. We have them for up to three months." Her face had hardened again. Then she smiled. "I hope it's all right. When I heard there were policemen on the fourth floor, I thought it would be just what the youngsters needed. The Block agreed right away. He takes them for two hours on Tuesdays and English is with them on Thursdays. He's different, but they love him just as much."

Seventeen

AT 1000 HOURS ON WEDNESDAY, FOUR DAYS AFTER THE shooting, Denise told me that Louis was on the phone.

"I called in to take a couple of more days off and Margaret told me you've been trying to get hold of me."

"Louis, where the hell are you?"

"Beverly Hills. Wait until you hear me sing."

Shit! "Louis, Nicastri was murdered Saturday night. The mayor has been bugging me about why you're not here. I told him that we had been in touch."

"The mayor, why he . . . What happened to Nicastri?"

"He was shot by a mobster. You better get back right away. This is very big and very bad. Call me back with your flight number and I'll meet you at the airport. I suggest you duck everyone until I brief you."

He sighed, but didn't argue. "OK, I'll get right back to you with the airline information."

An hour later Paul English came in. I knew he had taken Joan, the receptionist from Middleston Electronics, to dinner the night before and I was waiting for his report. "I trust that your dinner last night was a success? I mean as tiring as it must have been," I said, glancing at the clock.

"It was quite successful. Joan is charming, an altogether exemplary representative of her sex. However, I wish you to know that I'm spending all of this time with her strictly in the line of duty.''

''Don't bother putting in an expense voucher for dinner. I won't approve it and you're two hours late for work.''

''Pity. Well, at least she provided breakfast.''

''Paul, as much as tales of your sexual prowess intrigue me—''

''Fraleigh, as usual, your sarcastic interruptions are causing you to miss the point of my report. Joan has provided us with a way to get someone inside Middleston Electronics.''

''I'll reconsider on the dinner.''

''That seems only appropriate.'' He began to pace up and down, gesturing like he was lecturing a college class. He went on, ''It seems that for a year the company has been contracting outside for cleaning and minor maintenance. And the cleaning company is owned by Barney Smith.''

Barney was an old friend. A former FBI agent, he had left the Bureau after ten years, quickly becoming a millionaire by providing contract cleaning for Silicon Valley companies. His law enforcement interests had never waned, however. More than once, we had put undercover people in his operation with good results. It would be tricky, maybe fruitless, but . . .

''What do you think, Paul?''

''It's worth a try. I spoke to Barney. He has a meeting set up with Middleston Electronics at two o'clock today to answer their complaints about poor service. It would be natural to bring whoever is going under with him. The question is who? Either the Block or I would be recognized. And we're not sure of our personnel right now.''

''Nobody knows Raoul. He just came on board Friday and we kept him out of the press in the hospital shooting.''

"It's asking a lot of him after what he's been through in the last year."

"I know. I hate to even ask him, but there's no one else. We'll lay it out to him. If it's a no, we'll accept it."

We got Raoul on his home phone. He was still sharing guard duty with the Block. I spelled out the play to him. "What about Janice?" he asked.

"She's leaving the hospital. We can take you and the Block off and use uniformed men."

"Fraleigh, one thing. You know I never turned down an assignment, but I'm getting back with my wife and kids. Things are coming together for me now. I just can't take on an undercover job and patch up my marriage."

"I understand, Raoul. Don't worry about it, we'll get someone else."

"Who? You don't have anyone. And I really appreciate you hiring me. If you hadn't, I don't know what would have happened to me."

"Hey Raoul, forget it. I don't want you taking the assignment on that basis."

"Fraleigh, I'll tell you what. I'll do it for a week or two, then you owe me a week's compensatory time. It will give me a chance to make amends to Momma."

"I don't know, Raoul. Maybe we should forget it. You get back with Maria. This thing will work itself out."

"No. I want the assignment. Janice is quite a person. I want to be part of nailing the people responsible for getting her shot. Besides, it's a real whodunit."

"Are you sure?"

"Yeah. I'd like to do it for a week or two."

"OK. I already owe you a week. Let's make it two weeks off. At fourteen hundred hours Barney Smith will take you over to the plant. You know where his office is. Get over there about a quarter to. You'll go in as an apprentice helper so they won't expect you to know much."

He laughed. "I was a little worried about that. I'm not exactly the handiest guy."

I hung up. "Paul, give Barney a call. Explain some of what—"

"I already did. It was just a question of who and when. I'm glad that you agreed that my dinner costs last night should be reimbursed."

"Wait a minute. I didn't say it was approved. I said I'd reconsider and I have. The dinner was productive and under ordinary circumstances we should pay. However, since you informed me that you were provided breakfast the next morning it's a wash. You're even."

The investigation was moving forward. I went to my car to pick up Louis at the airport. Once again I almost missed the flyer under my windshield. Another corny icepick. It reminded me that I had forgotten to call Tony White. Well, it looked like Ned Dorn had some competition on taking me out.

Louis came into San Jose International Airport on a PSA flight from Los Angeles. I got a firm handshake and a big smile, but there was a shadow of something I couldn't read in his eyes. I drove us to the nearby Red Lion Inn. The buzz of traffic on the adjacent US 101 joined with the noise of airport jets to provide irrefutable evidence of the Valley's prosperity. The area surrounding the hotel had been some of the most fertile farmland in the world. Within the last decade it had been born again as the home of hundreds of computer-related businesses. The ornate lobby and multiple chandeliers were as new as Silicon Valley's electronic affluence. We went into the coffee shop and found a secluded table. The lunch crowd had just about cleared out.

I hadn't said anything, but Louis spoke like I had asked a question. "I didn't look at a paper for three days and only caught part of the TV news one night. I'm not sure that Nicastri's death was all that big a story in Southern California, but it was shitty luck. I missed it. And Margaret didn't say anything when I called."

Instead of reminding him that it had been more than three days I said, "She did a job on both of us, Louis. She knew I was waiting to see you, but she deliberately didn't tell you. She thinks she covered her ass in case we charge her with violating civil service regulations and under the circumstances I don't think we want any publicity on you not being aware of the case."

He nodded in agreement. "Bring me up to speed."

I waited until the waitress took our order then showed him a copy of the anonymous note on Captain Petrie. The original was in my safe.

"Why didn't I know about this?"

"I found it on my desk just before I left Friday night. I had been at the DA's office after I left you trying to get them off their ass on the Kelp murder case."

"What's the problem with that one?"

"Oh, it's some kind of turf war between the coroner and the county lab people. The result is her body never got examined to see if sexual intercourse had taken place. The DA is feeling sorry for himself because Chaney, the guy we busted for the homicide, has a pattern of rapes and now the prosecution won't be able to introduce it."

"Want me to call the DA?"

"No. It looks like they got together on it finally. It won't help in this case, but hopefully in the future the machinery of justice will function a little better than a Model T Ford. But I did go up to your office with the note, about 1800 hours. You were gone."

"Right. The Chamber of Commerce and United Way were meeting to plan this year's fund drive. I'm going to be chairman. I had to be there."

"Yeah. Well, I decided to stake out his house. We borrowed a DEA van from their San Francisco office. The Block, English, and I did the surveillance."

"Good idea. Come up with anything?"

I took a breath. "Did we? You're not going to like this, Louis. We observed Nicastri, Carol Mansell, and Alex Fortono visiting Petrie."

Louis frowned. "You mean to say you had the mayor's aide under surveillance without telling me?"

"Wait a minute, Louis. I didn't dream Nicastri was going to show up."

"You should have informed me immediately."

"You might recall that I called you right away and you refused to tear yourself away from the mayor's party. And Carol Mansell. She's bad news, Louis. I can't believe you got involved, knowing her background."

He was furious. "That's no goddamned excuse and you know it. You should have come right over to get me. She was supposed to be through with Alex Fortono for a long time. If you had told me you saw them together . . ."

I bit my tongue to keep from reminding him that he had said no way. He hadn't been in to mood to see me. His singing lessons were more important.

"All right, go on," he said.

I shoved some of Paul's pictures across the table. He looked at them briefly, frowning for a moment at Caruso carrying the suitcase. "The guy with the suitcase is the one who hit Nicastri," I said.

"What did you do after the surveillance?" he asked.

"They all left except Petrie. We didn't have enough for a warrant. The van had to be returned. Paul sat on the house in his car. Shortly after I relieved him, Caruso showed up. He went in and came right out carrying a package which turned out to be an Uzi, the murder weapon."

Louis sat there, absorbing. I began to feel a little better. He was a master at analyzing and directing an investigation. He nodded and I continued. "I followed Caruso to Lefty's Fun Palace, a male strip joint. They almost made me, but I managed to get out of there in one piece. A young woman, Janice Bell, helped me. Her brother is LAPD."

He frowned. "You brought in a civilian? How long have you known her?"

"Louis, I didn't know her. I sat at her table by ac-

cident. She hid me and led me out of the place. She
ended up getting shot by Caruso.''

"Shot? Jesus Christ! I don't believe this. I take a
couple of lousy days off and. . . . How did she get
shot?"

"She put the Hound Dog under Caruso's Cadillac."

"What? What the hell were you thinking of, Fraleigh, to let a woman you don't even know do that?"

"I didn't want her to do it. She just did. I thought
she was just . . ." I decided I didn't want to tell Louis
that she had wet the seat and I was afraid the equipment
was damp. "Louis, if you let me tell this, we can go
back over the whole thing. It will be a lot quicker."

"Yeah, I bet. Go on."

"OK. Janice sticks the apparatus in place. Caruso
and Nicastri are in the far end of the parking lot. Just
then I hear a burst from the Uzi and see Nicastri go
down. Caruso runs like hell. I yell for him to stop. He
goes right past me. The girl is frozen. I didn't dare
shoot for fear of hitting her. When he sees her, he cuts
her down. I empty my gun. Hit him once, unfortunately
not fatal. He takes off. I radio for help and rush Janice
to the hospital.''

Louis stroked his chin. "When . . . never mind. Go
on.''

"A uniformed cop stops Caruso based on my APB.
Incredibly, our valiant Captain Petrie, who is not working but is on standby, responds. In front of four witnesses he beats a confession out of Caruso, who
conveniently tells him where he threw the Uzi and other
little tidbits that get excluded the next day."

"What the hell! Petrie . . . ? Where were you, Fraleigh?"

"I was in the hospital giving a transfusion to the girl.
You might at least ask how she is."

"I used to have enough confidence in you to believe
that if she was killed or in critical condition you would
have included it in your report. But I better ask. How
is she?"

The two of us were ready to start swinging. "She's going to be all right probably, but she did undergo surgery. In any event, the next day the judge suppresses the evidence under Fruit of the Poisoned Tree doctrine. Petrie's violation of the suspect's constitutional rights mean that the gun as well as the statements were inadmissible."

"He wouldn't hold him based on your testimony?"

"I got there a little late. They had already cut him loose."

"You were late? Didn't you anticipate that without your testimony there was no case?"

"Of course. I sent word that I'd be delayed. Janice had a relapse, they thought they might have to operate again. I gave more blood."

"I won't ask why only your blood could be used."

I let that pass and went on. "Paul followed Caruso. After the judge cut him loose, his lawyer drove him in the Cadillac. It still had the Hound Dog on it, so Paul had no trouble. Crazy Phil, as he is know to the police in LA and Chicago, was driven right to Middleston Electronics. They used the executive entrance."

"Did you ask the mayor about this?" Louis frowned.

"I'm not in the habit of telling suspects about what we know in investigations and asking their advice."

"Damn it, Fraleigh. He's the mayor and he's innocent until proven guilty just like anyone else. You have nothing. The cocaine note must be bullshit. You know Fortono is too big to get close to dope and the mayor is one of the richest men in the state. You don't even have enough to get a search warrant."

"I guess the pictures of Nicastri and Fortono are my imagination."

"Fraleigh, I've tried to tell you a number of times, up at our level you have to get out of this habit of thinking of guilt by association. You're still talking like a street patrolman. People of the mayor's social station and wealth travel in all kinds of circles. And it's also possible that he didn't know what Nicastri was doing. So there may well be a reasonable explanation."

"I'd love to hear it." I held up my hand to stop his interruption. "The plot thickens. Two days after Caruso disappears, two hoods attempt to off Janice in the hospital. They lose the shootout. One splits, but the other dies. He was a small-town punk from Chicago. Raoul Chavez did a hell of a job."

"Raoul Chavez! What the hell was he doing in the hospital?" Louis was as angry as I had ever seen him, but I kept going.

"He came on board Friday. I assigned him to the hospital. He's a lot more trustworthy than Petrie and the others the mayor and Nicastri saddled us with. By the way, we may have enough for a warrant for the whole bunch of them tomorrow."

"How's that?"

"Paul and the Block seized the suitcase from Petrie's garage when they went to put him on administrative leave."

"You didn't question him either?"

"You know damn well he's a cutie. We'd get nothing and they'd find out everything we know."

"Doesn't sound like we know much right now. You went ahead and hired Chavez even though I ordered you not to?"

"He came in with a psychiatrist's letter giving him a clean bill of health. Listen, Louis, it's a damn good thing we have Raoul. Nobody knows him. I put him inside Middleston Electronics to see if he can spot Caruso or anything else going on."

"Inside? You put someone undercover in the mayor's corporation? Naturally, you told the mayor about all this?"

"As far as I'm concerned, right now, the mayor is one of the players."

"Let me remind you that I'm back and that the police in the United States are under civilian control. We don't live in a police state. How did you get him in?"

"Barney Smith's cleaning service. Louis, about Carol Mansell. I begged you on the phone to go home alone. I asked to see you."

"All right. I won't see her again. I guess it was too good to be true."

He was so down that I almost didn't say it. "Louis, think. They used her to get you out of town. Now they've got a hammer on you."

He didn't answer, nor did he say another word during the twenty-minute drive to headquarters.

Eighteen

I WAS TOO LATE TO MAKE DINNER AT THE HOSPITAL that night, but when I got there around 1930 hours, English and his new friend Joan were visiting. She was everything Paul had described. Janice gave me a big hello. I went through what had become a standard greeting, a hug and kiss. I was aware that Paul and company were taking it all in. When I turned around, I avoided his knowing smile. His girlfriend's mushy expression was right out of a happy ending on "Little House on the Prairie." I sat down a little sullenly, but soon was laughing along with them at Janice's mimicking of the doctor's description of the Block guarding the shooting scene. The physician hadn't minced words with her.

"Is there anything new on Caruso? I still dream about that terrible man and his machine gun." Paul and Joan had left and Janice wanted to be brought up to date. I told her about my difficult meeting with Louis. She was silent for a while, then said softly, "He must be under a lot of pressure. You two are very close and a little conflict between close friends produces a disproportionate amount of hurt. Did you always work together?"

"For quite a few years. We've been good friends."

"Oh, Fraleigh. Don't be so rigid. You say that with such finality."

"Louis has changed. I don't know him anymore. I once watched him direct a complex investigation for two years. It involved serial murders of young hikers. He was under fantastic pressure. The media, the brass, problems of coordinating with other agencies, and he was terrific. He was always solid, kept everyone else calm. Now he's split from his wife, drinking more than ever, involved with Carol Mansell . . ."

"But it's a different job. He's the brass now. And it can't be easy dealing with an ego like the mayor's. The pressure must be enormous. I don't thing you're being fair to him."

"Are you kidding? I've been breaking my back covering for him with the mayor while he was off shacked up with a broad he shouldn't be seen with."

"That's what I mean. You think you're holier than thou because you lied for him, but you're actually being terribly righteous in your judgment of him. You're so antimanagement. I wonder how you ever agreed to come with him and take the job as chief of detectives?"

Briefly I told her about our problems and the phony charges against the Block and English. She listened without interruption. "It's too bad. You were so close and now you can't communicate with each other. You have to try to be more understanding, Fraleigh."

"Mm. You know tomorrow is the big day. Are you up to getting out of here?"

"Are you serious? I can't wait."

By tacit agreement we changed to more pleasant matters. I had asked my cleaning lady, Mrs. Washington, to do an extra cleanup of the place and to get some flowers. I hoped it had been done.

"Fraleigh, tell me again about the note that you found on Nicastri."

"It was some computer gibberish. I guess the mayor was afraid that I was going to denounce him for using Nicastri for his private business. Actually, we would have paid to keep the weasel doing anything as long as he stayed out of our hair.''

''I majored in engineering with a minor in computer science. I got fed up with computers and became interested in business, but I'm curious to see what you call gibberish. Could you bring that note tomorrow?''

''Sure. I didn't know that that you were a computer maven. How did you get from there to studying strip joints?''

''I told you. I was bored with bits and bytes. And I'm not into strip joints. You're such a smart-ass. I'm also a member of an antinuclear group. You're probably horrified like my brother.''

''An antinuke, eh? Get busted and all that stuff?''

''Yes. Do you think annihilation of the human race is something to laugh at?''

''No.'' I eased off. ''You're quite right, it is a serious problem.''

''Don't patronize me. I'm not a child. If you think it's a serious problem, what have you ever done about it?''

''Let's talk about something else. I'm too tired to get beat up by a feminist tonight.''

''I happen to care about womens' rights, too, but it's interesting that you equate the two causes.''

''Look, if you're not going to be able to maintain your objectivity like I do, I can't trust you to help unravel the mysteries of this case. You'll be reduced to watching daytime television.''

She looked at me a long moment before saying, ''That's male coercion, but I'll let you win this time.'' The smile was back, thank God.

The next day we checked out of the hospital. It was a twenty-minute drive through suburban sprawl to my apartment. Endless rows of tract housing were interrupted only by intermittent shopping centers and nests of condominiums, all sandwiched between freeways. They had labeled it the New City, but it was the same old traffic congestion on any street that went halfway straight. I stayed off the freeways. Even this early in the afternoon it was bumper-to-bumper time. Houses located within a half-mile radius of the freeways were wrapped in the constant hum of traffic, while their inhabitants inhaled the automobile and industrial fumes that passed for air in this part of the country. And the only people not worrying about toxic spills from the electronics manufacturing companies were alcoholics and those who drank bottled water. Of course, the privilege of living in Silicon City made it all worthwhile.

Janice did a cursory inspection. The tiny kitchen had a breakfast counter that looked out on the living room. She opened the refrigerator door.

"Golly," she said. Mrs. Washington had been good enough to shop for me. The refrigerator was full. I was glad Janice was impressed. I had been when Mrs. W. told me how much it all cost. Jan moved from the kitchen into the living room, glancing at my collection of books, mostly paperback, lining the living room wall around a small fireplace.

"A real fireplace. But I don't see any wood."

"It's still August, remember."

"I was afraid you were going to say that you used paper logs."

She walked into the bedroom, inspected the queen-sized bed and the bathroom without comment. Back in the living room, she briefly checked my record collection, then plopped into the chair across from the small coffee table.

"It's comfortable. I can see you sitting here in front of a fire, reading Elmore Leonard to improve your professional performance."

"Actually, I read sex manuals for that."

"Promises, promises." She laughed.

"This move has probably tired you out. Why don't you rest a while."

"No. I'm sick of resting. I had to walk every day in the hospital. Now I want to."

She took my hand and we went out the sliding glass door, past the small brick patio, and onto the lawn. There was a light wind, bringing with it the distant hum of the freeway. We walked toward the jogging trail. I kept one eye out for Lorraine and the other for Icepick Ned, but there were only a couple of kids on the path.

"God, it's a beautiful day. Why is it that you have to get sick to appreciate the ordinary?" she said.

She walked very slowly, but I worried about her stumbling on a rock or hole concealed by the grass. After a short distance I said, "Janice, maybe you should take it easy at first. How about we go back and sit on the patio for a while. I'll make you some tea."

"All right. I'll let you baby me for a while, but even the hospital gave me a glass of wine with lunch. I noticed a bottle of Mirrasou Chardonnay in the refrigerator."

"I'll call the doctor to see if it's OK," I joked.

"They're all so glad to get rid of me and Block, they'll agree to anything."

The wine wasn't cold enough, so I stuck it in an ice bucket. She raised her eyebrows in mock admiration. "Class."

"To a quick recovery." I raised my glass to hers.

"Delicious. And that bouquet of flowers on the coffee table is just for me? You've totally destroyed your hard-guy reputation, you know. If you start annoying me, I can ruin you. I'll simply tell the Department the truth."

I took a copy of the puzzling computer note we had found on Nicastri from my pocket and gave it to her. "Don't think you're going to laze around here without earning your keep, sister."

"Even talking out of the side of your mouth won't save your tough-guy rep. But it is funny. You can't act at all, you know. They better not ever let you do undercover work." She frowned at the slip of paper. "This intrigues me. You don't think it's important, do you?"

"In an investigation, anything may turn out to be

important. But you have to set priorities. The analysis of that suitcase is what I really want to see as soon as possible."

"And this is low priority, right?"

"Are you kidding? Look at the lengths I'm going to to get expert analysis."

The glass of wine did what I expected. "It's only four o'clock and so pleasant sitting here, but suddenly, I can't keep my eyes open," she said.

"Come on. I'll show you where everything is."

"I'll just lie down for a few minutes." She stretched out on the bed. She was dressed in dark blue slacks and a lighter blue short-sleeved blouse. I put a blanket over her. "The service isn't bad, so far," she said. A minute later she was breathing deeply. I watched for a while, then went to sit on the patio, unsuccessfully trying to identify what I was feeling.

Nineteen

ANOTHER WEEK SLIPPED BY. LOUIS AND I MET BRIEFLY several times. He said nothing further about discussing the case with the mayor and I certainly wasn't going to bring it up. No news was good news as far as I was concerned. Raoul was working at Middleston Electronics. He was to contact us only if there was something to report. The lab promised an analysis of the suitcase any moment.

Uniformed men guarded Janice during the day. I took over when I got home. The beat officer gave us extra attention at night. We had long, leisurely dinners. Most nights I grilled fish, steaks, or chicken on the patio barbecue. She teased me about the simplistic barbecue recipes I followed religiously, although twice I wrung out of her exclamations of "delicious"—once for my barbecue lemon-onion-basted swordfish steaks, and another time for lamb chops marinated in dry sherry with a touch of olive oil, oregano, onion, and a dash of salt and pepper. We shared a taste for artichokes with a lemon butter dipping sauce, flavored with just a touch of tarragon and served with chilled Robert Mondavi Fumé Blanc. Other nights Janice tossed a salad for us with a tasty dressing.

One night over dinner she pulled out of me the story

of my failed marriage. The following day I told her about my disastrous love affair with Sandra.

"It's too bad you didn't have children by your first marriage."

"I was only married once. Sandra and I never even talked about it. And that is the craziest thing I've ever heard. The one thing I'm grateful for is that I don't have to worry about kids whose lives I messed up."

"I don't really disagree. It's just that you're really an affectionate person and I think you still love Sandra."

"Wrong. And please don't start analyzing me. I have to put up with English and the Block doing it all day."

"Paul is very handsome. Has he ever married?"

"No. But if you're interested . . ."

"You can relax. I have no romantic interest in Paul. I'm just curious about the interaction. You're all so different from each other. I've gotten to know the Block and you, but Paul has only visited me once. Raoul told me what the three of you went through in the Stone ambush. Was it the head injury that made Paul a little . . . you know, a little strange?"

"He was captured in Vietnam and went through a bad time. Actually, he's been more normal since he got knocked into a coma."

"So-o-o tough. But you're not fooling anyone. You're really a team of little boys and despite the teasing you're very protective of each other. The Block told me you were, in his words, ga-ga for Sandra and crazy about her children. I still don't understand why it didn't work out. God, you do have a temper after all. You're furious."

"I don't appreciate those guys spilling their half-assed theories to you."

"You really can't stand anyone getting too close." She smiled. "I'm sorry. I guess I am being terribly nosy and analytical, but after all I've never lived with a man before. But tell me this. Do you think Paul is serious about Joan? I saw the way they were looking at each other when they came to visit."

"I doubt it. Somehow it's hard to imagine Paul putting himself in a position where he had to work to support a wife and kids."

"That idea is so ridiculously old-fashioned. Both parents work nowadays and with comparable worth catching on, women don't have to be apologists." She narrowed her eyes. "You do believe in comparable worth?"

"Sure. If a woman does the same job as a man she should get the same pay."

"Fraleigh, are you putting me on? No. You're not. You're so damned smug, complacent. You don't even know what comparable worth means do you?"

"Whatever it is, I'm for it," I said, but I could see that my reasonableness wasn't going to help.

"Women shouldn't have to be truck drivers and cops just to get a decent wage. The male-dominated world has it set up so that secretaries, nurses, and other traditional female occupations are on the low end of the wage scale."

"It seems to me that the marketplace, supply and demand, has something to do with it."

"Is that so?" There was color in her cheeks and she was damned appealing even with angry eyes. "I guess the male chauvinist school of economics can explain why truck drivers, who certainly aren't that highly skilled, earn twice what clerical workers earn?"

"It's probably more than double, but in that case you're right. It's not demand that jacked those salaries up. It's an organization called the Teamsters Union. Pure power tactics. If women want the dough they can join the Teamsters."

"Brilliant. Just brilliant, Fraleigh. All this time a cop when you should be in the University of Chicago's School of Economics. And stop grinning at me or I'll hit you with my dinner plate."

"Hey. You're violent. Maybe you could be a union organizer."

"Very funny. But, dear chauvinist, you inadvertently

defined the issue. It's power, whether union or political. The women's movement is our clout and it's going to overcome all the male nonsense about the marketplace supply and demand just the way the Teamsters and other unions did.''

"Just don't cut my pay, OK? It's kind of expensive wining and dining you in the style you're accustomed to.''

"Once more you're saved by the bell, Fraleigh. You're spared my devastating comments on the last crack because those two glasses of wine with dinner were just too much in my delicate condition.'' She postured, rolling her eyes skyward and holding her stomach, which was slightly swollen. "Good night, my body guard and chef.'' She came close and kissed me full on the mouth.

It was a mistake. I put my arms around her and kissed back. Both of us were breathing deeply. She pulled away, flushed. "Remember the doctor's advice, Fraleigh.'' She attempted lightness but didn't make it. We had only known each other for days, but it had been intense. The danger. Her injury. The laziness of the summer evenings. There was something going on between us and I had mixed feelings about that.

"Good night, Jan.'' I watched her walk erectly into the bedroom. I guessed from the stiffness of her walk and the way her right hand was pressed against her stomach that she was feeling some pain, but she never complained.

A couple of hours later I began to doze over some case reports I had brought home. I got into a pair of pajama shorts, my hot-weather sleeping attire. I used the bathroom as quietly as possible and walked back toward the living room, where I bunked on the sofa bed. As I closed the door, I heard her whimpering. I went over in the dark and touched her forehead. It was wet with perspiration. I touched her face and felt tears. "Let me get you something for the pain, Jan.''

"I just took pain pills. Come and hold me.''

I slipped into bed next to her. I put my left arm around her and moved up against her back. She was on her side and snuggled her rear end into me, taking my hand and cupping it over a breast covered by the thin nightgown. I got hard. It was almost painful, yet there was a peaceful pleasure in the intensity, knowing that sex wasn't possible. After a while she fell asleep and I stayed cushioned against her warm flesh, my face in her hair, inhaling her smell. When I woke in the morning my right arm was numb and cramped.

My days were full during the next week. The Uzi bandits had pulled another daytime robbery and this time a liquor store clerk was dead. The Downtown Business Association had met with Louis and me, but they were demanding to see the mayor. The mobile park rapist was on vacation, but the gray van rapist had hit for the thirteenth time in four months, mostly in neighborhoods where he wasn't supposed to. Six of his assaults had been in the usual places, on the fringes of the university, the downtown minority and low-income sections, but the rest had taken place in the high-rent district. Homes upward of three hundred thousand. Lawyers, engineers, budding entrepreneurs, lower-strata venture capitalists, money managers. Silicon City's third tier. They weren't quite up to their idols, who had made it to the extent that security patrols and live-in help kept their estates and surrounding streets free from strangers. But if the new elite hadn't quite caught up to the betters economically, they were no slouches at screaming when their wives and daughters were attacked. And the van rapist hadn't helped. He was increasingly vicious, sometimes brutally punching his victims into unconsciousness.

We needed a task force of sex investigators and patrol people to come up with him. The problem was that Curtin, my best sexual assault investigator, who was so gentle with victims that they ended up loving him, didn't particularly get along with other cops. And Patrol Captain Toll, who was to coordinate deployment of uniformed personnel with the task force, had never been a dick and was known as a prussian in the patrol bureau. The citizens alert group wanted a meeting with us the next day, prior to their formal protest to the mayor and City Council.

"LaRouche needs to see you."

I looked up. Paul had come into my office unannounced, as usual.

"He'll have to get on line."

The Block followed Paul into the room. "Fraleigh's down on shrinks," he said.

"His ill-fated love affair with Sandra Fortune, the female Darth Vader of the profession, is no doubt a factor," Paul said.

I looked down at my yellow pad. If I put Toll and Curtin together at the citizens meeting, all hell would break loose. On the other hand, if Captain Toll got the idea that he had been cut out . . .

"Seriously, Fraleigh. Dr. LaRouche is concerned about Raoul. I know you don't like LaRouche, but Raoul is having flashbacks over the hospital shooting," Paul said.

"What? The hood he killed had a manslaughter conviction, two aggravated assaults, one extortion, and an attempted murder with a deadly weapon. He has also been associated with Splioto's organization in Kansas City," I said.

"Nevertheless," Paul answered, "he was a human being."

"Yeah. Nobody's perfect." The Block laughed so loudly that Denise poked her head in the doorway.

"Did you call, Chief?" She knew I hadn't, but she was terrified of the Block. His cackle probably sounded like a war cry to her and she was being superloyal, checking to see if she needed to call an ambulance for me. I kept forgetting to tell her that Janice found the Block "sweet."

"No, Denise." I smiled to show that I was unafraid.

"You're due at the indoctrination for new investigators in Room 307," she said, anxious to get me away from the Block.

"Will you see LaRouche?" Paul asked.

"You gotta help Raoul, Fraleigh," the Block added. He smelled of barbecue sauce and . . . beer! It was ten thirty in the morning. There was a suspicious spot of red sauce on his chin.

"Block, goddamn it. Have you been having barbeque and beer?"

"Don't get your balls in an uproar just because I'm trying to help a fellow officer. I can file a grievance on that. Right, Paul?"

Captain Toll walked into the office. Few patrol officers wore hats. It had been optional for a couple of years. Toll's hat was on letter perfect. His uniform was impeccable. His shoes had been spit-shined. He was frowning, but momentarily he forgot what he had come for. His nose wrinkled and he turned suspiciously toward the Block.

"What can I do for you, Captain?" I said before he could ask questions.

He turned toward me. "Chief Fraleigh, sir. I believe I should select the personnel for this task force—"

I saw knowing glances flash between the Block and Paul. I moved quickly. "Captain, I'm heading for a meeting. Would you walk with me? We can discuss it on the way." I nodded to Paul. "I'll see you two later and you can set up that appointment with LaRouche."

"Yes, sir, Chief Fraleigh, sir," Paul said. The Block stood at attention and saluted as we left. Toll glared at them. Within two minutes, they would have turned him into a raving lunatic.

When I returned to the office Denise said, "Someone named Raoul called. He wouldn't leave a message, but said he was having lunch at Gus's around twelve o'clock tomorrow. He hung up before I could tell him that you're scheduled for lunch with Chief Robinson."

"Call Margaret and cancel the lunch. See if I can meet any other time during the day with the chief."

Later in the afternoon, I met with Toll and Curtin about the task force. For forty-five minutes I reasoned, cajoled, flattered, and did all the things that I had observed Louis do successfully. All that happened is that Captain Toll sat straighter in his chair and got more rigid. Curtin, sexual investigator par excellence, slouched deeper in his chair. His responses and facial expressions got more sullen as Toll's increased in military stiffness.

My phone rang. Looking at the clock, I immediately remembered. Janice was fixing a celebration dinner of sorts. We had known each other for two weeks. Mrs. Washington had done the shopping. All I had to do was show up around six. Goddamn it. The clock told me I was already twenty minutes late, and these two sat, silently rebuking me for taking a call during our conference.

"Fraleigh."

"You forgot."

"No. I've been tied up in a meeting. Hold on a minute."

I put the phone down and faced them. "Now listen, you two. Thirteen people have been raped. If this character hits on one more victim in this town I'm going to have your asses. Do you understand?" I slammed the desk. Toll jumped slightly out of his seat and Curtin perceptibly eased out of his slouch.

"Toll. *I'll* pick the personnel and you'll goddamn well coordinate it smoothly with the dick bureau. Got it?"

"Yes, sir."

"And you." I pointed to Curtin, whose expression was alert, without a trace of sullenness. "You'll address that citizen group and I want them purring with satisfaction over the police department's efforts by the time they get to City Hall."

"Gotcha, Chief."

"OK. That's all."

Toll actually saluted. Curtin, being a dick, gave a careful half wave, half salute, and they got out quickly.

I picked up the phone. "Wow. What was that all about?" Janice asked.

"Progressive personnel administration. I'll pick up the wine and be home in fifteen."

"Yes, sir." I heard her laughing before I hung up.

Twenty

EARLY THE NEXT MORNING PAUL HANDED ME A SINGLE sheet of paper, the lab report on the suitcase. "It contained microscopic traces of element number seventy-nine."

I looked down at the report. One of the enterprising lab boys had drawn a little square. In the upper left-hand corner I saw the number 79. Directly opposite in the top right corner was the drawing of a rectangular cube with a period in the middle of the cube's face. Below the rectangle, **Au** was printed in boldface. Under 79, numbers were listed in a column in lighter, smaller print: 2970, 1063, and 19.3. Square in the middle of the box in bold black, but smaller print, was the number 196.967 and the word "Gold."

"Gold? No cocaine?"

"Correct."

"What the hell are all these numbers and symbols?"

"You needn't be irritable just because the lab report didn't conform to your expectations." He pointed to the 79. "This is the element's atomic number. 'Au' is its symbol; the cube represents its crystal structure, 196.967 is its atomic weight. Its going point is 2970."

"Paul, enough, damn it. What does it mean?"

"For one thing, that your own boiling point has been

reached, but these are merely the scientific characterists of the basic element of gold, a yellowish, precious, malleable, ductile metallic element. The lab analyst was cautiously noncommittal, but finally admitted to me that he thinks the traces did not come from jewelry or gold nuggets. He believes it quite likely that the particles came from gold bars rubbing together. He would not certify any of this officially.''

"Gold bars. We can't get a search warrant on that basis. There wasn't any trace of drugs?''

"None. However, I do have news from my own investigation. The luggage, as we suspected, is expensive—Vuitton. Only three stores in the area carry the brand. I investigated the one nearest to the Middleston estate and obtained this charge copy.''

I looked. The suitcase had been part of a set purchased on the account of Lorraine Middleston. The copy of the sales slip was signed by her and the date was eight months ago.

"Had it been drugs, we would have had Solly tight.''

"True. Now all we seem to have is a thickening plot,'' Paul said.

"I have to meet with Louis. Would you like to come along?''

"I think not. You two are the protagonists in this drama.''

"Thanks, Paul. I'll keep that learned comment in mind until the right moment.''

He hesitated, then sighed. "The Block is the one who should be reporting this. He took his mother out for her birthday and saw Carol Mansell and Louis leaving Alexander's restaurant last night.''

Alexander's was one of the *in* places. Expensive, glamorous and frequented by Silicon City elite. The entrepreneurs, venture capitalists, and members of the top banking and law firms. Naturally, yuppie engineers and mid-managers came to gape at the high-tech celebs.

I went past Margaret, the frowning female dragon,

without comment. Louis was on the phone, but he waved me to a chair. "Yes, Claude. I'll take care of it. Yes, I understand."

Claude was probably Claude Romain, the mayor's new legal counsel. He had been Nicastri's underling. Louis listened carefully. He seemed tired. "I said I'd take care of it." He scowled and there was an edge to his voice. This wasn't the usual let-it-all-roll-off-your-shoulders Louis. He hung up.

"How's it going?" he asked. No smile. No handshake. He wasn't even trying to hide his preoccupation.

"We got the lab report on the suitcase. No drugs, but traces of gold, possibly from gold bars rubbing together. The suitcase was purchased on the charge account of Lorraine Middleston and that name was signed on the sales slip."

"Do you have the lab report?"

I handed it to him. "I don't see any reference to gold bars. How do you know it didn't come off jewelry or something?"

"The analyst gave a verbal opinion, but wouldn't confirm it in writing."

He leaned back in his chair. His eyes were hard. "And Raoul Chavez?"

"I'm meeting him at noon. That's why I cancelled lunch, but don't worry, Louis. I still owe you a meal. I'll buy next time." I smiled.

He was frowning. "So despite this intensive investigation of the mayor, we still don't have the elements of a crime and we have an undercover cop with an itchy trigger finger planted in the mayor's corporation. This would look like great Keystone cop stuff, Fraleigh, if the media got hold of it."

I swallowed and shoved the crack about Raoul out of my mind before I spoke. "We still have the murder of Nicastri by a mob flunkie who, just hours before the hit, was with the mysterious Captain Petrie, who was hired by the police department at the mayor's insistence."

"I think maybe it's time to have a frank discussion with the mayor and then interrogate Petrie."

"I don't agree, Louis. You're quite right. We don't have evidence of anything yet. If we question them, we achieve nothing except listening to a bunch of bullshit and they learn what we know."

"I'm trying to get through to you. I report to the mayor. He's my boss. You seem to have convicted him in your mind, although you're not even sure of what. But I can't justify withholding information from him any longer. He may have a perfectly reasonable explanation of his contacts and we're not giving him a chance to clear the air and maybe help get this investigation moving. Also, I have to tell him about Chavez. He'd be justified in firing me right now for keeping that from him."

"How about giving it a couple of more days before you brief him?"

He stared at me. "Two days. But I'm telling him about Chavez today."

"I'll have to pull him out, Louis. I can't let his cover get burned and keep him in there."

"I'll emphasize to the mayor that he's not to tell anyone."

I got up to go. "I hope you'll reconsider that and not tell him at all. In forty-eight hours we'll lay the whole thing out for the mayor. We can tell him then."

Back in my office, I did what I had shrunk from. I called Daddy Warbucks. "Fraleigh, how are they hanging?"

"No lower than yours, Daddy. Are you free for lunch tomorrow?"

"You know I'm never free, Fraleigh. You usually buy dinner, though."

"Can't make dinner. Where should I meet you?"

"How about Perry's? Around twelve. I'll adjust my schedule so that I can get the full benefit out of our law enforcement conference."

It was his way of saying that senior FBI agent George Warbucks would eat and drink up a storm in exchange for whatever tidbits of information I was able to win from him. I then called Pete Haskill, the regional federal drug enforcement chief, for a breakfast meeting in the Palm Court in the Sheraton. I was wryly conscious that my past meetings of this kind in San Francisco had lasted into the wee hours of the morning. Now I had to get home for dinner.

I went to meet Raoul at Gus's, a working-class bar not too far from Middleston Electronics. It served a halfway decent lunch. I shed my jacket and tie before entering. Raoul was in a corner booth, but I took my time in acknowledging him. No one seemed to be interested in him or me, so I approached slowly. He waved me on. "Nobody to worry about, Fraleigh, except maybe her." He grinned at the young waitress, who seemed totally uninterested in us except as customers.

"Something from the bar?" she asked, running a greasy rag over the table.

"A Coors light. How about you Raoul?"

"A Bud light."

"Make it two Bud." I forgot Raoul had a chip on about Coors.

"You're beginning to get the message, Fraleigh."

"Yeah." It brought to mind Janice's reaction to the nuclear thing. It was getting so you couldn't talk to people without a sensitivity scorecard. The waitress returned with the beer. We ordered combinations of Chili Rellenos, Cheese Enchiladas, and Chicken Enchiladas.

"Have you seen anything interesting, like a fugitive named Crazy Phil Caruso, in between changing light bulbs?"

"Hey, don't knock hard work, Fraleigh. It's good for the soul."

"If this is what you have for lunch, it's bad for the body."

He laughed. "I've been running at lunch. I'm just bulking up because of you."

"Have you seen anything?"

"No sign of Caruso, but I'm stunned by the coke. It's so open. Half the employees don't have coffee breaks, they have dope breaks. It's a drug flea market in the parking lots during lunch time. Two of the top executives actually put the stuff up their noses right in their office while I was working five feet away. Of course, I'm just another wetback to them, but still . . ."

"We haven't been able to find even a trace of Caruso. Do you think he might be hiding at the plant?"

"No. But an interesting thing. You know how at any given time there's half a dozen cars in the parking lot covered with canvas?"

I shrugged my ignorance.

"They let employees leave cars there during vacation, whatever. Their sports cars have to be protected. Well, the second day I came to work the Caddy was there and it was covered."

"Are you sure it was the same car?"

"Oh, yeah. I looked under the canvas."

"I'm not sure you should be taking those kinds of chances, Raoul. In fact, I'm thinking of pulling you out. These guys don't play."

"Believe me, I'm just another Mexican to them. I'm invisible."

"How are you doing personnally? You had a close call on the shooting. Is everything OK?"

"Everything except that loco shrink, LaRouche. Get that guy off my back, Fraleigh. I went to him because the Department requires it and he keeps hassling me about dreams. I don't have none, but he won't accept it. And he keeps scheduling me for more sessions. I'm tired when I leave here. I put in ten or twelve hours a day. I don't have time for that bullshit."

I smiled. "It's for your own good, Raoul. Blowing that poor underprivileged hood away caused trauma. You're not even aware of it."

"I was aware for the first two days because I knew I waited a couple of seconds too long to shoot. I kept kicking my ass. If you hadn't drawn fire he would have blown me away. But the doctor thinks I feel guilty for shooting the goon. I try to tell him that he's wrong and he keeps saying that I shouldn't repress my feelings."

"Raoul, I want you to be alert. If there's the slightest sign that they're looking at you a little different, I want you to get in your car and drive right to headquarters. Agreed?"

"Sure. But I don't think it's likely. And something's up. Those two top cats I told you about, the ones doing coke in front of me, have been rushing around this morning. I went right into their offices. They were arguing about molecules or something. Usually they ignore me, but this time what they were talking about must of been something special. They shut up, but not before I heard one of them mention Caruso. I still have another week to go and I think we may come up with something."

"He mentioned Caruso? What did he say?"

"I don't know. I just caught the tail end of their conversation. But they were talking about computers. I never seen so many terminals in my life. The secretaries have them. The receptionists have them. The executives use them. What do they all need them for?"

"To keep track of their dough and the dope. How do I know? You're the undercover man."

"Yeah. I'm kind of enjoying it. They got some fine-looking women there, Fraleigh."

"Don't forget Maria. How's the family?"

"Hey! Maria always said I can look as long as I don't touch." His teeth flashed and I noticed that this time the waitress passing by smiled at him. "Things are looking good. I talked to Maria. We're going to do a second honeymoon with those two weeks you promised me. In Ensenada. She has relatives there. They all think I'm El Jefé. It should be fun."

Twenty-One

THE 101 FREEWAY WAS STOP AND GO, ADDING TWENTY minutes to my trip. I was fifteen minutes late when I entered the Sheraton Hotel's Palm Court. The elegance of the stately old room was always impressive. Pete Haskill sat sipping coffee. He looked like he belonged. He was thin, about forty-five, with a full head of black hair. In his three-piece dark pin-striped suit, he looked more like a successful lawyer than a twenty-year federal cop.

"You must really need information to have picked this place, Fraleigh." He glanced at columns reaching upward to the lofty ceiling where sunlight flooded through the huge skylight. "Although it always used to be dinner when you needed help. Get married or something?"

"How are you, Pete? You're certainly looking prosperous." I shook his hand.

He fingered the suit self-consciously. "Marshall's on sale." He picked up the menu. "Too bad it's not Sunday. Did you ever try the brunch buffet?"

I was damn glad that it wasn't Sunday. Not only did ordering from the menu give me more time to feel Pete out, but I remembered yesterday's lunch calories with Raoul. And the Sunday buffet was loaded with Eggs

Benedict, bacon, sausage, home fries, croissants, danish pastries, all the foods I took pains to avoid. Naturally, a guy like Pete would load his plate. I would gain weight just from sitting next to him.

He ordered a large fresh orange juice, corned beef hash, two poached eggs, and a basket of croissants. I had grapefruit juice, bagels, and lox. We chatted. I had known Pete for about five years. He had transferred in as the assistant agent in charge. Unlike most of the people picked to head up the DEA and FBI offices, he was more cop than bureaucrat. But he still played them close to the chest. That was why I avoided him and Warbucks unless I was stymied. You always felt like you had given up more than you got in return.

"I'm curious about coke, Pete. It seems to be epidemic in Silicon City."

"Welcome to the club. Do you know anyplace where there's big money, celebrities, and no cocaine? The Valley is probably no worse than the entertainment and sports industries."

"What I'm wondering is whether any big shipments are coming in now? Last I heard, we were getting moderate amounts from Colombia. And it was a Cuban-Colombian group doing the importing and major distributing."

"What makes you think it's changed?"

"Well, some rumors. We hear that there may be new action with some of the electronics industry big shots and the old-line mafia bosses."

"Not the Mexican Mafia?"

Pete was into his usual fishing, but I wasn't about to discuss our note and surveillance in detail. "Pete, you know as well as I do that the Mexican Mafia and the Hispanic Nuestra Familia are knocking each other off. That is, the few left, the ones who aren't doing long sentences in the joint. They can't handle big action right now. But somebody is."

"Is this why you borrowed the surveillance van?"

"Yes and no. We may have a cop involved."

"I wondered why you would get into it, now that you're a big shot." He allowed himself an official DEA half-smile.

"You know, Pete, it's great of you to let me take you out to breakfast so that you can pump me for information and break my chops at the same time."

"Just our way of showing gratitude to you local taxpayers. We're sent from Washington to solve all your problems. This wouldn't have anything to do with Alex Fortono showing up in your territory lately, would it?"

"I guess that answers my question. If you guys have risen out of your stupor long enough to be aware that he's here, it must be big stuff."

"Who's the cop? It can't be some street patrolman to get you to spring for this kind of ambience."

"Ambience? I always knew you were a college man. How come they wouldn't take you into the FBI? It's a two-way street, Pete. Tell me what's going on. Maybe we can work together on the cop. If it's as big as I think it is, you guys should be in on it."

"And the Bureau?"

The Reagan administration had put the Drug Enforcement Agency under the FBI over the protests of local law enforcement. DEA people were now subservient. They didn't appreciate headlines on how the FBI had broken up huge dope rings when they were really cases worked by DEA agents. "You know how I feel, Pete. The Bureau doesn't know its ass from its elbow about dope. We don't want to waste time with them. We've always been able to work well with you guys."

"OK. Our intelligence indicates that high-tech is a major target for cocaine. It's an easy one. Many of the assholes running it are just like movie stars. The glamour bit, sophistication, unbelievable amounts of money being made in the industry, life in the fast lane. You know what I mean."

I nodded.

"We hear that the Western mob, especially Fortono,

is going after the distribution market. Up until now, they've been strictly financing, playing it safe," he said.

"What about the electronics whiz kids?"

"Well, we know one who had a fortune go up his nostrils before he got into politics, don't we?"

"That doesn't make him an importer."

"No. But one hears that it takes a war chest of at least fifteen million green ones to run for the United States Senate from this state. And it's the same price tag for glamorous mayors as for anyone else. A few shipments of size could do it."

"Fifteen million for that family is peanuts and you know it, Pete."

"They belong to the superrich, all right. Who's the cop, Fraleigh?"

"All I have is an anonymous note about a suitcase full of dope. We used your van, but came up empty as far as dope. He did meet with Fortono, and the guy who carried the suitcase was Crazy Phil Caruso, a button man from Chicago originally, but also busted in LA. He ended up blowing away the mayor's aide, a shyster creep named Nicastri. The suitcase contained nary a trace of drugs, but the lab found particles of gold from gold bars."

He whistled. "A suitcase full of gold bars. That would be up in the millions. Do you ever get tempted, Fraleigh?"

"Who doesn't? But I worked around these punks long enough not to have any illusions of what it must be like to look over your shoulder for the rest of your life."

"You're right. In five more years, I draw my pension. The wife and I are building a place up near Lake Tahoe."

"Stay away from the casinos. The cop's name is Richard Petrie. We hired him as a detective captain."

"You screened him and he's dirty on dope?"

"He came highly recommended. From the mayor's office, if you know what I mean. But one thing that might interest you guys; he's an officer in the Army

Reserves, spent a lot of time during the past ten years in foreign ports.''

Pete's eyes narrowed. I knew DEA compiled profiles on frequent travelers. ''Let's leave this one open, Fraleigh. It sounds like you have a real whodunit. We'll do some discreet checking and get back to you. If you need the van or any personnel, let me know.''

I wondered what else he wasn't telling me. Pete Haskill had never offered me equipment and personnel.

Perry's was an FBI hangout on Union Street. There were plenty of attractive young women to ogle. Warbucks was doing more than his share of that when I approached the bar. He was a big square-shouldered man. His bald head and last name had made the nickname Daddy inevitable. It was hard to judge age from his appearance. I knew he had been in the Bureau for fifteen years. I guessed he was around forty. He introduced me to a young agent even bigger than he was. And Daddy was six two and weighed in at a muscular two hundred twenty pounds.

His colleague was around twenty-eight and spent half the time assessing the women and the other half checking his own dark good looks in the mirror behind the bar. Daddy had a half-finished martini in front of him. ''Hey, another round, and put it all on his check.'' He gave me a bear hug to make sure the bartender would know who to sting. Daddy slugged down the other half of the martini.

His companion said,''Back me up.'' He was drinking a Bloody Mary. I had a light beer.

''I was trying to tell junior G-man that this fucking city is as corrupt as New York.'' Daddy was hard of hearing from too many years on the firing range without ear protectors. His booming voice soared over the cafe noise and people looked around. Taking in Daddy's size, they quickly glanced away from his hard stare.

''You're a disgrace to the Bureau, Warbucks. How can you stand him?'' the younger agent asked me.

"That's the only thing about him I can stand."

"Hey. That's pretty good, Fraleigh." Daddy laughed loudly. "Come on, let's get away from this asshole. He couldn't even find a queer on Castro Street."

Having spoken at the top range of his considerable voice, he had now really turned some heads. "I can see the Bureau still regards you as a model for their public relations program, Daddy."

We found a corner table. "Well, got Silicon City straightened out yet?"

"Almost. Just a couple of little problems."

"Yeah. Like the mayor playing footsie with Alex Fortono and the police chief banging a mob broad. Who the hell does Louis think he is, Jack Kennedy?" I shrank back from his booming laugh. "But I'll tell you the truth, Fraleigh, a little piece of that bird would tempt even a patriotic American like me."

A young waitress came and took our order, never getting too close to Daddy or taking her eyes off him. I wasn't enjoying my trip to San Francisco. It was clear that Silicon City's goings on had been the subject of conversation in federal law-enforcement circles.

"What the hell happened to Louis? He used to be some cop. I was surprised when he accepted the job to begin with." He shook his head from side to side.

"Don't forget where we were working and what that power structure was like." The Bureau agents fell into two camps. The majority were hired because they had law or accounting degrees. But a number of others were brought in without college backgrounds because they had served in local law enforcement. They were called the cops and it wasn't a laudatory term. Most people assumed Daddy had come in that way. Actually, underneath the bravado was a shrewd man who had made the law review at Boalt Law School at Berkeley, one of the finest law schools in the state. His father, though, had been a cop and risen up to inspector, one of the top ranks in the NYPD. His casual question to me was anything but. They had been wondering why honest cops would voluntarily get themselves linked up with Silicon City politics.

"Tell me what you hear about Fortono, Daddy."

"We have reason to doubt his integrity."

"Come on, you asshole. This doesn't go any further than me."

"What's going on at night that caused you to change your M.O. ? You used to bribe us agents of the Federal Bureau of Investigation by buying dinner. Now it's lunch. Anyway, tell me what brings you to town."

I repeated what I had told Haskill.

"What's the cop's name."

"Richard Petrie."

"Oh-oh. Don't tell me. Assigned to Army G-2 in the reserves, right?"

"You know him."

"Of him. And that's all I can say. But you guys better watch your asses real good. You're playing with some big power."

"Does he work with you people?"

"No, Fraleigh."

"That leaves only one other agency unless you're lying to me again. I thought they weren't supposed to be into anything domestic."

"You've been reading the papers the last couple of years. Some of their people have been in business as much for themselves as for the Agency. Then, too, we've never been terribly happy about the way they interpret that domestic charter stuff. And I ain't bullshitting ya. We wouldn't touch Petrie with a ten-foot pole."

"But Fortono and Middleston?"

"What's your guess?" he asked, eyeing me speculatively. Was I pumping him for my friend and boss, who might just blab to the mayor?

"The mayor wants to be a U.S. senator and the campaign next time out is likely to cost upwards of fifteen million. I guess the mob can deliver labor money and maybe a bunch of entertainment celebs for endorsements and rallies. Middleston can deliver the gambling monopoly if the initiative passes," I said.

"What about the gold bars?"

"We can't figure it out. But the mayor's aide got wasted right after the delivery, so it's got to be connected."

"Cocaine payment?"

"It just doesn't figure, the way it went down with the suitcase."

"Let me toss you another thought." Daddy paused to drink half of his third martini. The only sign of his intake was a slight ruddiness in his cheeks. "The biggest game around Silicon Valley isn't cocaine, despite Pete Haskill's bullshit. It's industrial secrets. They're ripping each other off. The companies themselves are stealing and some of the bastards are breaking their asses to see how much new technology they can sell overseas. It's prohibited under federal law, but to them it's just another market."

"And you hear the mob is taking a piece of the action?" I drank my beer. It could be, I thought. Over the years they had certainly developed the networks to smuggle everything from people to narcotics. Why not high-tech secrets? The mob and the CIA were old buddies. The World War II alliances, the plot on Castro. We had heard plenty of those stories. "I can see them anywhere where there's big money to rip off, but why would the spooks be in with them?"

"Only the Shadow and the Bureau know what evil lurks in the minds of men." He winked and ordered another martini.

Haskill and Warbucks hadn't solved any mysteries for me, but their comments sure gave me more to ponder. And I did just that, taking scenic US 280 back to Silicon City until I noticed a white Plymouth staying a quarter mile behind me. I zipped off an exit ramp, jumped out of my car and waited expectantly at the stop sign. But all I netted was a slightly nervous female, a schoolteacher type who looked scared when she saw me standing, hand in pocket, beside my car. I got back in and pulled to the side. Within a couple of minutes it was clear that I had come up empty.

Twenty-Two

WHEN I GOT HOME, A YOUNG PATROLMAN WITH A WOR-
ried face greeted me. His face was almost as red as his
fiery hair. "I guess I goofed, Chief. About two hours
ago, I had to use your bathroom for a couple of minutes. When I came out I found this." He handed me a
note.

> Dear Officer Toggle,
> Please forgive me for tricking you. Don't be con-
> cerned about me. I assure you that I am perfectly
> safe. If the Big Chief comes home before me, tell
> him I just wanted him to worry about me a bit.
>
> Janice

"Stop glaring at the poor boy," Janice breezed in the
door, pecked me on the cheek, and waved goodbye to
Toggle. He looked at me. I shook my head affirmatively
and, much relieved, he took off.

"Don't be cross." She put her arms around me and
hugged. "You'll be proud of my detective work."

"Janice, are you crazy? Don't you understand that
you're dealing with people who would kill you without
a second's hesitation?"

185

"Where I went, they wouldn't dare. Not in broad daylight."

"You're wrong—they'd do it anywhere, anytime. And they could have been watching this place." Not only Caruso's pals, I thought, but Icepick Ned as well.

"I checked. I really did. The parking lot was clear. And I took a taxi. He came right to the front door."

"They would have killed four taxi drivers to get you. Promise me you won't do anything like that again."

She still had her arms around me. She smiled. "I promise. Now give me a squeeze. A real squeeze. Don't be a sulk. Don't you want to know where I've been?"

She looked amazingly healthy. It hadn't been that long since she had been shot. Yet here she was, in a pretty white blouse and a billowing skirt. She noticed my appraisal. "Do you like my outfit?" She whirled around. "But don't get any ideas." She shook her finger at me. "You can't hide under my skirts whenever you like."

"Feeling pretty chipper? You must have solved the case."

"Oh, God, I hope you're not one of those macho bores who hates women to outdo you."

"No. I'm one of those macho cops who hates to see a good-looking woman get shot because she doesn't listen to me."

"I want you to call Lee's for Chinese food. I'm famished. Detective work is so invigorating. I'll brief you while we're waiting. See, I'm already picking up the jargon."

"Just so you don't pick up any more lead." I went to the phone.

"I want pot stickers, beef with snow peas, shrimp with garlic sauce, and lemon chicken," she said.

"Don't I get to select any dishes?"

"No. But you can pay. I'll let you exercise your masculine instincts."

"The doctor said no sex for four weeks."

"You're pretty crude for a chief of detectives."

"It's all show. I'm really a teddy bear."

"Is that why you asked him about my having children?"

"What . . . ?" She sat there, chin in hand, laughing at me. "Big-mouthed doctor." I turned away from her and gave the food order just as she had dictated.

"I needed a state of the art computer library, so I called Joan."

"Janice, you didn't go there!"

"They have the best. Joan got me right in and after she was finished work she drove me home. Did you know she's working on a masters in management training? Isn't it a shame that because she's an attractive woman she gets put on a reception desk? Do you think she's beautiful?"

"I didn't notice. I'm much more interested in a woman's intellect than physical things. But maybe it wasn't sex at all. Maybe she just doesn't snort enough coke to get into the inner circle of management."

"You're such a smart-ass. In fact, they've tried to hit on her a number of times. It's probably true. She didn't get stoned and leap into bed with the bosses, so she's still a receptionist."

"Fascinating. I can see why you're so elated over discovering all this sex discrimination."

"If we didn't have Chinese food coming, I wouldn't tell you a thing."

"Oh, yeah? The police have their methods, you know." I moved next to her on the couch and put my arm around her. "I was worried. No kidding."

"I know. I guess it was a dumb thing to do." She touched my cheek. "I wish . . . I wish this ugliness was over. The danger, my injury." She kissed me and we stayed close without a word until the delivery boy with the food rang the bell.

Pretending not to, I watched her deftly using chopsticks to place a piece of shrimp in her mouth. I had never mastered chopsticks. She chewed slowly. "Mm, delicious. Anyway, Fraleigh, the library refreshed my memory and Joan, who is one sharp lady, expanded it. Size, power, speed. That's the computer game. The first ones were as huge as houses, consumed a lot of energy, and were slow. But they've shrunk from big vacuum tubes to smaller transistors, then down to unified circuits and then to a chip of silicon with circuits etched on that aren't even visible without magnification. Are you following me?''

"Sure, everyone knows that stuff.''

She sneered at me while savoring another shrimp. "Humph. Typical male stubbornness in refusing to acknowledge superior feminine knowledge. Anyway, simultaneous with the diminution in size, energy consumption was dramatically lessened and speed of transactions enormously increased.''

She paused and sipped the wine. "God, this is good. What made you pick it?''

"The ambience.''

"I'm not sure you're using the word correctly. In any event, the question of what next in computers is intriguing the world right now. Not only corporations, but governments are looking for the ultimate scientific breakthrough. The prevailing guesses are that the new discoveries will involve processes similar to the functioning speed of the human brain and use components the size of billions of minute brain cells. Synthetic molecules would resemble tiny transistors, which could be seen only under an electron microscope. The energy running along these molecules are solitons. Remember this is theory. Another idea involves protein molecules made up of smaller amino acid molecules.

"No doubt you're aware that the term bit refers to binary digit. And a byte is a measureable portion of consecutive binary digits, for example an eight-bit or six-bit byte.''

I nodded like I knew what the hell she was talking about.

"The current wisdom of bits and bytes will be regarded as quaint history if Middleston Electronics' discoveries are implemented.''

"You got all this out of the library?''

"No. I was exposed to some of the theory in school and in some periodicals I browsed recently. What's exciting is that Middleston's library had some cross-references to their research and development in this area. Of course, the material is available only to the few people who work on it. I couldn't see their research, but it looks like they are on to something. You see, the whole area of gene and bacterial research makes this so exciting. It seems that Middleston Electronics has come up with the prototype of a system for developing genes in growing bacteria cells—bioengineering—which, in effect, would lead to a molecular computer.''

"Are you saying that note we found in Nicastri's pocket may mean something.''

"I'll say. Do you mind if I finish the lemon chicken?''

"How come you eat so much and still have that figure?''

"Knock off the sexist talk and the cracks about how much I eat. Let me tell you what Joan said. Apparently Solly has incurred his father's wrath by investing so heavily into the research I told you about. It's no secret that the company will be in trouble if it can't pull something out of its R-and-D hat soon. Now, the final item is that Middleston senior is Chairman of the Board. He structured Solomon's CEO compensation so that the mayor's fortune is directly linked to the value of company stock. He's not exactly poor, but his net worth decreased by sixty percent over the last two years. He has a personal cash flow problem.''

"How the hell does a receptionist on the front desk know about the CEO's salary and the company's financial health?''

"A receptionist doesn't. A bright alert young woman who takes business courses and reads *The Wall Street*

Journal knows a lot of things that would surprise certain male chauvinists."

"What did Joan have to say about the mayor's loving wife?"

"You used the right word, loving."

"Just typical la dolce vita stuff of the superrich, eh?"

"You know, you can be obnoxious at times."

"Huh?"

"You're so smug. Antifeminist. Antibusiness." She wasn't smiling over Chinese food now.

"You lost me, Janice. I thought it was common knowledge that Lorraine bedded anyone she wanted to. And having seen Middleston in action I can understand his lack of sex appeal."

"You thought . . . Damn it you're so ignorant. Did you ever think of Lorraine Middleston as a woman?"

I decided to pass on that one.

"Lorraine Middleston graduated magna cum laude from Smith and operated one of the most successful public relations firms in the Valley until she had the misfortune to meet Middleston. It was supposed to be the glamour marriage of the decade. Two young, attractive business people whose careers would complement each others'. But Lorraine hadn't figured out that her father-in-law didn't approve of career women and that her jellyfish husband was incapable of standing up to his father. Solomon reneged on his promise to Lorraine. When his father quietly blacklisted her firm in the industry, he sat it out. No wonder she hates them."

"You done good, Watson. I'll even wash the dishes in your honor."

She frowned at me. "No male counterattack?"

"On the contrary. You've helped explain some things."

She only half-stifled an enormous yawn. "It was a more active day than I've had in quite a while. Will you think it terrible if I say good night?"

I stood and put my arms around her. She squeezed back. I watched her walk into the bedroom, confident and agile. I remembered how well she had moved in putting the Hound Dog on the Cadillac. And then Caruso so casually firing a string of rounds. Another couple of inches one way or the other and even the best surgeons wouldn't have saved her.

What had her brother Ken said? Someone had to be held responsible and he hadn't meant lawyers' justice. I wasn't concerned about Caruso. Either I or his own colleagues would sooner or later bring him his due. But what about those behind the scenes who were responsible? Would there be any justice for them? It was a long time before I joined her in sleep that night.

Twenty-Three

I PULLED MYSELF AWAY FROM JANICE TO TURN OFF THE
alarm. She turned toward me and, still asleep, put her
right arm across my chest and her cheek onto my shoulder. It felt good. I stayed in bed, coming awake slowly.
Finally, I disengaged myself gently and made for the
bathroom. Twenty minutes later I let the same freckle-
faced, uniformed man into the living room. He looked
sheepish. "It won't happen again, Chief," he said.

He was anxious for reassurance, but until my third
cup of coffee I hated the world. It was better all around
that I didn't talk to anyone. I waved at him and hit the
road.

Denise, bless her soul, had the coffee ready. I scanned
the watch commanders' reports. The gray van rapist
has taken the night off. But a young man had been
stabbed and set on fire in his own apartment by two
men he had brought home to discuss literature. The
crime had occurred at 0200 hours. The case would
make the day for the media ghouls. He was still alive
but in serious condition. It was a toss-up whether he
would survive. My bet was that the follow-up investigation would reveal once again that the path of gay love
had not been smooth.

At 0830 hours I called Warbucks. As usual he wasn't

in—out catching spies, no doubt. I left word for a callback. I looked at a report from Phil Short. The secret witness program had yielded up Tina Vasquez on the barroom murder. She was a hype with a record of petty theft and drug offenses. The newspaper employee who was the go-between in the anonymous witness program was given the information that Tina had risen to the big time in a burst of PCP. She had walked into the tavern and blasted away college student and part-time bartender Michael Castraldi.

Her elation over this achievement led her to brag about it at a party on the following evening. The young gentleman who wished to remain anonymous while collecting one thousand bucks had observed her displaying a .38-caliber Beretta while boasting about offing the bartender. She hadn't mentioned that the robbery netted only seventy-two dollars.

Homicide detectives arrested her two hours after the information was received at headquarters. The murder weapon was recovered at her pad under a pile of Hollywood gossip magazines, along with a picture of her at the party proudly holding up the gun. It was an excellent picture. Tina was puckered up to kiss the murder weapon and the tattoos on her arms, described by the murder witnesses, were crystal clear.

She had made no statement other than to tell her questioners to fuck off.

I read a memo from the commander of the sexual assault unit. Lieutenant Cathy Stevens's dry prose informed me that the mobile park rapist had been arrested. It seemed that a gentleman from Los Angeles had been resettled in Silicon City six months previously by the California Parole Department. He had failed to register as a convicted sex offender and, unfortunately for his victims, his mug shots and fingerprints had been stuck in a bureaucratic quicksand. They had finally arrived last week and within twenty-four hours the squad had an eyewitness ID, an arrest warrant, and the suspect, Lewis Sarett, in custody. His apartment was searched under a warrant and several items taken from victims were recovered.

I noticed a stir of excitment in the squadroom. Lieutenant Stevens sat at a desk to my immediate left. Her back had stiffened and a flush spread along the back of her neck. Looking past her into the squadroom I saw that Junior League vice-president Mary Desmond was making her bimonthly visit. As coordinator of the volunteers for the county victim witness assistance program, she made sure to come by every couple of weeks. She fancied tight linen skirts and had nice legs, but that wasn't what made her visits memorable. It was the silk blouse with the four top buttons undone over the thirty-six inch bosom.

She smiled at the friendly greetings and whistles. She glanced in my direction to see if I was following her progress through the squadroom. I hastily turned to look out the window as I observed Cathy swiveling in her chair to face me. The Junior League vice-president stopped to chat with Lieutenant Short, who had volunteered to be laison for the project. Two other detectives immediately moved to the wall map next to his desk and began to move colored pins back and forth while chatting away with good old Mary. The squadroom filled with laughter. The chart had been put up two months ago for a robbery pattern. The gang had been apprehended within a week and the map hadn't been used since.

Lieutenant Cathy Stevens barged into my office, hands on hips, shoulders square. She wasn't a thirty-six by a long shot, but she was an attractive woman in her thirties with a good figure. During her first week in the squad she had been approached by Mark Felt, regarded as an asshole by everyone and by himself as a lover. He asked her for a date. She held up her wedding ring. He held up his and said, ''I'll tell you what. We won't tell our mates any new bed tricks we learn from each other.''

"Do you want it verbally or in writing?" Cathy asked.

"The sex stuff?" he asked with a broad smile.

"No. Your reprimand for conduct unbecoming an officer." He had settled for a verbal reprimand, but the real punishment came when the story spread through the grapevine. Cathy didn't have any supervisory problems after that.

"When are you going to do something about that . . . that exhibitionist and this juvenile behavior by our so-called professional detectives?"

"What's going on, Cathy?"

"Chief, you know perfectly well what's going on. Every time she appears the same thing happens." Cathy turned to point at the coordinator of volunteers. Fortunately, friendly Mary had moved on to visit the other squads.

"She does get a lot of Junior League women to do volunteer work in the courts, Cathy."

"That doesn't mean you ought to sit here and watch those baboons foam at the mouth. Why don't you do something about it?"

"It seems to me that they work for you, Lieutenant. I don't see why you run to me to demand supervision. That's your job."

"Oh, it is, is it? OK."

A number of the investigators had seen Cathy storm into my office. There was an expectant hush. She stalked out and in a loud clear voice that carried the length of the room said, "All right, children. It's time to get back to work."

A week before, a new sergeant on duty at the entrance desk downstairs had made an unfortunate error in judgment. He allowed two little old nuns into the building to solicit funds for their order. Cops are the easiest touch in the world. All of the dicks in the room had contributed. Unluckily, the good nuns had given each donor a token in return for his gift. It was a tin cup with the order's name painted on the front. "Handy to keep your pens and pencils in," they said sweetly.

A couple of days later one of the cops discovered that the cup made a distinctive sound when tapped against his metal desk. Now the cups were tapped in unison and the chant, "Grievance, grievance, grievance," filled the room with a noise reminiscent of the inmates in an old Jimmy Cagney prison movie banging their metal trays to protest something done by the evil warden. The din swelled throughout the room and into the corridor, where people gathered to see what was going on.

Cathy motioned to her only female investigator. "Let's go for coffee, Kim. Maybe the zoo will quiet down by the time we return." They looked sternly at me as they left.

The phone rang and Daddy Warbucks's booming voice asked, "What can the FBI do for you, Fraleigh?"

"I have about two dozen answers to that and they're all obscene," I said to Warbucks.

"Obscenity against the Bureau or any agent thereof is treason. You know that, so be careful or a pack of us will come down to visit you after we finish lunch at Perry's. What the hell is all that noise I hear?"

"It's a detective version of a prison uprising."

"What did you do to the poor bastards?"

"I hired a female lieutenant."

"The Bureau doesn't go for that crap."

"Just wait. Listen, Daddy, you got me. I won't commit an obscenity against the Bureau. The threat of you guys driving in my town after you've had lunch at Perry's is enough to terrify anyone. Daddy, you remember that shooting I told you about? I forgot to mention that the dicks took a note off the stiff. It had some computer gibberish on it. We figured that the mayor was using his aide to run errands while on the city payroll."

"That's a pretty serious allegation to make against an elected official," Warbucks interrupted.

"Yeah. Well anyway, I know a computer expert. She

thinks that the note may well refer to some kind of a research breakthrough. I remember what you said about high-tech espionage."

"Ah, this expert. Is she the reason that you're suddenly unavailable for dinner nowadays?"

"Daddy, that's one thing about you. You can never focus on anything but crime and your work."

"Can you send someone up to the office with a copy of the note? Abe Abramowitz is our whiz on the computer stuff. He's crazy as hell, but brilliant, you know what I mean?"

"You probably mean that the guy has more sense than to drink with you bums."

"No. That's not it at all. He does drink with us. It's just that after four drinks, Abe begins to drink champagne."

"That's bad?"

"Sure is. You see, once he gets on champagne he starts ordering free drinks for the whole bar. Of course, he never pays and it causes some problems if no one has put the bartender wise to him."

"I'm sure J. Edgar would have been proud of the way you guys keep the Bureau traditions going. I'm a little short on people today. How about you having someone drive down for the note?"

"We can't. The whole office is going out to a bachelor party for Malone, that asshole you met last time we had lunch. Can you imagine a broad dumb enough to think he can love her as much as he does himself? We got some joke lined up for him."

"Don't tell me. I don't want to get indicted as an accessory. I remember the time you guys thought it would be hilarious to steal your boss's family station wagon. And it was hilarious until one of you totaled it and the San Francisco cops discovered that you had taken the wrong car. Remember how pissed that Greek shipping executive got when he found his wrecked car?"

"Hey, you can't let an occasional foul-up dampen

your sense of humor, Fraleigh. Why don't you drive up yourself with the note. You can come to the party.''

"I'll send it up. Don't let Abramowitz drink too much champagne. I want to know if that note means anything.''

Twenty-Four

"THERE'S AN OFFICER STEVE TOGGLE TO SEE YOU."
Denise interrupted my fifth reading of the case chronology. The anonymous note had started a series of
events that were still unresolved. Every time I went
through the list it became more and more difficult to
imagine bringing the key characters into court. Ken
Bell's demand for justice outside the courtroom kept
haunting me.

Toggle was the young patrolman who had allowed
Janice to disappear. He seemed like a good kid, but I
hadn't have time to listen to any mea culpas. "What
does he want, Denise?"

"All he'll tell me is that it's about an arrest he made
last night."

"I don't remember consulting the chief of detectives
when I was a rookie making arrests."

"Oh, don't be so mean." She giggled.

"I guess he's cute. Is that right, Denise?"

"Chief Fraleigh! You're terrible. Shall I send him
in?"

"Of course. Who am I to interfere with young people's desire to socialize."

"Morning, Chief. I know you're busy, but you'll be
interested in this guy I picked up last night." I could

see why Denise had accommodated him. He was a lean and narrow six foot two, with bright red hair and a freckled open face. He filled his dark blue uniform well. "I stopped a car around 0300 this morning. The driver was stoned on marijuana. But the guy in the passenger seat was shook. He tried to shove this under the seat." He handed me a folded sheet of paper.

I opened it to see a map drawn of a jogging trail and apartment complex. The hair began to rise on the back of my neck. I turned the paper sideways and sure enough 1F, my apartment number, was listed with an arrow pointing to the patio entrance.

"I never would have spotted your address if it hadn't been for those two days of guard duty."

I flipped the drawing over. My address was printed right on the front of the paper. There wasn't any name, but 1F was written neatly below the street number.

"I figured this might be something important so I called for a fill and got both suspects out of the car on felony stop procedures. This was under the seat also." He held up a .45 automatic.

"Loaded?"

"The full clip."

"It's a good thing you were careful, Toggle."

"You bet. This guy, Vincent Rodriguez, is Mexican Mafia. He's on parole for a 211 armed robbery of a gun shop."

Our intelligence unit had distributed a list of local members of California prison gangs to patrol personnel. The gangs had been formed within California prisons, but were soon controlling drug supplies and involved with other organized crime activities in the cities. The Mexican Mafia was the largest and deadliest of the groups. Toggle had been paying attention.

"I think I'll have to chat with this lad. Where is he?"

"I have him lodged in preprocessing."

I buzzed Denise. "Get hold of the Block. I need to see him pronto."

"I couldn't get a word out of him," Toggle continued. "He's doing the no comprende act. But I was careful not to let on I knew who lived in the apartment."

The Block came in. "Officer Toggle here picked up a guy with a map of my apartment. he's a 211 parolee and a member of MM."

"What's he got to say about all this?" the Block asked.

"He's doing the *no habla ingles* number," Toggle said.

"Maybe we can refresh his memory, whatcha think, Fraleigh?"

"We'll try," I said, getting to my feet. "But you know these guys in either the Nuestra Familia or Mexican Mafia are into the macho bit. There's supposed to be a death code for talkers."

We were in the doorway when Toggle said, "I know about the macho stuff. That's why I was so surprised to find these when I searched him." He held up a pair of pink lace panties.

"Where was he carrying them?" I asked.

"Carrying them? He was wearing them."

Wearing them. That changed things. I took the panties and tossed them to the Block, motioning for him and Toggle to come back into my office. We sat down. "How much time does he have left on his robbery parole?"

"Three years and he's probably got two more coming on the gun charge."

"We got him by the nuts, Fraleigh. Or I should say by the ass." The Block laughed.

"What about the driver, Toggle?"

"He's a lightweight. Only a couple of driving under the influence busts. He's not in the organization. It looks like Vincent just picked the wrong guy to get a lift from."

"Did the driver see Vincent wearing the panties?"

"No. At least not after I took them into custody."

"Thanks for bringing this in, Toggle. It could be im-

portant. The Block and I are going down to interrogate
Mr. Fancy Pants.''

Toggle asked, ''Would it be OK if I watched you
through the one-way glass when you question him?''

''Be my guest.''

We went down two flights of stairs and put our weapons in the lockers outside the detention area. Toggle
opened the door with his key. I spoke to the sergeant
on duty. ''We want to talk to the prisoner in number
four.'' He handed me a master key chained to a smooth
piece of wood six inches long.

The key opened a holding cell only eight feet by eight
feet. The padded walls gave the space an even more
confining feel. Vincent didn't even look up when we
entered.

''Buenos días, Vincent.'' I gave him the Miranda
warnings in Spanish. His record showed him to be
twenty-one years old. He was slight, about five foot
seven, one hundred forty pounds. He wore the white T-
shirt and blue slacks that were almost a uniform among
his peers. His jet-black hair was razor cut in conformity
with MM standards. There wasn't the slightest hint of
a beard on his face. Many of his gang were troubled by
acne, but Rodriguez's light brown skin was clear. He
probably shaved about twice a week.

The Block sat on the opposite side of the table from
the prisoner. The table, bolted into the concrete floor,
was bare. Vincent ignored me until I asked him in
Spanish why he had the map. His eyes flicked briefly
at me and hesitated a second on the Block. He sat with
his legs crossed and hands laced over his kneecap, his
head downward. Silence had worked with Toggle. Rodriguez wasn't about to abandon it easily, but sweat
showed along his hairline.

The Block shifted his gaze to me. I inclined my head
slightly in his direction. ''Get up Rodriguez.'' Vincent
stayed still for a moment, then thought better about ignoring the Block's hoarse command. The vision of being yanked to his feet by the monster sitting opposite

him probably had something to do with his decision. He stood slowly, his head bowed, eyes downcast. "Turn around." He turned but his eyes looked at the floor. "All the way around." The Block's voice sounded like a truck changing gears on a steep hill. Rodriguez completed the turn so that his back was toward the Block.

"You got nice slim hips, Vincent," the Block said. I saw Rodriguez stiffen. "And a nice ass." The Block got noisily to his feet. Rodriguez's eyes flashed at me with a touch of panic. I looked away. "You got three years you owe the state on the 211 beef and we got two more for you on the .45. A felon carrying a loaded piece. You really ain't up on your rehabilitation act are you, Vincent?" The Block moved ever so slowly around the table until he was directly in front of Rodriguez, who hung his head even more. But there was no way he could shut out the ominous voice and the massive presence confronting him.

The Block just stood there for a moment. Then he took the panties from behind his back and held them in front of the boy's bowed head. "Wait until the guys at Soledad hear about these, Vincent. That nice-boy ass of yours is going to look like a manhole cover. And I hear a few of those guys who like to gang-bang sweeties like you got AIDS."

Rodriguez jumped away from him. *"Por favor, señor."* He was on his knees in front of me, his hands clasped as if he was saying the Our Father.

"English only, Vincent," I said. The Block sat and folded his arms.

"Please, officer," Vincent said to me, glancing over his shoulder at the Block. He was somewhat relieved to see him seated, but the Block's stare had its usual impact. He turned back to me, pulling at the sleeve of my sports jacket. "Don't let him tell on me."

"Why was my address on that paper, Vincent?"

"The paper? I found it. I—"

I turned toward the door. "Please, officer!" It was a scream. He was still on his knees.

"If you give me just one more word of bullshit, I'm walking out. He'll handle your case."

"The captain. I'm his snitch. He wrote on the paper. All he asked was that I scout your place. I wouldn't do nothing bad."

"Who is the captain?" We had a real breakthrough.

"He works here. You know him. Captain Petrie."

"When did he ask you to do this?"

"Yesterday."

"What else did he ask?"

"To see if there was a woman and *policia*."

"What did you tell him?"

"Nothing. I swear. I haven't seen him. I would go to his house tomorrow."

"Have you been to his house, Vincent?"

"*Si*. By the ocean."

"What else did the captain ask you to do?"

"Officer, will you help me?"

"The panties? Don't worry. We'll keep that quiet if you're honest with us."

"And the new charge? The gun?"

"You haven't given us anything yet, Vincent."

"But I will tell you about the machine gun. If you help me."

"What machine gun?"

"The captain knew Mario had a stolen machine gun. He told me when Mario would not be home. I stole the gun and brought it to his house. But Mario is bad. He'll kill me if he knows."

"Who is Mario?"

"A *teniente* in my organization. The captain arrested him once for drugs. They made a deal. Mario never went to court."

"OK. Mario won't hear any of this from us. But tell me about the gun. When did you bring it to the captain?"

"Eight o'clock in the morning two or three weeks ago. A Saturday. He makes me stay. A lot of whites came in a Cadillac. They brought a suitcase. The captain put me in a closet with the gun. I think he thought they would rob him, but they didn't.''

"How many gringos, Vincent?" I asked.

"Una mujer hermosa." He stared at Block's frown. "A beautiful blond woman and three men.''

That was the group we had observed. I waited for Rodriguez to continue.

"They talked. Friendly, shaking hands. They left. The captain told me to wait. One would come back. I watched TV, drank beer. Later the man who had carried the suitcase came again. The captain thought I was in the television room, but I was looking through the crack.'' Rodriguez pointed to the crack of light coming through the door jamb. "I heard them. The captain and this Italian laugh and hug each other. The captain called him partner, but this hombre got mad. Wanted *oro,* gold. He took the machine gun and I started to run. But the captain was cool. He said he needed time to pretend the gold had been stolen, but the other man could keep the gun. He wrapped it for him. He kept calling him partner.''

"The other guy. What did he look like?" I asked to make sure he was talking about Crazy Phil.

"Taller than the captain. Strong. He wore a blue jacket like an admiral and gray slacks.''

That sure sounded like Caruso. "What else, Vincent?"

"I swear that's all. That's all I know.''

"What did the captain say after the man left with the gun?"

"He call me out to the front room. The other man was getting into his car. Captain Petrie tell me I be very rich if I help him steal the gold and the man in the car have an accident, disappear into the ocean.''

"And.''

"I do not do these things. I told the captain the man would have the machine gun. No one could hurt him. But he laughed. Said he would help and get the gun away from him.''

"What kind of gun was it?"

"It said U-Z-I." He spelled the letters.

"Where did Mario get the Uzi?"

"All I know is what he told everyone. He and a group of brothers drove a truck through a gun store window. They grabbed whatever they could and ran."

"Where?"

"In Los Angeles."

"When?"

"Last year. I think in the summer."

"What were you going to tell Petrie about my place?"

"I was to go there tonight and to report tomorrow."

"You've never seen my place?"

"I swear on it."

"You better not be lying, Vincent."

"I swear. I was going to look tonight."

I caught the Block's eye. He shrugged that he didn't have any questions. "OK. We'll keep your little secret as long as you keep quiet about us. If you remember anything else we may even put in a good word with the judge."

"Gracias, gracias."

"You two work together like pros," Toggle said.

"We are pros." I took a deep breath and with an effort pushed Rodriguez's fear about the panties out of my mind. "This investigation is in a highly sensitive stage. I don't want you to breathe a word of this to anyone."

He looked hurt. "You don't have to tell me that, Chief. I won't even tell my wife."

He had a wife. I'd have to break the news to Denise. "Let's go upstairs to my office, Block."

Paul was waiting. "Petrie and Caruso musta been pulling some kind of double cross. Do you think that's why they whacked Nicastri?" the Block asked.

"New developments?" Paul said.

I told him about the arrest and questioning of Rodriguez.

"Petrie and Caruso thought of each other as partners? I wonder. What do you think, Fraleigh?"

"I think that if I had a partner like Petrie I'd have trouble sleeping at night."

I went by Louis's office, but neither he nor dragon Margaret was there. I scribbled a note asking him to call me.

"God. You must have terrified that boy."

I had prepared succulent chicken breasts for dinner. They were soaked in garlic butter sauce and then shaken in a paper bag full of white flour and herbs. Janice whipped up a delicious Caesar salad while I got the chicken ready. I poured the two remaining glasses of a 1983 Chateau St. Jean Chenin Blanc to go with the salad, which we ate while the chicken was slowly cooking on the outside grill. For the chicken, I pulled a bottle of Mirrasou Golden Chardonnay from the freezer. It was just right. I had picked it up unchilled in the same supermarket where I had stopped to purchase the Romaine lettuce and chicken. Janice pumped me about the newest case developments over dinner.

"You don't suppose we ought to open a restaurant together, do you?" I said.

"Every once in a while I get a glimpse of the world you work in. Lying, violence, manipulation, terror, and betrayal. It's such a terrible environment. Then you come home and prepare delicious, albeit primitive, food and talk about literature and art."

"I know about football and baseball too. And don't confuse simplicity in cuisine with quality. You feminist snobs can't see beyond quiche."

"But that's really the way it operates isn't it? You pressure them into betraying each other."

"When we're lucky. Sometimes it doesn't work."

"I guess you mean when they have a lawyer. No wonder cops always complain about Supreme Court decisions."

"Actually, some of the best deals get made when the

guy has a lawyer. The lawyer tells them don't be a schmuck. Give up your mother if you have to.''

"But what does it mean? Is Petrie as evil as Caruso? What plot are they into? It seems to me that the suitcase couldn't have contained enough money for all this violence.''

"If it was filled with gold it was plenty of incentive for the killings that we normally see. But you're right in a way. It seems premature for them to kill a low-life like Nicastri. It's puzzling. But maybe it was some kind of a warning.''

Twenty-Five

I HAD MIXED FEELINGS ABOUT TRAVELING BACK TO OUR old jurisdiction. I knew the depositions would be a drag, but I was looking forward to seeing the Robinson twins. I was hoping that it wouldn't be awkward with Sarah.

My two depositions were scheduled for the afternoon. The law offices were close to the old courthouse. I made the short drive, marveling at the growth of the electronics industry. Defense work had been a real boon to the industry. There were many new buildings just opening or under construction. Some had little patches of grass or skinny young trees planted on the edges of their ever-present outdoor parking areas. It was an electronics sprawl, stretching out mile after mile. For an innovative industry, it showed a remarkable lack of imaginative architecture.

I was there to testify on old homicide cases, fairly open and shut, but the defendants were minor-league cocaine dealers and still had enough dough for private counsel. It was clear that the lawyer's meter was running. He asked what I did before I became a policeman. I was a lifeguard. Did it involve any law enforcement? No. Were you trained to investigate incidents? No. To make reports? Yes. On rescues. All the while the deputy DA sat picking his teeth. He had already disclosed to me that these depositions weren't so bad. His supervisor allowed lunch expenses for sessions that took all afternoon.

The stenographer had to make a pit stop. We took a break while she was gone. "I've seen lawyers draw out cases, but this is too much. Can't you stop him?" I asked the DA.

He was a lifer. Twenty-five years in the office. Once in a while they let him try an obscure homicide. "By the time I drew up a brief, got on the judge's calendar, and presented a verbal argument, it would take three times as long. My colleagues don't have the luxury of being on the public payroll. When one of them has a live one, he has to make up for the no-pays."

The second lawyer's office was in the same building. He didn't have a legitimate question to ask as far as I was concerned, but he drew it out agonizingly. It was almost 1800 hours before he finally ended it. I wondered if the late hour enabled him to nick his client for dinner.

I called Sarah to warn her that I was on the way. I had picked up two sets of hand weights as presents for the twins. I stopped at a florist shop near the lawyer's office and purchased a dozen roses for Sarah. A liquor store sat conveniently next door. I bought two of their best bottles of Italian Chianti. It was a high-class place. The Chianti ran $4.90 a bottle.

They lived in an older section—full-grown trees, larger lots, and a variety of homes as opposed to the ubiquitous tract housing. The Robinson place had a large backyard, which provided total privacy for their hot tub. I pulled into the driveway, parking in back of a new BMW. The divorce settlement must have been expensive.

"Sarah!"

"Fraleigh. You look like the same tough rascal. How are you?" She was beaming as she pushed me back from our embrace, hands on my shoulders.

"You're as beautiful as ever, Sarah."

She grimaced in wry disagreement. But she did look terrific—as always. Her black hair was short, styled close to her head. She reminded me of a much younger Lena Horn. Her figure was better than ever. She must have been into aerobics or something. Her red blouse complemented the matching pleated summer-weight skirt.

"Don't say anything critical, Fraleigh. My self-confidence is a little fragile right now." Her eyes had been apprehensive during my hasty inspection.

"Ninety-five percent of the women in this world should be lucky enough to be as fragile as you. Stop fishing for compliments."

"You're impossible. Come have a glass of wine." She led me by the hand to the breakfast-nook table where the family and I had often eaten together. In keeping with the delicious Italian smells wafting out of the kitchen, the table was topped with a brightly colored red and white tablecloth. Two old Chianti bottles held unlit candles. Soft rock came out of the living room speakers.

She took the roses from me and put them into a vase after filling it with water. "These are beautiful. Thank you, Fraleigh." Her eyes lingered on mine and I got uneasy when hers misted a little. The roses went onto the middle of the table and their fragrance floated over me. She lit the candles and poured two glasses of Chianti from a bottle in a wine cooler. "To old friends," she said. We clinked our glasses together, smiling.

I sat opposite her on the wooden wall bench I had always occupied at dinner. She took a straight-backed chair, unselfconsciously putting her feet up on my thigh to be rubbed. It was habit. Sarah had always worked hard as a nurse. When I came to visit, she stayed on her feet hustling up dinner while Louis, the twins, and I played basketball in the driveway, trying to make impossible shots into the hoop above the garage. When Louis and I had come inside, collapsing around the table for beer or wine, Sarah had routinely put her feet

on me for a rub. She wore nylons and the smooth tex-
ture and slight smell of perspiration triggered pleasant
memories. But Louis wasn't sitting next to me tonight.

"Where are the twins, Sarah? I bought them a little
present."

"Fishing."

"Oh. What time will they be getting home?" The
veal parmigiana smell reminded me that I had skipped
lunch.

"It's just you and me, Fraleigh. They're camping.
They won't be home until day after tomorrow. Ouch!"

"Sorry." I had abruptly dropped her feet.

"You mean I don't get my feet rubbed because the
boys aren't here?" She smiled. I filled our wine glasses
even though we had only taken a couple of sips. "Stop
looking at your watch. You just got here."

She put her feet back on my thigh and raised her
eyebrows. I started rubbing them, but I had a cold feeling in my stomach and sweat was on my forehead. "Are
the boys taking it all right, Sarah?" My voice didn't
sound normal, but she gave no sign of noticing.

"They're young, unlike me—their whole life is ahead
of them. They'll adjust."

I didn't have anything to say to that.

"I saw her on television. She's very beautiful." I had
stopped rubbing, hoping she'd remove her feet, but she
nudged me. I started squeezing again. "God, that feels
good on the old feet. You didn't answer. She's gorgeous, isn't she?"

"Who?"

"Oh, Fraleigh. Lorraine, of course. I got to keep
this, as part of divorce settlement." She took her feet
off me to reach over to a file sitting on the kitchen
counter, pulling out a note and handing it to me. It was
a typed note to Louis on Lorraine Middleston's stationery. It contained some flirtatious and playful innuen-
dos, but nothing incriminating—unless you knew
Lorraine the way I did.

"I don't think you have to worry about her, Sarah.

She's not in your class." I handed the note back and moved my leg closer to the table leg so that she couldn't rest her feet on me. She slipped clumsily when she tried, looked at me quickly, and then rose to replace the note. A slight flush tinged the light brown skin around her throat and I wished I was anyplace else in the world. Then it hit me. "Sarah, the note. Can I see it again?"

Sarah had picked up the excitement in my voice. She handed it to me and watched curiously. The anonymous note about Petrie had been typed on a machine with a bent "e." Lorraine's note had the same "e."

"What is it, Fraleigh?" Sarah had put on a new tape and the sound of blues and trumpet filled the room.

"There are some strange things going on in Silicon City, Sarah." I was unsure of how much to tell her.

"I don't want to sound corny, but Louis and I had a pretty good marriage going until he met the Middlestons with their coke-snorting habits."

I waited, but she was staring into the candle. "How's that, Sarah?"

'Oh, I don't know. I'm so confused. So hurt. But, hey, I promised you a good dinner." She poured the rest of the wine. "Come on. You used to dance with me." She pulled me to my feet and we, or at least she, danced lightly around the floor. She was a good dancer and swirled away from me a couple of times, lightly spinning and swaying to the music, occasionally singing the lyrics in a surprisingly pleasant voice. I wondered how I could get her back on the subject of the Middlestons. "Lighten up, Fraleigh. Come on, let it go. You'll feel better."

I tried and for a few minutes she had me moving to the music with rhythm that usually escaped me. "Enough. It's time for the feast," she said. We were both flushed from exertion, but she was right, it had been fun. I opened a bottle of Chianti while Sarah served the veal and spaghetti with tomato sauce. "Confess. You're really Italian," I said over the salad, which we were having Italian-style after the entreé.

"If only I was, maybe I could have held my man. Tell me what's happening up there, Fraleigh."

The mellow time over dinner was gone, but I had a feeling that Sarah was ready to talk about Lorraine.

"First tell me a little about this note, Sarah, then I'll fill you in."

I refilled our glasses, reminding myself to ease up.

"There isn't much to tell. I think she wanted Louis to take that job as much as her husband did. And Louis . . . I saw the way he looked at her. But at first, I think he was sincere. That he really wanted me to come along. He stressed how we would enjoy the social life going with the job. I was strongly opposed. We had just been getting comfortable financially. I wanted the twins to finish junior high and go on to graduate. Our high school is one of the top-rated in the state. And those people scared me. Phony whites."

"Go on."

"Not like you." She reached out and put her hand on my cheek, warmed from the wine. Her hand didn't cool my face off a bit. "I mean it. You're not black, but you have a touch of soul." I realized that she was sloshed.

"How did they entice Louis?"

"I think she did it the oldest way in the world. That white pussy. She didn't have soul, but Louis had white fever. They were class, he would tell me. Now I read in the gossip column that he's chasing Carol Mansell. Do you have any idea what it's like to be a black woman in this mother-fucking country? Civil rights, ha. A license for those chalk bitches to take our men away. And only white male trash is interested in black women. Look at you. You can't wait to get away from me. It's the other way around, Fraleigh. White men rape black women. You're perfectly safe."

"Sarah. We've been friends for a long time . . ."

She reached for the last of the Chianti. I went to pour it at the same time. The bottle slipped and fell to the floor. "Shit," she said, picking it up quickly and going into the kitchen to get some paper towels. I stood. She had more to tell about the mayor and his wife, but it was already past time for me to go. She wiped the floor, throwing the wet paper towels in the trash. The little domestic chore seemed to settle her.

"You're right, Fraleigh. We've been friends for a long time and I ruined a good evening for you. I'm sorry."

"Forget it, Sarah. Friends?"

"Right on. Now dance with me once more and then get the hell out of here."

The music was soft and dreamy. Maybe I was only kidding myself, but Sarah in my arms seemed to give me a feel for the music that I couldn't remember having before. The trumpet soloist began to hit some high notes and Sarah moved closer, brushing against me with her breasts. She put her lips against my throat. I wondered if I could leave in the middle of a song. Suddenly her left hand reached down between my legs to touch my rock-hard penis.

"Sarah." I jerked away from her.

"Thank Christ, you're hard. I was beginning to feel that I wasn't a woman anymore. It's OK," she assured me, resuming her light-footed dancing. My face was flushed and pounding blood made me light-headed. The tape was nearing its end and Sarah spun away from me, humming softly, swaying from side to side, taking tiny steps in keeping with the beat.

She reached out both her hands and we touched lightly.

"Let me ask you one last question. Did Louis ever say anything personal about the mayor?"

Still swaying as the music wore down, she said, "He told me the mayor had been candid with him about having a cocaine problem, but . . ." She moved closer to me and brushed my lips with hers, "But, Mr. Detective, my former husband said the mayor assured him that he was cured."

I thought about it afterward in confusion. Almost not believing that it had really happened. Sarah moved in slow motion. One moment she was swaying to the music, talking conversationally, then in one fluid motion came to me, went down on her knees, unzipped my fly and had my erect penis deep into her mouth before I knew what was happening. Her agile tongue sent a wave of pleasure through me so intense that my knees trembled. How could it be? My reflexes were still sharp enough for the ring, but I had frozen, my hands had reached for her shoulders too late. And my plea—"No, Sarah, no"—echoed pathetically around my ears. With a sinking feeling I realized that things could never be the same again.

Gently, I stopped her from bringing me to a climax. I picked her up and carried her into the bedroom. It didn't matter now. After a brief frenzied foreplay we made love, if you can call it that. I had never been with a woman so violent. She shuddered, bringing herself to climaxes so fierce that she raked me with her nails. I stopped her from that and from biting her knuckles so hard that she twice drew blood, but I couldn't stop her screaming and thrashing. The whole thing was so distracting that I peaked a number of times only to subside. Each time that threw her into a new frenzy. Finally, I did come. She was pounding me on the shoulders with her fists.

I held her and she cried for twenty minutes without stopping. I stared at the ceiling. For some peculiar reason I was able to numb my mind. A time would come when I would have to face what had happened, but now I was able to stare blankly at the ceiling.

Sarah got up and went briefly to the bathroom. When she came back, my eyes followed her nude body, the slender hips and firm round breasts. She paused at the foot of the bed. Her eyes were locked on mine. There was no smile. No trace of affection or intimacy. Just an intense excitement.

"Come, let's go in the hot tub," she said.

I followed, watching her shapely buttocks. The water was heavenly. I was sore all over. I felt some of the tension begin to ease. Tomorrow's conscience hadn't arrive. Sarah sat catty-cornered from me. She was strange. No conversation or smile. Her eyes never left mine. I couldn't read anything in them. Still without expression her foot under the water sought my groin and she lightly began to toe my balls. I didn't think it was possible, but I got hard again.

Then I saw a change in her eyes. "So, Fraleigh, how does it feel to go down on your best friends's wife and to get head from her?"

In the ring, good fighters are able to read their opponents eyes to see the beginning of a punch. That's what saved me. Sarah's heel had squared off to my testicles and she drove savagely forward. I had already moved and her heel slid off my thigh. She fell under the water and came up screaming, her nails bared, but I vaulted the redwood wall and ran for the sliding glass doors. I knew she was following. My fervant hope was that Louis hadn't left an old service revolver around. She was berserk. I went through the open door full speed and locked it behind me. In the bedroom, I scooped up my clothes, slipped into my moccasins, and ran like hell for the car. I heard the glass door shattering. She must have used a chair. Bare-assed naked, I gunned Silicon City's unmarked police car out of the driveway, hoping that no enterprising patrolman was going to appear at four in the morning.

Pulling over in a park area a quarter of a mile away, I quickly dressed in the darkness. My mind didn't function during the short drive to my place. Only as I got close to it did I remember that Janice was sleeping in my bed and a uniformed cop was in the living room.

In no mood to see anyone, I decided to skip going home and to use the electric razor and spare toothbrush I kept in my desk.

I drove to headquarters in a daze. When I got there I went to the locker room and put on my running clothes. In the soft California predawn I pushed myself, running ten miles.

I stood under the warm shower for fifteen minutes, leaving only when some of the troops came in to change for the early day shift. Listening to the jokes and cop talk in anticipation of patrol, I didn't like to think what my day would be like. Only when I dressed for the office did I realize my badge was missing from my suit jacket. I was pretty sure that I hadn't dropped it.

Twenty-Six

DENISE FLOATED CHEERFULLY INTO THE OFFICE AND
told me I looked terrible. Fifteen minutes later Paul
English handed me the rest of his report on the mayor.
He told me I looked terrible. His report confirmed the
little bits and pieces of financial information that had
come to me. My head was pounding. I took a couple
of aspirin. Somehow I got through the morning. By
1600 hours I was thinking of leaving early. But then
Denise buzzed me on the intercom to say that the chief
wanted to see me. The Block came in as I was leaving.
"You look like shit, Fraleigh. Hit the chief up for
tomorrow off. It will be a great day for jogging. You
know what I mean?" He winked. I wiped sweaty hands
on my trousers and headed down the hall to the chief's
office.

Judging from Louis's demeanor, I wondered if he was
about to give me not a day off, but unlimited leisure.
He looked worse than I did. His eyes were puffy and
he was gaining weight again. Last month's diet was a
thing of the past. I pushed Sarah firmly out of my mind
as his eyes looked up from the report he was reading.

"That citizens group is driving the mayor's office
crazy about the gray van rapist. How is it that we haven't
nailed that guy after fourteen rapes?"

"He wears a ski mask, so none of the victims have been able to ID him. And he's been lucky. A couple of times we got calls to 911, but our units just missed him. Most of the time he wears gloves, so we haven't even got a good latent."

"Still, we should have something on the van. And a guy like this isn't just starting his career. He's got to have a record."

"Louis, we've checked every sex parolee and everyone on the sex offender register in this area through DMV files. None of them owns a gray van. We pulled in five who own gray cars for questioning, but none of them look good. They're all at least three inches shorter than our descriptions."

"It's easy for rape victims to be off by a couple of inches."

"There are other discrepancies—general build, past M.O., and so on. We just don't think any of them is good for it. All we can do is hope someone turns him in or that he'll make a mistake—that the next case will do it for us."

"It may well do it for me and you, Fraleigh. Do you have any idea what the media is doing to the Department over these cases?"

"I've got an army of people working on it."

"Too bad you didn't use the army before, instead of wasting them on the mayor."

"Have you told him yet about Raoul?"

"He's in Washington. He's coming back at noon tomorrow and I'm going to brief him immediately on this case." He glanced down at his desk. I was dismissed.

Opening my notebook, I was about to tell him what Rodriguez had said when he looked up. "Oh, Fraleigh." Somehow I knew it was coming. My heart was racing and I felt clammy sweat soaking my shirt. "I think this belongs to you." He tossed my badge forward on the desk. It was the longest eight inches in the world reaching to pick it up. His eyes never left mine. "It came air express—same day delivery." He turned the mail receipt toward me so that I could read the large block printing. TO: Police Chief L. Robinson, FROM: Sarah Robinson.

"Louis . . ." He got to his feet and walked out without looking at me. I picked up the badge and put it in my pockets. There was no use trying to talk to him now. I'd see him in the morning before he got together with the mayor.

I was sitting at my desk reading Paul's preliminary report on the mayor when Petrie popped in for his forty-eight-hour visit. I looked at him with new interest. Since Petrie's last appearance Daddy Warbucks had titillated my imagination and the lab report on the gold residue in the suitcase had surprised me, to say nothing of Rodriguez's revelations.

"You could at least offer a disgraced member of your command a cup of coffee, Chief."

I buzzed Denise and she brought us coffee. "How do you fill your time on administrative leave? I'm curious," I said when he remained silent. It might have been my imagination, but he seemed a shade less cocky this morning.

"Oh, I read espionage thrillers. The trouble is that our country is always the villain. I miss the good old-fashioned patriotism of cops. They assume that intelligence agents are on the level."

"Sometimes that can be a hard assumption to hold on to."

"Not really. It depends where you start from. If you're suspicious to begin with, then you can imagine all kinds of things. Intelligence people aren't that different from undercover cops. They have to associate with all kinds of people—politicans, mobsters, and questionable others. Agents can get a bum rap. Secrecy is required. They can't always explain why their actions were warranted."

"It almost seems like you're trying to tell me something, Petrie."

"Maybe I am. I think you're a hell of a cop. We're not really on different sides." He stood. "Thanks for the coffee, Chief. See you in forty-eight hours."

Cathy Stevens came in. "Chief, we had another gray van rapist attack today, but this time I think the son of a bitch ran into the wrong victim."

I had never heard Cathy get emotional about the terrible cases that she handled day after day. She motioned to Curtin, who was standing in the doorway. He came in and took the chair next to her.

"I believe this is the one, chief," Curtin said. "He hit on a seventy-two-year-old woman, Bertha Katz. He wanted her wedding ring before he raped her. When it wouldn't come off, the animal pulled a razor-sharp knife and cut off her whole finger."

I winced. "What's her condition?"

"She's incredible," Curtin continued. "She's practically assigned herself to the case. It's probably good for her. She's concentrating on nailing him and not on what happened. The doctors say that the finger amputation isn't going to hurt her general health. Do you know what she told me? She wants him caught and the ring back to wear on her other hand."

"She's a gutsy gal," Cathy said. "When she saw he was going to cut her she grabbed his ski mask and pulled it off. I'm sure he would have killed her, but the phone rang and he panicked. She got a good look at him and she's going through the mug file right now. If she doesn't make him, we can at least get the artist to do a facsimile. Also, we have two good latent prints where he touched the door frame running out of her apartment."

"Not only that," Curtin added, "but the scrapings from under her nails will give us a blood type and some hair samples."

"Great. Don't let up on it and —" I stopped. Phil Short ran into the office. "Did you hear the radio? The Block and English took on the Uzi bandits all by them-

selves, downtown. They were crazy to do it. There's an
ambulance on the way.'' He paused for breath.

I was on my feet. My mouth opened by no words
came out. ''Are they all right?'' Cathy asked.

He frowned. ''Them? Yeah, they're fine.''

''You dummy. Why didn't you say so?'' she said.

'I'm sorry. I didn't think . . .''

''You OK, Chief?'' she asked, as I fumbled in my
desk for a stomach pill while my heartbeat slowly edged
back to normal.

''The ambulance is for the restaurant cashier they
shot, but she's DOA. Those two guys are 5150,'' Short
continued. Section 5150 of the Public Health Law was
what we used to confine mentally unbalanced people.

''They had spotted the gang, but couldn't get close
to them before the gunman opened up. English just
walked up to him and grabbed the barrel of the gun.
The Block was charging behind him like a rhinoceros.
They went down like bowling pins. English covered
them with the Uzi while the Block handcuffed them. Of
course they didn't follow procedure, but what cops!''

''If they had followed procedure we'd have a dozen
more DOA's,'' Cathy said.

''They're down in pre-processing right now. I'm going down,'' Short added.

''Phil, tell them good job for me,'' I said.

''You ought to tell them that yourself, Chief,'' Cathy
said.

''You're right.'' I got up to go with Short.

Pre-processing was mobbed. Cops, witnesses, reporters, photographers, television crews. I was lucky to
get a chance to shake their hands. Paul said something
in Latin to me. I patted them on the back again and got
out of there.

Back upstairs I returned to Paul's report on the Middlestons. It took me a couple of minutes to concentrate.
First the gray van rapist break, then the Uzi gang—what
a day.

Paul had followed Lorraine for a day. There was no

guarantee that it was typical, but she took aerobic dancing from 1500 to 1600 hours, then went browsing through expensive shops before having dinner with a lady friend at the country club. Paul had confirmed that she was enrolled in the aerobic program.

I was leaning against her Jag when she came out of the fitness center. "Fraleigh, what a pleasant surprise."

Sarah was right. She was blond and beautiful and she wore her expensive sports clothes well. "Good morning, Lorraine. Do you have time for a cup of coffee?"

"I always have time for a handsome policeman, but you offered me a shower last time." Her laugh was as deep as I remembered it.

"We've both had showers already." I motioned toward the fitness center.

"But one can't be too clean." She showed her white teeth.

"How about across the street?" I pointed to a croissant and coffee place, no doubt located across from the fitness center so that people could undo their real and imagined calorie loss.

"Fine." She took my arm as she had at the party, pushing her breast against me. I swore I could feel the nipple harden.

We split a croissant, "It's a good thing I have a singles tennis match this afternoon," she said, spreading butter on her bread. "What are we going to talk about, jogging or showers?"

"How about the anonymous note you wrote on Captain Petrie?" Since we didn't have Sarah's note and it hadn't been analyzed and there was plenty of chance that I was wrong. I held my breath.

"I underestimated you as a detective, Fraleigh. That's wonderful. Tell me how you knew."

"Only the Shadow and Fraleigh know what evil lurks in the minds of women." I was getting my full money's worth from taking Warbucks to lunch.

"Oh, come. It wasn't evil at all. Aren't you cops always demanding that the public get involved?"

"Touché. But we don't like to be sent on wild goose chases. There wasn't three million dollars worth of cocaine. In fact, there wasn't even a trace."

Her blue eyes were twinkling as if we were just having fun talking about this season's ballet program. "True. It was gold. But don't blame me. I didn't find that out until later. Everything else was correct, wasn't it?"

"Except for the time, there was nothing else. Did you know about the other people and who were going to show up?"

"The other people. You mean Alex and Carol. This is precious. You're being the close-mouthed detective interrogating me. Are you going to handcuff me and take me in?" Her eyes mocked me. "One of your colleagues once indulged my handcuffs fantasy. It was disappointing. Perhaps I shouldn't always indulge my fantasies. But maybe it would be different with you." She raised her eyebrows.

"Lorraine, this isn't a game. A man has been murdered. A young woman shot."

"Referring to that ingratiating flunkie as a man is a compliment he doesn't deserve. Whoever did it should get a commendation. But the girl. I heard that she lives with you. Is she pretty?"

"It's just for security."

"Of course." She laughed. "But you don't jog with me anymore."

"That's different. I didn't know you were working your way through the Department." This time she really cracked up, laughing for a full minute. She wiped her eyes with a tissue. I began to wonder if she was crazy.

"You're marvelous. Don't misunderstand me. I'm not putting down your chauvinism. It actually makes you more appealing. You guys all pride yourselves as studs and the biggest womanizers are heroes. But a woman who enjoys different men is a round-heels and fucking her isn't the achievement it's supposed to be. You have to be her whole universe before your male ego is satisfied.''

"Lorraine, you do happen to be married to the mayor.''

"My marital state is hardly a deterrent to other policemen. That's what makes it more delicious. They can't get over screwing the mayor's wife. It's a status thrill and fear of getting caught at the same time. I confess to getting kicks out of their kicks. Those dry engineers from Solomon's electronics days weren't nearly as much fun.''

"You must really hate him." For an instant her face lost its beauty and her eyes, which smiled so constantly, bit into me, hard. Then she smiled again.

"I forget. You are a detective.''

"Your note was clever. Where did you pick up the 'stepped-on' jargon? You had me thinking a cop wrote the note.''

"I find narcs are fascinating people and they just love to talk about their work.''

"Would that comment also explain the police department memorandum paper? And how the note appeared on my desk in headquarters?''

"Ah, but that would be burning one of your subordinates. Is that the right word, burning?''

"Yes. You've practically completed Police Science 101. How did you find out it was gold and not cocaine?''

"The same way I found out that they were meeting.'' She was being coy now.

"Petrie?''

"Richard, the enigma. I know you're guessing. But you're really good. I'm enjoying watching you work. Keep going.''

"I take that as a yes, right?'' She nodded in agreement.

"Even as devious a man as Richard is careless when

I'm naked in his bed. None of them guess that I love to listen on bedroom extensions."

I tried to remember whether I had gotten any phone calls that Saturday when she was at my place. "Let me ask you this, Lorraine. Is Solly's run at the Senate behind the wheeling and dealing?"

"Of course. His father cut him off, doesn't even speak to him. Solomon is a rich man in desperate need of money. When he asked for my money for the campaign, I just laughed." Paul had confirmed that Lorraine's family had millions from a frozen TV dinner company and a fast food chain. "But Fraleigh, I hope you're not going to arrest him before we get to Washington. Think how much fun I could have there. All of those handsome congressmen."

"Why Louis? Why did you mess up his marriage?"

"Louis is a very interesting man. Complex. What did he lose? A mundane existence with a neurotic woman in the stifling suburbs? And his being black made it infinitely more interesting for me. You see, my dear husband, despite his surface civil rightsism, is a racist. My being with Louis really got to him. At the same time, he wanted Louis. A black police chief guaranteed great national coverage. And Louis as chief diverted attention from the shoddy treatment of minorities in Silicon City. So, if my body was keeping Louis in line, Solomon would go along. But I didn't like being used. Louis was hurt when I moved along. He's sweet. But it was time."

The croissant was like lead in my stomach. I was careful to keep my face expressionless. "And Carol?"

"Yes. My clever husband hit on that little scheme the first time he met with Fortono. Don't you think these Italian gangsters are alluring? Their affinity for violence is so similar to you cops. Fortono views women as cattle, present company excepted. He calls me a blond Madonna. So with my husband's approval he dispatched Carol onto poor Louis. He's still seeing her. Did you know?"

"Was it Captain Petrie who set up the meet with Fortono?"

"Of course. Solomon and his staff of bunglers could never have arranged it."

"Lorraine, what is the transaction, is it gold or cocaine?"

"Oh, but that's no fun. You have to analyze, deduce, trick me into answering your questions. I'm not just going to pour out the information. In fact . . ." She looked at me speculatively. "I wonder just how far you'd go to get answers to your questions. Solomon is in Washington. Would you like to see the master bedroom suite at our mansion? No? I can see from your face. Pity. You do look terrible. Have you been tom-catting all night?"

"My own guess is that it's a mix of both coke and technology. But why give the gold to Petrie? I can't believe that setting up a meet commands that kind of dough."

"That's better. I like watching you detect. Someday we'll jog together again. Solomon's R & D people have come up with some kind of breakthrough. I think he plans to sell the technology to raise the money for the Senate race. He could sell his stock after they announce the discovery, but that won't be for several months and he has to have the cash within the next month or the party will give the nomination to someone else. Enter Alex."

"And Petrie has the foreign contacts to launder the gold and sell the secrets."

"Bravo! But as tough as you are, darling, don't get into it with Petrie." She shivered. "There's something about him. He's always planning three steps ahead, and . . ."

"What? Go on," I said when she stopped.

"He likes to see people in pain. And some very bad people are afraid of him, enough to do what he wants. Even Alex is wary of him. Solomon is terrified."

"Why did Caruso kill Nicastri?"

"Oh-oh. I'm late to tennis. I must go. Pick me up some other time to feel me out, or up." She laughed. Picking up her purse, she paused and put her hand on my cheek. "This has been fun. As far as why Nicastri? You might consider that my weak-kneed husband has the habit of wavering on key decisions. If it was a warning it certainly worked on him."

I watched her walk out, slim tan legs handsome under the white skirt. Her gold earrings glinted in the bright sun. One of Silicon City's gentry. A woman who wasn't content to divorce her husband. She had written an anonymous note designed to put him behind bars for a lot of years. On the other hand, the Mom and Pop homicide cases we got weren't exactly examples of the path of true love either.

Twenty-Seven

I WAS ONLY BACK FOR A FEW MINUTES FROM MY MEET-ing with Lorraine when Phil Short stuck his head in. "Chief, do you have a moment?"

"I'm just about to meet with the task force on the gray van rapist."

"I'll only take a minute. In the excitement over the Uzi bandits, I forgot to talk to you about this new homicide. I guess you saw the units at your place last night."

I wasn't about to let Short know that I hadn't been home. I lifted my shoulders in a shrug.

"The security guard that was stabbed to death at your place has an interesting background."

I sat down. "Go on."

"Well, he's got several past drug busts and the narcs think he may have been doing some small-time dealing in crack. Then too, he's just gone through a bitter divorce and custody fight over his two kids. Both he and the wife have filed charges with us that they think the other put out a contract on them."

"Jesus." That damn Bently telling me how great the security was.

"Well, it's still an open case. It's always possible it was a burglar or something, but you know what kind of people the security firms hire. Minimum wage, no

230

background check. We checked your apartment. No problems. I put two of my best men on it.''

"OK, Phil. I have to run to my meeting. Keep me up to date on the case.''

"Right.''

Of all nights for me not to be home. I dialed my number. Short had checked the apartment but I was relieved when Janice answered.

"Hello, Janice. What do you say to my stopping at Lee's to bring home Chinese food for dinner? It's been almost a week since we had some.'' I was a great conversationalist.

"OK.'' I could feel the chill over the phone.

"What would you like to order?''

"Whatever you wish.''

"I don't know if I can take all that responsibility on my shoulders.'' Silence. "All right, see you tonight.''

The rapist task force took half an hour to outline their plans on identifying him. I returned to my office and about an hour later Warbucks walked in. Denise made a half-hearted effort to protect me. I waved her away and closed the office door.

"I checked on the individual we spoke of. He's a scoundrel all right. Dishonest to the core,'' Warbucks said.

"Daddy, could you take it easy on all the scientific FBI jargon and tell me what the hell you found out?''

"Ah, you locals lack the romance, the ambience of our profession.''

"Ambience? Is that a required word now in federal training classes?''

"In answer to your question, Chief of Detectives Fraleigh, the subject has been persona non grata with the firm we mentioned, his former discreet employers for whom he moonlighted quite profitably for a number of years. It seems that he was of the Wilson school. Too much of the entrepreneurial spirit, if you get what I mean. They found that he had several of his own deals going on their money. Given their public relations program, they severed relations without prosecution. Rumor has it that the elected official we discussed has employed the individual to market the commodities I mentioned to you.''

''What did your computer expert Abramowitz have to say?''

''Alas, he got on a champagne kick at the bachelor party so his analysis was a day late. But he was quite interested. How familiar are you with Maui?''

''I don't have time for a Hawaiian vacation right now.''

''I should say not. You're up to your ass in alligators and someone is draining the pool. But I'm talking law enforcement stuff now. Let me tell you about an elegant resort—a place called Kapalua just past La Haina. Million dollar condos. Ritzy, ritzy, and owned mostly by Jap nationals, one of whom is Yoshomo Tanaka. He, you may remember, was the go-between for Hitachi and Mitsubishi on the sting we did for IBM. Tanaka was trying to steal IBM secrets for the Jap companies. We got convictions of the companies and indicted a couple of their executives for industrial espionage, but our lawyers screwed up the case and good old Yoshomo walked on us. Abramowitz is sure that this is the same Tanaka mentioned on the note found on your DOA.'' He paused dramatically. ''And one mayor of Silicon City, Solomon H. Middleston, Jr., spent the last three days at Tanaka's condo on Maui.''

''What? On Maui? He's supposed to be in Washington meeting with some senators.''

''Today he *is* in Washington. He flew back to San Francisco yesterday and got right on a flight to the District.''

''You put a tail on him?''

''No. No. This information is confidential, Fraleigh. I mean it. We don't want it getting out. Some ACLU congressman will start pissing and moaning. Ever since we took over the DEA our computers have been programmed to screen the airline reservations. You know the DEA used to monitor frequent travelers to drug hot spots, but it was a Mickey Mouse program compared to what we have now. I just routinely ran the mayor's name on it."

"There's no way his airline reservations told you about a meet in Kapalua."

"True. That did involve asking one of our people there to postpone his golf game long enough to see what Solly was up to. They do keep an eye out on Tanaka routinely, so it was easy."

"Any recordings?"

He raised his eyebrows in horror. "The State Department would be devastated that such a thought ever even surfaced during our conversation. My goodness, bugging a millionaire Jap's condo just when the president is asking them to lower their trade barriers."

"Are they good quality tapes?"

"Super, I hear. I haven't heard them yet myself, but I hear Tanaka and Middleston were talking about a deal on the sale of Middleston Electronics' R&D discoveries. When we get the tapes in the office, I'll give you a call. We can have dinner. I forgot. I mean lunch. Hey, by the way, Malone's engagement is off. At his bachelor's party we all got into a contest of drinking straight shots of vodka. Unknown to him, we were drinking water. When he passed out we dumped him in his skivvies on his beloved's lawn in the Presidio. Her old man is a wealthy banker muck-a-muck. Naturally, we called the police. Can't have bums sleeping it off on rich peoples' lawns. Malone was grouchy when the cops woke him up. Reportedly, he used foul language and tried to flee into the house of his financée. They wouldn't let the rowdy in. Too bad you missed it." He laughed so loudly that Denise looked in.

I tried conversation several times during dinner that night without results. Finally, I said, "Janice, about last night—"

"You're not required to explain anything to me." She was close to tears. "And before you start to lie, a woman called. She said she was Sarah. She was sweet, just inquiring if you had gotten home all right."

She was as sweet as a cobra. "Janice, I think I am required to tell you what happened, but I'm afraid to. We're just developing something and . . ." I took a deep breath. "I'm not proud of last night."

Janice looked me straight in the eye, but made no comment. Slowly, but honestly, I told her what had happened, how I thought the twins would be there, how I didn't leave when I should have. How I was still scratching for information on the mayor. She didn't encourage me to go on or ask questions. When I finished telling the whole unpleasant story of what happened with Sarah, including the hot tub and how I had left, she got up and went into the bathroom.

The phone rang. "Fraleigh, Raoul. Can you meet me at the side entrance of Middleston Electronics in fifteen minutes? I have some stuff you should read right away."

"OK, Raoul. Are you sure it's safe?"

"*Si*, but don't be late."

Janice hadn't come out. I went into the bedroom and spoke to her through the closed bathroom door. "Janice, that was Raoul. I have to meet him. I don't have time to get an officer here, but I'll set the alarm system. Don't open the door and call 911 right away if you get concerned. I'll be back in less than a half hour? OK?"

I heard a muffled yes through the door. I called communications and directed that the beat car give the condo special attention for the next hour.

Raoul and I made like spies. He presented me with copies of memos linking Solly to meetings with Fortono and to the possible sale of information on R&D projects relating to gene bacterial inserts, protein molecular side chains, and so on. All signed by Solly. It looked like it would fit nicely with the file Daddy Warbucks was putting together.

Given what we had learned from Rodriguez and what Daddy Warbucks had told me about Middleston and Tanaka, we were ready to move.

"This stuff is great, Raoul. Why don't you just get in your car and get out of here?"

"I'm still hoping to catch a glimpse of Caruso. He's a fugitive. We can move right in and nail him. If I see him, I call SWAT. We don't even need a search warrant, right?"

"Right, but you haven't seen him so far. What makes you think it any more likely now?"

"I don't know. A hunch. Or maybe I just don't like feeling I left the job unfinished. We said a week or two. That means another couple of days. I'll leave then. You can assign me to keep the dick bureau in toilet paper and light bulbs. It will be a snap after all the expertise I picked up on this job."

"OK. Remember what I told you about bailing out if you think there's any danger of being made."

"How about another beer, Fraleigh. I'll buy out of my undercover expense account."

"I can't Raoul. I left Janice alone. I want to get back."

"Was it safe to do that?"

"My place is well alarmed. Besides its only for a few minutes and the beat car is sitting outside."

"Well, get packing. Tell her I said hello. She's all right, Fraleigh. You ought to think about settling down."

I pushed against the traffic to get back. I didn't like leaving Janice alone. Pulling into my parking space I noted with satisfaction that the beat car was in front. I had been away only thirty-five minutes. As soon as I opened the door, I saw the note on the coffee table and knew she was gone. I picked it up.

Fraleigh,
I'm at my apartment. I don't think I still need protection, but if you believe I need a guard,

please make the arrangements. I'll let him in only
if he calls first. Please don't call me for a while.

                                                J.

I checked and her clothes were gone. She must have
called a cab and packed the minute I went out the door.
The beat officer had been looking for prowlers, not
someone leaving the complex. Only a slight trace of her
fragrance remained as proof that she had been there. I
picked up the pillow she had slept on and held it to my
nose for a moment.

I called and assigned a uniformed cop to her place
with instructions that he telephone her before respond-
ing, to make sure she knew who would be ringing the
bell. Then I sat down and let the emptiness of the apartment and my own life sweep over me.

Twenty-Eight

BY 0900 HOURS THE NEXT MORNING WE HAD A MAKE on the gray van rapist. We all met in the conference room. Lieutenant Stevens briefly presented an overview of the case, then asked Curtin to give us the latest developments. Captain Toll sat impassive, Paul English looked like he was daydreaming, and the Block stared holes in Curtin, who ignored him while he spoke. "Mrs. Katz did it for us. She picked Roger Webb out of the photos. At first we wondered if she was right because he's listed as only five ten and most of the witnesses described the perpetrator as six feet or over. But we immediately pulled his prints. He's a graduate of Atascadero Hospital for mentally disturbed sex offenders. At the time of his commitment, he copped to one rape, although he was really good for at least four. The hospital kept him for the usual three years, then discharged him. His cure didn't last very long; six months after he was discharged the attacks began."

"Why didn't you nail the dirt bag before?" the Block growled.

Curtin flushed a little. "I've been with this case for seven months; this is your first exposure—"

The Block opened his mouth to say something. I cut him off. "Let's get on with it."

237

"We looked at all the Atascadero releases and sex parolees." Curtin was steaming as he continued. "He didn't fit the profile. His M.O. was different on the original rapes. He went in bedroom windows. No car or van was involved. And, as I mentioned, the height and build were off. The fingerprint unit only took twenty minutes to match his prints with the latents from Mrs. Katz's door frame. We just got this." He tossed an arrest warrant on the desk.

"Where is he?" I asked.

"We have his home and work address. We don't want to miss him."

"Be careful. If he smells you guys, you won't get him."

"Right, Chief. I suggest that we split the SWAT team. Half at the computer company he works at, half at his residence," Curtin said.

'I don't think that's feasible.' Toll didn't like others making suggestions for his beloved SWAT warriors. "To properly deploy and secure the computer company during work hours will require the entire twenty-man team."

"What about the B team?"

"At Fort Ord. Semiannual training exercises this week."

"Do you think it's possible to scout his job to see if he's there before we commit the team?" I asked Curtin.

"Ordinarily, I'd say yes. But this guy is sharp and slippery. I'd like to have the place covered so there's no chance of him running if he gets wind of us."

"The problem is that is we surround the company and he's home sick or something, someone may give him a call and we lose him," I said.

"My partner and I will sit on his house until we hear from the SWAT team," Curtin said.

"I'd rather have you with the SWAT people and the Block and English sit on his house," I said.

"Are you saying that you don't trust me to get him?

Or maybe you and the Chief think I'll crowd you away from the television cameras.''

He was overtired. His fuse was short and the Block hadn't helped any. "You're too close to the victims on this one, Curtin," Toll said. "Chief Fraleigh is right. The SWAT team firearm discipline is perfect. No emotion gets in the way.''

I thought Curtin would explode. Denise stuck her head in the door. "Chief, Lieutenant Short is on the phone.''

"For God's sake, can't you see we're in conference,'' Toll barked. Denise winced and her eyes got watery.

"Tell him I'll call back in—''

Denise stuck to her guns. "He said it's about Janice Bell and it may be important.''

"Take the call, Chief. I'll handle this,'' Cathy Stevens said.

I hesitated. "Tell him I'll be right there.'' I turned to face three pairs of angry eyes. Only English and Cathy seemed to understand that I had to take the call. I went into the office.

"I'm at the coroner's. He just did the autopsy on the security guard.'' Short sounded a little out of breath. "The cause of death was puncture wounds to the heart. Probably an icepick or similar instrument.''

An icepick? "That's for sure?'' I asked stupidly.

"Yeah. The Doc is certain.''

"Phil, a few years ago I put a punk into Quentin who used an icepick. He's been hassling me lately. Left some threatening notes under my windshield both here and at the apartment lot. Tony White is his probation officer. Get his number from Denise and after you get enough information have him picked up.''

"You think maybe the security guard saw him casing your place?''

"I wouldn't be surprised. And tell the dicks to be careful. He's flaky.''

"Right, Chief. You better watch your back until we nail him.''

"Yeah. Keep me informed. And give Dorn's description to the uniformed detail guarding Janice Bell."

Short agreed and hung up.

Dorn. Unbelievable. Dorn was after me, not Janice. Still, he was unpredictable and he was probably aware that she had been living in my condo.

I motioned Paul and the Block out of the meeting and told them what Short had reported.

"That little worm. I'd like to get my hands on him. He'll get born again, all right."

"Don't underestimate him, Block. He's demented, but he's fast and cunning," Paul said.

I glanced at my watch. Damn. It was already 1015 hours. I had to speak to Louis before he picked up the mayor at the airport. Now that I knew about the Solly/Tanaka connection I couldn't let him brief the mayor. Caruso would never come out of hiding and Raoul's cover could be in lethal jeopardy. I ducked back into the conference room. Clearly Lieutenant Stevens had handled the bureaucratic squabble a whole lot more smoothly than I had.

"Here's what we agreed to, Chief," she said. "If it meets with your approval. Officer Curtin, Captain Toll, and the SWAT team will cover the plant where the rapist works. I'll go with the Block and English to his house. When we come up with Webb we'll hold a press conference. Curtin is most familiar with the case, so he'll brief the press. We want the SWAT team to get credit for all the help they give us in these cases, so Captain Toll will represent them."

"It sounds great to me. Let's get moving on it." I got up and went back into my office. "Denise, call Chief Robinson's office. I need a half-hour with him before he leaves to pick up the mayor at the airport."

"Chief Robinson is at the mayor's office picking up some papers for him." I was scribbling some notes on what I had to tell Louis. Denise watched until she was sure I was listening. "He says to come over right away. He's leaving to pick up the mayor in thirty minutes."

Thirty minutes. I grabbed my jacket and the file, not even taking time to remove my gun from the drawer and strap it on.

This time I moved down the stairs even more quickly. I had to have twenty uninterrupted minutes with Louis. It wouldn't be pleasant meeting with him. But we were both cops and we were going to have to put Sarah out of our minds to concentrate on Middleston. We were going to have to ignore the tensions between us. I was going to have to update Louis on all the newly obtained information about the Uzi, about Rodriguez scouting my apartment for Petrie, Raoul's findings at the electronics company and how it all dovetailed with the FBI's theory.

A short, stooped old man in a sombrero, of all things, passed me in the police parking lot. It was off limits to civilians, but as I had frequently complained to Captain Toll, half of the people going to court or to visit someone in the county jail trooped through our lot. I wondered a moment about the old guy's dark sunglasses under the sombrero. They looked expensive, out of synch with the rest of his outfit.

Routinely, I looked to my right where my car was parked. It was still there. Our police department was doing a hell of a job preventing car theft today. I stopped and looked more closely. The sun was causing a bit of a glare off the windshield, but it looked like a piece of paper was tucked under my windshield wipers. Dorn wouldn't dare. Would he?

I walked to the car. As I reached for the paper I heard Paul English screaming, ''Fraleigh! Fraleigh!'' It brought a chuckle. Cool, laid-back Paul screaming and now running full speed toward me. I watched him as the little old man approached, mumbling something, probably wanting directions. The Block had come out of the building and, seeing English on the full run, walked after him.

''Look out!'' English yelled. His sprint had carried him to about twenty yards from me. Too late, I saw

Ned Dorn discard an old man's mannerisms. The ice-pick in his right hand flashed in the sunlight. His sombrero flew off as he made his move. He was shorter than I and his thrust was aimed upward through the stomach to the heart. And it probably would have been on target if my clipboard hadn't been in my left hand. The pick's razor-sharp point cut through the board and I felt a momentary sting as it broke the skin over my ribs. Dorn drew it back, ready for another lunge at me.

Paul English was a machine now. He wasn't a cop or a philosopher. His officer's survival training in the marine corps had taken over. As his hands closed over Ned's throat, I kicked Dorn in the balls. It wasn't the best of kicks because I was twisting away from the ice-pick while clasping my right hand over the spot where it had stuck me. In the distance I could see the Block break into a trot. It was reminiscent of a locomotive's first few wheel turns before getting up a head of steam.

Dorn was helpless now in English's grasp. The ice-pick fell to the ground while his hands futilely sought to break the throat hold. "OK, Paul. You got him. Put the cuffs on," I said.

But English wasn't hearing; his eyes were glazed. He was back in the Nam jungle, about to break a sentry's neck. "Paul, for Christ's sake don't kill him." I didn't give a shit for Dorn, but I knew that a grand jury might not be as understanding as I was. I staggered away from the car and tried to help Dorn break the death grip. Over his shoulder I could see the Block now at full speed, closing on us. I realized he thought we were struggling to disarm Dorn. The Block put his head down. "No, no," I yelled, knowing that his huge bulk was going to crash into us full speed. I felt myself driven into the side of my car, slipping to the ground and into fuzzy unconsciousness.

I awoke in the emergency room. "The puncture wound doesn't look like much, but they say you got a concussion on your head." The Block was embarrassed.

It began to come back to me. "Concussion? Damn you, Block. You almost killed me. How's Paul?"

"He's OK. He ain't hurt, but he's in one of his weirdo moods again. He acts like he's in a daze. He even tried to choke me after you guys went down. I had to slap him. The poor guy's been through a lot lately. Still, it's a good thing he was following you. When Dorn turned to come after you, he slipped for a second on his old man act and Paul picked it up. Otherwise . . ."

"And Dorn?"

"He's got a few bruises. I can't get over you guys not being able to handle a skinny punk. It's all those crappy salads you eat instead of real food."

"We had him handled until you crashed into us. Paul was going to break his neck. I was trying to stop him."

"Paul should know it's all right if you smoke those punks when they're armed with icepicks or knives, but the citizens get upset if you croak them with bare hands, even though it saves money."

A doctor moved in and gave me an injection. "Hey, what is that?"

"Tetanus. Routine with puncture wounds. You have to undergo X-rays of your stomach wound and head injury. That's quite a bruise." He touched my left temple.

"I don't want any sedatives. What time is it? I have to get out of here."

"The X-rays won't take more than an hour, but I suggest that you take the rest of the day off even if they are normal. You earned your pay today."

"Block, what time is it?"

"1220 hours."

1220. "Did anyone talk to Louis?"

"No. We all been tied up trying to save your ass."

I needed to get a message to Louis, in his car, at the airport, anywhere, but I knew it was too late. I was groggy and I let them wheel me out to be X-rayed without protest.

Two hours later, a fat detective I had never seen before drove me back to headquarters. He chewed a tooth-pick and never said a word. I took the elevator up to my office. I was too tired for stairs. Denise fluttered around until I asked her to leave me alone.

The Block and English had left to stake out the gray van rapist. Other cops took charge of booking Dorn for attempted murder and filing the preliminary arrest reports. Our reports would have to wait.

"You should be home in bed. Look in the mirror. That bump on your head looks like a grapefruit. And you got stabbed." Denise had come back into the office.

I had looked in the mirror. The Block must have thought he was a middle linebacker. "The icepick barely broke the skin. And I have a hard head. How about doing me a favor and getting me a cup of soup from the cafeteria?" I knew she'd never leave me alone unless I got rid of her.

"OK. Now you just sit quiet."

Twenty-Nine

"CHIEF FRALEIGH'S OFFICE." DENISE WAS ANSWERING the phone after she had deposited a container of unwanted lukewarm soup on my desk and returned to guard my office door.

I heard her high heels clattering. She stuck her head in, apparently afraid that buzzing me on the intercom would worsen my condition.

"What is it, Denise?"

"Janice Bell is on the phone."

Janice. I hadn't spoken to Jan since she left the apartment.

"Take the call, Chief." Denise's big eyes were earnest.

It had been less than twenty-four hours since Jan left me, but my heart was thumping. I picked up the phone and tried to sound calm. "Hello, Janice. How are you?"

"I'm . . . What do you mean?" She sounded confused.

"Is your stomach OK?"

"Yes, I've been to the doctor. Everything is going well. I thought you were asking about security."

"No. I was afraid something had gone wrong with your wound."

"Fraleigh, I've been meaning to call you. I just

couldn't be around you. I know it was cowardly to leave without talking to you, but . . . I guess physically I just couldn't face it.''

"I really miss you, Janice," I said, afraid of what she might say next.

"I know, but I just couldn't stand to be around you. You were so full of self-hate. That's why I called you. I didn't want you to think that I left because I hated you. In fact, after you told me about Sarah, I realized I was falling in love with you. I couldn't handle that. I can't handle that. I thought we could have a relationship. I know I'm not explaining this well, but I thought we could have fun. You were nice, but I didn't think there was any danger that I would fall in love. You're such a predator in your work. Fanatical about getting anyone you're after. But after that story about Sarah I realized you're so terribly . . . terribly vulnerable. Like the rest of us. And I don't have any absolution to give you for what's been happening. I haven't even sorted out my own feelings. I'm sorry, but right now I have nothing to offer you and I don't want to be around your pain.''

"Janice, could we go out to dinner? We don't even have to talk.''

"I'm going down to stay with my brother Ken for a couple of weeks. Maybe when I get back.''

"Have a good rest and take care.''

"Fraleigh, one other thing. Joan called me from Middleston Electronics about an hour ago. She said there was a scuffle or something. She'd like you to call her.''

"A scuffle?''

"Yes. In the parking lot. It looked like they arrested someone.''

"OK, I'll call. Take care of yourself, Janice.''

Two weeks. I had Ken's number from when I notified him of the shooting. If she didn't call within a week, I could check to see how she was.

I dialed the number Janice had given me for Joan.

"Fraleigh. How are you? I'm probably being silly, but something funny happened. About two hours ago, a fight broke out in the parking lot. Two men struggled with this maintenance man. I guess they were plain-clothes security."

"What did the maintenance man look like?" There was a catch in my voice, but she missed it.

"He's kind of cute. He doesn't say much, but he had a real boyish grin. He's new, only here a week or so. He's Hispanic. About five ten and strong."

"Joan, this could be very important. Tell me again what you saw in the parking lot."

"Well . . . this large car has been in the lot for a couple of weeks. It's covered with canvas. The maintenance man got underneath like he was doing something. I don't know much about cars, but he was under the rear bumper. I . . . the car is a white Cadillac. The license number is 1HMK853."

I took down the registration even though there was no need. It was the Caddy. "Joan, how could you know that if it was covered?"

"Well, they took the cover off about five minutes ago and drove off. It was weird. When I first saw them, they were really fighting. I'm pretty sure they weren't fooling around. But five minutes ago, they seemed like they were stoned and laughing. They could hardly walk. And the maintenance man was the worst of all. They just about carried him to the car."

Jesus Christ! They had taken Raoul. "What direction did they go?"

"Left, you know, south."

"Hold on Joan, this is an emergency. I have to put out an alarm for the car, but I need more information from you." I dialed the dispatcher and put out an APB on the Cadillac, giving the possible direction of travel. Remembering Caruso's fondness for Uzis, I told the dispatcher to broadcast that units should follow, but not attempt to stop the vehicle. The perpetrators could be assumed to be heavily armed and that an undercover policeman was a hostage. I hated to do it, knowing that the media would immediately pick it up on their scanners and we would have the usual circus, but there was no choice.

Joan's descriptions of the other two men fit Captain Petrie and Crazy Phil Caruso exactly. Janice was right. Joan was wasted as a receptionist. I updated the alarm, giving Caruso's and Petrie's names and descriptions along with the advice that they should be considered extremely dangerous. I directed that the fixed-wing aircraft be notified if it was airborne and if it wasn't to get it in the air as soon as possible. I started to order the SWAT team to assemble until I remembered they were grouping around the computer plant staking out the gray van rapist.

I had to let Louis know. Margaret answered the phone. "The Chief isn't here and I'm not sure when he'll be back. He went to meet the mayor at the airport this morning. He waited for you, you know. And I must say he didn't seem happy when he called from the mayor's office to ask where you were. I haven't heard from him since."

Of course. Louis had called just when I was dodging Dorn's icepick. He'd gone to meet Middleston, unaware of the incident.

"Margaret, do you have any way of getting hold of him? We have a real emergency."

"He didn't take his pager, but he told me he'd call right after he had lunch with the mayor."

Lunch with the mayor! What were Louis's words? "I'm telling him as soon as he gets back from Washington." And now, a few hours later, Raoul was in big trouble.

"Please have him call me as soon as you hear from him." I hung up, walked to the police radio receiver in the corner and turned it on loud. Back at my desk, I sat and sweated, waiting for what had to come.

Toggle stuck his head in the door. "Chief, did you hear the news on Rodriguez?"

"We've got an undercover officer being kidnapped, Toggle. I don't really have time for anything else right now."

"I'm sorry. I didn't know." He paused uncertainly. "As long as you're here, what's the news?"

"There was a screw-up in court. They never even called me and the parole officer had some family problems. His little boy was killed in an automobile accident. He never got around to revoking Rodriguez's parole on the gun charge. The judge let Rodriguez go on his own recognizance pending trial." He shook his head.

"We'll pick him up. Guys like him have no place to go."

"It's not that, Chief. I mean, the news isn't that he got out. It's that the Santa Cruz police just found his body. He was shot through the back of the head. They stuffed him into the trunk of a car parked in a shopping center. Some passerby noticed the leaking blood. He was probably killed within an hour of his release."

"God damn. And in Santa Cruz." I shook my head. I wondered how far from Petrie's house he had been found, but I couldn't really get my mind off Raoul. "Thanks for letting me know, Toggle."

"Happy to do it, Chief. I hope the hostage thing turns out OK. I won't take any more of your time." He strode out with the confident swagger that cops adopt after being on the job a while, the same swagger that I had often observed in Raoul Chavez.

Paul called me. "We picked up Webb. He walked right into our arms, or I should say the Block's fist. We caught him coming back from the grocery store. I got word to Curtin. We'll let him handle the scene, interrogation, and press release."

"Good. As soon as you deliver Webb downstairs come up to my office. The bastards have Raoul."

"We're on the way."

I called the communications van that Toll had been

using as a temporary headquarters at the computer company.

"We heard the good news, Chief. I'm debriefing the team."

"Don't dismiss them. We have an undercover cop who has been kidnapped. All patrol units are looking for the car. We'll need you guys right away if they hole up."

"We're already mobilized. We can respond anywhere in the city within twenty minutes."

Exactly seven minutes after the APB was broadcast a beat unit on the southeast side of the city spotted the Caddy. Ninety seconds later an unmarked detective unit took over the tail. Within a minute our Cessna single-engine plane had the Caddy in view. We ordered the unmarked car to stay out of sight and to follow directions from the aircraft. It was just a matter of time.

For half an hour the Caddy circled back and forth. Finally it pulled into Brisby Drive, a cul de sac in a middle-class residential area. An automatic garage door opened and swallowed the car. My line to the dispatcher was open. I ordered beat units to do a standard barricade operation. All vehicular and pedestrian traffic was stopped well out of the firing range. Neighboring houses to the front, rear, and sides were to be evacuated. The aircraft was to circle the area and assist patrol units in securing the perimeter.

I sent Toll to set up a command post in the area. Their ETA was twelve minutes.

I beat them by five. I crawled up to a forward temporary command post manned by the district sergeant, Bogan, just as the advance SWAT units were pulling into the designated assembly area—a Presbyterian church parking lot an eighth of a mile behind us. Bogan was totally bald and very black, a cigar-chewing motorcycle veteran who wore a bar on his breast indicating that he had received the Medal of Valor, policedom's highest award. But he had underestimated the shooting skills and probable weaponry of the inhabitants. We moved back another twenty yards, where a decorative brick wall outside a city park provided us with some shelter.

Now routine took over. One of the SWAT officers had secured an area map. If we were lucky, he'd soon return from the city planning office with an architect's plan for the house itself. Within thirty minutes SWAT personnel, clothed in flak vests and outfitted with gas masks, would gradually replace beat personnel. Some team members were designated to carry tear gas launchers, others carried automatic Uzis, most carried automatic shotguns and nine-millimeter automatic pistols. Two marksmen carrying high-powered rifles with special scopes would be strategically deployed. Two new weapons had been added to their arsenal: a rifle with a night scope and one with a laser scope. Because it might be a long operation, arrangements were being made to obtain fire department emergency lighting equipment. If necessary the house would be floodlit all night.

Trained hostage negotiators were working on getting the unlisted telephone number for the address. As soon as they obtained it, we would block the phone line just in case some enterprising reporter tried for an exclusive interview. Ordinarily, the negotiators would establish contact as soon as the SWAT people were in place. But this wasn't an ordinary case.

It was a bad time for me because there was nothing left to do. Time to think. To think of Raoul inside the house. To think of the whole crazy series of events that had started just three weeks ago with the anonymous note. Or had it started long before that? What had Paul said about Louis and me? We were the protagonists. Was it true that even years ago, the seeds of this misadventure were germinating in our characters?

"Here comes the chief," Bogan muttered behind his cigar.

Louis walked erect. Bogan and I had been squatting behind the wall. When he made no attempt to join us, I stood up. Uncermoniously, Bogan stood and took

Louis's arm, leading him a few steps to the left where the wall was higher than our heads. I followed. The sergeant then gave an amazingly accurate summary of the events. All the time Louis stared straight ahead. He didn't even acknowledge when Bogan had finished. He simply turned to me.

"Is Chavez dead?"

Our eyes were locked together. There was so much pain in his that I couldn't speak.

"I can't see any reason why he wouldn't be," Bogan said.

Louis moved to the point where the wall was lower and stood staring at the house a hundred yards distant.

We heard the crackle of the radio. It was the aircraft observer. "I have binoculars on the backyard. There seems to be a man down on the patio. He's wearing a maintenance uniform. It appears to be Officer Chavez."

Toll cut in from the headquarters van. "Does he show any sign of movement?"

We could see the plane circle behind the house. Then the whine of the aircraft came through, indicating that the observer was transmitting again. "No . . . no movement, sir."

"I'm going back to the van. I want Toll to direct a tear gas assault as soon as the team is in place." I turned and left Louis staring at the house and Bogan chomping on his dead cigar, frowning at him.

"Fraleigh." Louis called me back. "Play this after the operation here is over." He handed me a cassette tape. Then he squeezed my shoulder and turned back to the wall. I stuck the tape in my jacket pocket.

The van was in glum silence when I got there. The Block had tears in his eyes and English sat with his head lowered.

"Captain, how much longer will it be before the team will be in place for a tear gas assault?" I asked.

"A frontal?"

"I'll leave that to you."

"I'd rather do a frontal. If that's Chavez in the back we don't want to do it there. Just in case he's still alive.

He brought me to a table where the map was spread, and next to it the house plans. He pointed. "I figure we'll take out the living room picture windows. We'll shoot the tear gas in through there. It will be a good diversion. Point men eight and nine will actually lead the assault through this side kitchen door. One Uzi, one shotgun. Twelve and thirteen will move up to eight and nine's spots, listening to radio instructions from eight and nine on whether to go in. In the rear, number seven will stay at the window he's at in the neighbor's house. He's got a high-powered scope rifle. Four and five have spotted a hole here in the back fence. Once they hear the assault begin, they'll go through. It's a twenty-yard sprint. Four has a nine-millimeter automatic pistol. He'll check Chavez. His partner with the Uzi will cover him. Seven will cover both of them with the scope rifle."

"I don't know how much good any of this will do. You know Petrie is a pro. He won't be fooled."

"I won't argue with that, Chief. But if you want to go in, I figure this is the best way to go."

"Where's the other marksman going to be?"

"Number one. He's going to be right at that wall you were at. Hold on, that's him now."

We heard a remarkably young-sounding voice say, "Number one in position."

"He sounds young; how old is he?" I asked.

"Naylor? He's only twenty-three, but he's the best we have. Shoots a perfect one thousand every time on the range and pisses ice-water in action. You don't have to worry about him."

Toll was wrong. I had to worry about all of them. Good men. No lives to be lost. I moved back to the table. We heard Bogan's voice over the radio. "Hey, Chief! Chief, for God's sake!" Every head in the van snapped to attention. I felt a cramp in my back the size of a baseball. I had trouble breathing. "Hey, you guys, hold your fire." Bogan, the calm veteran, was shouting into the radio. "That's Chief Robinson charging the house. That's the police chief. Don't shoot him."

"Number three to command. I see the chief, he's got an automatic. He's running full speed for the front door. Man, he can really move."

Of course he can, I thought, he was a track star.

We heard the blast of automatic fire. "Number three here, the chief is down. He's not moving, about twenty yards from the front, lying in the grass. I'm not sure where the shots came from. The top windows, I think. Request permission to put some rounds in there."

"Denied," Toll said without expression. "We don't know if there are hostages in there. If you spot anyone trying to shoot at Chief Robinson, you are granted permission to fire. Other than that, follow procedures."

I turned and charged for the door before he finished speaking. The Block filled the doorway. I hit him with my shoulder, actually bouncing him sideways, and would have been out the door if Paul hadn't grabbed me from behind. He slowed me up enough for the Block to regain his balance and wrap his arms around me. Together they wrestled me back into the van.

"Enough good guys have died already today," the Block grunted, releasing me, but standing loose. Toll stared at his radio set. His hat was still perfectly straight.

"Number three to control. There's been more gunfire in the house. Sounded like a burst from an automatic weapon. Maybe six or seven rounds."

The phone rang. Everyone jumped. Toll answered and handed it to me. "It's for you." He had a funny look on his face.

"Fraleigh."

"Fraleigh, it's Petrie. I'm glad we still use the same telephone number in the van. I tried to save the chief and the undercover cop, but Caruso had the drop on all of us. I just got to him, though. I got his weapon away from him and killed him with it. I want to come out, but I realize the guys might be a little high strung."

"You're going to the gas chamber, Petrie."

"What? Hey, you got it wrong." He gave his familiar confident laugh. "You got it wrong, Fraleigh. You and the mayor are going to give me a medal. Think about it. I've been working with the mayor and the federal government to stop the theft of secrets. I was almost killed today, along with the chief and the undercover man. Another thing. J. Gotting, my lawyer, is on the way. I know there's plenty of news media covering the house because they kept asking Caruso for interviews on the phone. So don't get any ideas. I'm coming through the front door in exactly five minutes. I'll have my hands up and my badge in my right hand. Bye-bye."

I looked to the side, where Paul had been listening on an extension. He was shocked. "I didn't realize until I listened to him that almost all the witnesses are dead or in his camp. We don't have that much on him. And his lawyer, Gotting, he's the best. He'll beat the whole thing." His face was pale.

"Well?" Toll didn't appreciate Paul's whispering.

"Petrie's coming out in five minutes with his hands in the air." I took a pair of binoculars. "I'm going back to the wall. I want to watch."

"Should I broadcast that he's coming out, Chief?"

I took a deep breath. "Yes."

The Block and English came with me. Sergeant Bogan was still crouched behind the wall with his cigar. The young marksman, Naylor, was next to him, his rifle resting on the wall. He never took his eye off the scope but he knew I was there. "They say he's coming out in five, sir."

"Yeah, just watch the dirt bag. He's tricky as hell. And Chief Robinson is lying right out front, wounded," the Block said. Paul looked at me. I could feel sweat on my forehead.

"Chief, ordinarily we have to request permission to fire, but our previous order was to fire if Chief Robinson is in danger. Is that still the order? Do we still consider the subject dangerous?'' Naylor asked.

"I didn't hear Captain Toll countermand the order,'' I said. My voice was hoarse.

"Fraleigh,'' Paul gripped my arm. "You heard Petrie on the phone.'' I shook him off and kept the binoculars trained on the front door.

Number three had been designated as radio voice. "The front door is opening slowly. Subject Petrie is coming out. His hands are in the air,'' he said, monotone.

I watched Petrie through the high-powered glasses. He was nervous, his usual confident smirk gone. He advanced slowly. When he was about fifteen feet from Louis's motionless body he made a mistake. He looked at the body and stumbled into a hole in the walk. Anxiously, he jerked himself back, but the motion caused him to swing his arms. His badge caught the late afternoon sun. "In his right hand. I see metal shining.'' Number three spoke quickly.

"I'm going to fire,'' the marksman next to me said.

"Fraleigh, for God's sake!'' Paul cried, full of emotion.

In my binoculars I saw Petrie's head shatter, his torso fly backward, and his badge bounce tinnily on the walk behind him. The noise from the rifle next to me came a split second later than the visual image.

"Jesus. It wasn't a weapon. He had a badge in his hand.'' The young cop stood up. I felt English's eyes on me.

"It was the only thing you could do, Naylor. Not your fault at all,'' I said. I walked toward the house. There was no hope in my heart that either Raoul or Louis was alive, but the ritual had to be played out.

Thirty

BACK AT HEADQUARTERS, REPORTS HAD TO BE DIC-
tated, typed, and signed. I had refused all interviews
with the media. Toll had done the ones at the scene.
Downtown, Paul and the Block were super. Paul did
the interviews with enough smooth double-talk to prove
that he was of police executive caliber. The Block's
presence and fierce stare intimidated the unruly reporters. I sat protected in my office, my mind swirling in
confusion, but with a growing determination that no
matter what happened, Middleston was going down.

His lawyer, Claude Romain, came in. "Chief, the
mayor sends his condolences on the loss of two fine
officers and his congratulations to you on a superb operation."

So that was one answer. The mayor wasn't going to
encourage the few reporters who were asking why Petrie had been shot down with his hands in the air and
his badge held high. Come to think of it, the mayor was
probably glad to see the end of Petrie. What had Lorraine said? Petrie terrified him.

"Thank you, Claude. I thought the mayor would
come over."

"He's taking this quite hard. First Nicastri, then
Louis. You know, he was quite fond of Louis. He's

really in a state of shock. But he was determined that you know that he thinks you've done quite a job."

I smiled. More likely, he was probably afraid that if he came over I'd book him. "Thanks, Claude. The mayor's support means a lot at a time like this," I said, knowing that I had to stay in office for a while longer.

"Er, Chief. The mayor was wondering if I could look at the press releases the Department has issued. As you can imagine, his office is deluged with calls."

"Sure. Here they are." I pointed to the desk and he picked up the marvelous releases Paul had written. Petrie was AWOL, a rogue cop. He and a gangster named Crazy Phil Caruso had killed two valiant policemen, Raoul Chavez and Chief Louis Robinson, and had died trying to escape the police dragnet. There was no mention of Middleston Electronics, Fortono, Carol Mansell, or the mayor.

"These are well done. Did you write them?"

"Along with my staff."

"May I use the other office to make a call?"

"Help yourself, Claude."

Ten minutes later he was back. "Chief, the mayor is asking if you could assume the position of acting chief. He feels that only someone with your leadership qualities can hold things together right now. Also, he thinks that it would be most appropriate if you presided at the funeral, knowing how friendly you were with Louis. Naturally, you are the favorite candidate for the permanent appointment if you should desire it." I had passed the exam.

"Claude, tell the mayor that I'm honored by the offer and look forward to showing him what kind of a job I can do."

He smiled. "I'll tell him. Here's to a long and happy relationship." He shook my hand.

It was 2200 hours before the Block and English came in. I locked the files in my desk. "How about a late dinner?" I wasn't hungry, but I suddenly realized that I dreaded going back to my apartment. Both of them agreed to dinner. I slipped into my jacket, automatically checking to see if my badge and car keys were there. I felt the cassette in my side pocket. I had completely forgotten it.

"Block, bring your battery tape recorder along. Louis gave me this tape and I haven't had a chance to play it."

On the drive to the restaurant we heard a radio news interview with the mayor persuasively claiming that the murder of his police chief and aide wouldn't affect his determination to crack down on crime.

"Christ, he'd be a natural in the Senate—if you weren't sending him to the can, Fraleigh," the Block said.

I grunted.

Paul looked at me. "You are unusually silent on the subject of the mayor, Fraleigh."

"He's a goddamn eel. An eel who's going to have the best lawyers money can buy. And all of the key witnesses are dead. How much hard evidence do we really have against him?"

For a change neither of them had anything to say. I snapped the radio off as the reporter gushed over the mayor's courage and we drove the rest of the way in silence.

The day's events hadn't daunted the Block's appetite. He had the steak house's largest T-bone, a plate of french fries, a salad, four bottles of beer, and emptied the bread basket twice. Paul and I had salads and split a carafe of white wine that tasted like the soap hadn't been rinsed out of the glasses. I was exhausted, sunk in a leaden daze, but I knew sleep would elude me.

Over coffee, I put the tape on. We heard the mayor's cultured voice. "I'm glad that you told me about Officer Chavez's interesting assignment, Louis. Why don't you look over the menu for us while I call my office. You know how messages pile up when you're away for a few days."

"Geez." The Block paused over his apple pie. "Louis must have wired himself."

The tape went off. My lethargy was gone. We leaned forward to listen. Louis had been wearing our latest equipment, a voice activated recorder. The sound came back on. "I'm sorry it took a little longer than I expected on the phone. Have you spotted anything edible?"

"They have grilled salmon on special, S.H." S.H. We had always wondered what Louis called the mayor in private.

"Fine. I'll have the same, miss."

"Er, miss. What time do you have?"

"It's 11:30 A.M." Louis was a good cop. He had established the time. It was clear that the mayor had been told about Raoul, made a phone call, and then a short time later Raoul had been snatched and drugged at the plant.

"S.H., please, you have to understand that I'm deeply concerned. It looks as if Carol Mansell and your administration were actively conspiring with organized crime members. Carol was at a party at your house just hours before she was seen with Alex Fortono at Captain Petrie's home. Your aide, Thomas Nicastri, and a gangster named Crazy Phil Caruso were also with Petrie. And that same night Caruso killed Nicastri. I know there must be a reasonable explanation."

There was a pause and then Solly glibly said, "You really hit it off with Carol, Louis. I know you don't suspect *her* of any wrongdoing or you wouldn't have stayed with her in Beverly Hills." When Louis didn't respond to his barb about Carol, the mayor continued. "Mm, this fish is good, isn't it? Who was it that saw them?"

"It was a routine surveillance. Apparently Petrie was under suspicion of some illegal drug transactions."

"I see." His voice was smooth on the tape, but I could picture his mind churning. He was up against one of the best interrogators I'd ever seen and Louis had parried his question about who had seen them.

"Did you know that Petrie had an odd background?" he asked before the mayor could regroup.

"Yes and no. He came highly recommended from people I know in Washington and Nicastri thought he was just what we needed. I'd recently started to worry about how he was working out and meant to discuss him with you when you returned, Louis. He seems quite . . . Machiavellian and capable of violence. I'm sorry that I became involved with him, yet I assure you there was nothing dishonest about it."

"I'm certain of that, S.H. What was it? Some kind of business deal?"

"Yes, exactly. As you know, many people are urging me to run for United States senator. Unfortunately, it takes a great deal of money. My advisors believe that I'm assured of the nomination and the election. And that's the frustration. If I don't come up with strong financial backing, the party will give the nomination to some hack who has the money."

"So it involved Middleston Electronics?"

"That's a shrewd guess. And you're right. I'm not going to burden you with the details. For your own sake. Claude has been working on the legal aspects of this and he doesn't think we have a problem. But just in case there is, Louis, what you don't know can't be used against you. I can tell you, however, that the whole thing is outrageous. Middleston Electronics through the years developed new techniques that are worth fortunes—twenty-five to fifty million dollars. But federal bureaucrats interfere with our rights to market them. I need that money for my Senate race. That's how Petrie came in. He has a reputation through his overseas army service of knowing discreet channels through which certain sales could be made without triggering the enormous government red tape."

"Like Fortono?"

"Precisely." The mayor's voice grew even slicker. "Louis, you're a good man. That's why I picked you as police chief. But sometimes it's hard for people outside of business and politics to understand that there are gray areas in the real world—business deals that are best made in secret. Associates that one must deal with who ordinarily would be shunned.''

"Like Fortono.'' Louis's voice was flatter, harder.

"He had never been convicted of a crime, you know.'' Clearly Solly told himself this at night. "He controls two powerful unions and all that bad press has rubbed off on him. He's a businessman who is interested in building gambling casinos if the state initiative goes through. I know you're opposed to him on that basis, and, of course, I have no objection to you voicing your professional opinion if and when Fortono gets as far as a hearing. The only commitment I gave to him was to a fair hearing. A man is innocent until proven guilty.''

"I've always felt the same way, S.H. So how did Petrie and Fortono help you?''

"Nicastri and I realized that selling the R & D product was the only answer to our financial problems. Petrie suggested that a man named Tanaka, who represents certain Japanese companies, would be a good buyer. Of necessity, the currency of such transactions is gold. Fortono, through his union funds, has the ability to move vast sums without attracting attention. He will get ten percent of the final purchasing price. It's just a clever way to get around all the time-consuming and wrong-headed restrictions on business.''

"I see, S.H. It's clearer to me now. Maybe you should tell me what went on in the meeting at Petrie's house.''

"Well, I wasn't there. And I'm not sure I understand you.''

"S.H., I'll be blunt. Somebody might think drugs were involved. Was there anything taken into the meetings? Anything that might have appeared to an over-zealous drug agent to have been a shipment of drugs?''

Solly laughed. "A shipment of drugs? Oh, heavens, no. But I see what you mean. Innocent things can appear suspicious. There would have been a suitcase. Phillip Caruso, one of Fortono's hired hands, would have been carrying a suitcase. But I can assure that it did not contain drugs.''

There was a pause on the tape. Louis let the silence build up. He knew better than to ask about the suitcase. He waited Solly out.

"This business deal is complicated," the mayor finally explained. "The group from Japan agreed to advance some gold bullion through Alex Fortono as a sign of good faith. The gold was to be held in escrow. It was delivered to Captain Petrie, who was to keep it in his safe temporarily.''

"But it didn't work out as planned did it?''

There was a long pause as the mayor chose his words. He continued smoothly enough. "On the afternoon that the gold was delivered, Caruso called me. He's not a sane man, Louis. And I can tell you that Alex is extremely upset over Caruso's foolishness. He's a nephew, not very bright, and has been in some minor trouble. Alex promised his mother that he'd look out for him.'' I could picture Warbucks in his FBI office chuckling over that description of Crazy Phil.

Solly continued. "I took the call. Caruso was quite agitated. He'd gotten this insane idea that Petrie intended to steal the gold. He kept asking me questions about Petrie's background. I tried to reassure him that Petrie was being paid a fee and was loyal.''

"Why did it matter to Caruso? Even if Petrie stole the gold, he was presumably being paid only a small percentage of Fortono's ten percent. It wouldn't have been that much money.''

"That was never clear to me, Louis. He seemed to think that if Petrie took the gold, Fortono would hold him responsible. I told him that it didn't make sense. I was the one who was responsible now that Fortono had delivered the gold to Petrie. But I couldn't calm him down. Finally, I agreed to send poor Nicastri to meet him at the nightclub. But Caruso became uncontrollably paranoid. He was even convinced that one of Petrie's men had followed him to the club. The argument cost poor Nicastri his life. And now it's all a terrible mess. Fortono's in Europe, hiding out. The Japanese have backed off. And Captain Petrie has become a very dangerous man. God knows what he's capable of. Why, he might even go to the newspapers.''

I had to laugh. Even now Solly was probably planning a way to mend relations with Tanaka and put his Senate career back into high speed. I flicked off the tape and we all stared at each other. Finally I said, ''The mayor's story is pretty consistent with the information we have. Both Lorraine and Janice confirmed that Middleston was the sniveling little rich boy who despised his father. The old man thought it would build character not to let him have any dough. Selling Middleston's R & D secrets was Solly's only chance to become a senator. And I can confirm Caruso's phone call. He stopped at a gas station to call and I did see him leaving Petrie's with the Uzi. And at the club I saw Nicastri trying to convince him that he was wrong about thinking he was being followed by a cop.''

Paul spoke. ''A seat in the Senate would have given Solly independence from his father and no one gets poorer as a United State senator.''

''A crook like Middleston would have made all the campaign dough back pronto. Remember ABSCAM? The Feebees just uncovered the tip of the iceberg of what those bastards in Washington are stealing,'' the Block said.

Paul ignored him and continued. ''What were Caruso and Petrie really trying to do?''

I looked around the deserted restaurant before speaking. ''From what that Mexican Mafia fancy pants Rodriguez told us, we know Caruso and Petrie were doing a sting not only on Middleston but on each other. Crazy Phil may have been crazy but his fears about Petrie were completely justified. Petrie was planning to fake a burglary and send Caruso for the big swim in the

Pacific. Then he'd blame the theft on Caruso, whose whereabouts would remain unknown. In a few years Petrie would pick up the gold from wherever he stashed it. Guys like him always dream of the big score."

"Where do you think the gold is now, Fraleigh?" Paul asked.

"In Petrie's safe. I don't think he had time to move it before he came under suspicion."

Paul frowned. "When you interrogated Rodriguez, did he have any explanation as to why Petrie casually handed over an Uzi to an unbalanced individual like Caruso?"

The Block answered. "Hand it over? Christ, Caruso picked it up. Petrie must have shitted, but somehow managed to wrap it up and get Caruso safely out of his house."

I turned the tape back on.

"I can promise you that it will be handled most professionally," Louis said to the mayor and the tape ended.

I spoke slowly, thinking it out as I went along. "After Crazy Phil panicked and shot Nicastri, Petrie tried to pull it all together. He deliberately beat a confession out of Caruso, knowing that a judge would have to set him loose. Petrie couldn't take the chance of Caruso being crazy or angry enough to talk to us. Somehow Petrie and Caruso must have struck a deal—and decided to trust each other again. Petrie hid him in the house on Brisby Drive, which he probably rented under an assumed name. For a while, Caruso was probably convinced that Petrie was going to work with him. They both must have been anxious to have Janice and me out of the way before Fortono got back from Europe and began asking questions.

"And I'm pretty sure that the hospital hit men were Caruso's. So he was doing his part. The one that ended up dead was a minor-league crook from Chicago, the kind of punk that hangs around the edge of the mob.

Caruso couldn't use anyone that might talk to Fortono. Luckily for us he picked a free-lance clown.''

"Yeah, luck. If it hadn't been for the mayor's nympho wife and the note she put on your desk you never would have been following Caruso in the first place. I call that bad luck,'' the Block said.

I shivered, remembering the intensity of Lorraine's hatred for her husband and the ease with which she manipulated people.

Paul spoke. "Lorraine seemed to enjoy her life in the limelight. What motivated her on this journey to destroy her husband?''

"Janice told me that Solly and his father double-crossed Lorraine and screwed up her successful business career. I'm sure there were other reasons. She's a strange one. If I could figure her out I could open my own shrink shop and wouldn't have to put up with you two anymore.''

"Ha,'' the Block cut in. "If we knew what sex games you and Lorraine played, Paul and me could cure you of all your hang-ups. Right, Paul?''

"Or at least write television soap operas,'' Paul answered. "What set them on Raoul?''

"Well, we know it happened right after Middleston's warning call. Solly's not the type to have explicitly suggested violence, but he definitely wanted them to know that a cop was around. Raoul was probably trying to put the Hound Dog under the bumper. Maybe Crazy Phil lost his head again. Or maybe Petrie was desperate by this time and was afraid that Raoul had learned something that could hang them. We'll never know for sure.''

"Louis really nailed him, didn't he,'' the Block said. "But didn't he know better than to tell a crooked asshole like Solly about Raoul being undercover?''

Paul spoke slowly. "Louis was an honorable man. The mayor had appointed him. He owed him a certain loyalty. As long as the man wasn't clearly guilty, he was innocent.''

"Bullshit," the Block said. "Any cop would've known that Solly was dirty."

"In a sense, Louis stopped being a cop. He was caught between the police and political worlds. And because of his position he wasn't quite at ease with the values of either—a distressed ambassador, representing two separate nations," Paul said.

"All that crap aside, I don't get why he gave up Raoul's undercover status."

Paul continued his lecture. "As a matter of principle, unless he was convinced that the mayor was in league with killers, he had to tell him about Raoul. His doing the tape on Solly is evidence that he was uneasy. Fraleigh's hammering at him was not without impact. But my guess is that Louis assumed he'd have time after the taped interview with the mayor. It must have been a terrible shock to him that he was too late to save Raoul."

"It sure led him to act like the Charge of the Light Brigade. Louis was too good a cop to charge like that. It was crazy," the Block said.

Crazy? No. The Block and English didn't know about me and Sarah. Louis had known what he was doing, all right. I remembered his eyes when he handed me back my badge from Sarah. If only we had talked then. And even later if Icepick Ned hadn't stopped me from seeing Louis. I could have convinced him not to tell Middleston. Or I could have gotten Raoul back. Either way, both Raoul and Louis would be alive now. We could have pulled it together. Louis and I could have repaired our friendship, maybe . . . but what had Paul said? Ambition, lust, and avarice. Hadn't both Louis and I fallen into those madnesses? My own actions had put a wall between us leading inevitably to the fatal events on Brisby Drive. I remembered the way he looked at me, handing me the tape, telling me to play it later.

"You have a very strange look on your face, Fraleigh," Paul said.

I pulled my thoughts back to the case. "What's bothering me is that we have four dead people and not much evidence to tie Middleston to it. The tape may well be inadmissible with Louis dead."

"Fucking judges!"

"Yeah, Block, but what did Middleston actually admit on the tape? Only the stuff about selling R&D. And he was kind of cagey. Even that evidence isn't so strong. I think Lorraine would testify for us if we had the goods on him, but not with what we have now. Even if he got convicted of industrial espionage he'd get a year's probation and a ten-thousand-dollar fine. All the key witnesses to the serious charges are dead. Middleston is still mayor and a candidate for the United States Senate. You heard the wire service stories he's putting out. Gutsy mayor cracks down on crime despite personal danger. He'll win big."

"Fraleigh. One thing," Paul interrupted. "When I took Joan to dinner—don't sneer Block, it was line of duty—she mentioned that some of the R&D research was done for the government under defense contracts."

"Big fucking deal, English. If your mind hadn't been so much on pussy you'd know that half the Silicon Valley companies would be out of business if it wasn't for defense work. Right, Fraleigh?"

"Right. I'm beat; let's get out of here." I looked for the waitress to get the check.

"Ah. But don't forget the public is like Caesar. They may love treason, but they hate traitors," Paul said.

The waitress finally came over and I gave her a credit card. It was after midnight, I was totally exhausted, the case looked lousy, and English was quoting Caesar. Somehow we couldn't let Middleston skate. Louis and Raoul had died because of his ambition. He had been a traitor all right. He had betrayed Louis.

"You guys are going to get sick if you don't start bulking up with real food." The Block finished the last crumb of his strawberry shortcake.

Traitor! I looked at English. "You know, Paul, there

have been a few espionage cases in the last couple of years and they all involved the sale of technology and the people were convicted and got long sentences. The courts didn't screw around like they usually do.''

"Ah. I was beginning to feel like a prophet without honor in his own country," he answered.

"Selling secrets to a foreign power is the real thing—espionage. If any of that R&D material is classified, Middleston could get life in prison," I continued.

"Spying. That dirty mother-fucking traitor! And to think he's got the nerve to run for senator. What the hell took you so long to think of it, English? You should have put me on Joan, Fraleigh. I take a little snatch in stride, don't let it hypnotize me." The Block spoke loudly enough to galvanize the waitress into returning my credit card and the bill.

"Paul, first thing tomorrow get together with Joan. If we can establish that even a sliver of that R&D work Middleston was dealing was defense secrets we can put him away for a long time. I'll call Warbucks. Maybe we can use you, Block. Some of those executives out at Middleston Electronics must have known what was up. I wonder how cool they'll be when you and Warbucks start questioning them about selling secrets to a foreign power. And it won't matter a damn under federal law that the secrets were going to a friendly nation, not Russia. The penalties are the same.''

"Executives. Why the hell should Paul continue with Joan after the way he's screwed up? He should get the executives, not me." The Block scowled, but his heart wasn't in it. We had been going through the motions of cop banter all evening. Raoul's and Louis's presence had been too much with us. I patted Paul on the shoulder. He had come up with a good idea. It almost made listening to all of his screwy quotes worthwhile.

Thirty-One

THE NEXT DAY PAUL TOOK JOAN NOT TO DINNER BUT to breakfast. He was on the telephone to me before they left the restaurant. "We were on target, Fraleigh." For a change his voice showed excitement. "Joan confirmed that a significant part of the R&D gene research at the plant was Defense Department-funded. In fact, researchers needed top-secret clearances."

"Great, Paul! The Department will pay for breakfast. I'll get right on the horn to the FBI."

Daddy Warbucks had listened somberly to my concerns over defense secrets being sold. "Fraleigh, you guys are full of shit. You know damn well that Middleston, scumbag that he is, never intended to sell defense secrets to any foreign government; he just wanted to sell it to another corporation under the table and the Jap corporations are always ready and willing to buy."

"Daddy—"

"Let me finish, you ignorant local sleuth. The fact is that his intent is his problem. We'll be delighted to have him admit that he was selling to Tanaka since the law doesn't distinguish between friendly and hostile foreign nations. You guys may have blundered into a juicy tidbit for me. I'll bring it to the attention of the illustrious U. S. Attorney, provided the pompous, publicity-seeking-asshole can get off his throne long enough to see me. If all goes well our guys on Maui will be visiting the luxurious dwelling of one Yoshomo Tanaka and I'll be coming your way to chat with some of the appropriate business types at Middleston Electronics about their duty to their country and what the penalties are for treason nowadays." He paused. "Hey, Fraleigh. I'm sorry about Louis and Raoul Chavez." Daddy's voice had suddenly gotten hoarse.

"Yeah. Thanks, Daddy." My own voice didn't sound any better. "Let me know what happens."

It was three days before the joint funerals of Louis Robinson and Raoul Chavez. Captain Toll was in full command of the ceremonies. Somehow he managed to find a tailor who would put together a uniform for me within two days. It was going to feel strange. I hadn't worn one in ten years. Toll had a habit of calling for funeral conferences. He would assemble large numbers of us in various meeting rooms. No one dared be absent. Not being respectful of cops killed in the line of duty was an image no one could survive.

Toll would appear with his hat on perfectly straight and inevitably unwind one of those collapsing pointers. Sometimes he would use a chalk blackboard. At other times he would employ maps. Maps of the church. Maps of the cemetery. Maps of the funeral route. I wondered if I was the only one who was confused. Being the new chief, I didn't have the nerve to ask questions, merely nodding my head in agreement when Toll asked, "Is that OK with you, Chief?"

At one point he made the mistake of telling me he would be next to me at all times. After that I no longer tried to comprehend the different formations. I sat and thought of the past month and the future. I thought much of the future while Toll went through the elaborate plans.

In between funeral preparations, the Block, English, and I worked on the case. Even though Petrie was dead we waited until the IRS had a court order. Then we had an expert open his safe and there it was. Stacks of gold bars. We didn't take possession of them, however. Three men from the IRS were there along with a panel truck. I had told them we believed that three million in gold bullion was in the safe and would probably be unclaimed. Render unto Caesar . . .

I did take possession of neatly typed documents in the safe indicating that the gold was to be picked up by a shipping company for delivery to a Paris firm. Other papers were made out to ship the gold from the Paris address to a numbered Swiss bank account. The manifest indicated that the gold was being transferred from a large New York bank to the Paris company. One of the IRS men came back to headquarters with me to get copies of the documents. He guessed that the papers were good enough to get the gold through customs and that the French firm was a front for a drop-shipping operation.

"You mean it's really that easy?" I asked.

"Not for you and me, but there are billions that never get traced. Sometimes even when we find out we're just told to bug off—national security. And who knows . . . ?"

Finally, we put together a complete case file. It included Lorraine's note and my supplemental report on what she had told me about writing it. Also included were a full account of the surveillance of Petrie's house, all of the pictures Paul had taken of the players, and my report on tailing Crazy Phil and witnessing the murder of Nicastri and the wounding of Janice. The lab report on the suitcase from Petrie's house and the documents Raoul had secured from Middleston Electronics were in the file, along with Louis's tape of his conversation with the mayor and the tape transcript. Naturally, all the crime and coroner reports were inserted into the thick folder along with the IRS receipts for the gold.

The medical examiner had concluded that Louis died of multiple gun shot wounds (seven). The ballistics unit matched the slugs to a nine-millimeter automatic pistol that had been recovered inside the house. The weapon had been wiped clean of fingerprints. Raoul had been killed by a single .45-caliber bullet entering through the back of his head. Evidence technicians stated that this weapon had also been wiped clean of prints. Vincent Rodriguez's wounds were consistent with those caused by .45 caliber bullets, but no ballistic confirmation was possible because the projectiles had passed through his body and were never recovered.

It was also clear from evidence inside the house on Brisby Drive and statements of neighbors that Crazy Phil Caruso had been living there since his release after shooting Nicastri. The county deed of trust indicated that the house was owned by Meta Productions Inc., Hollywood, California—Carol Mansell's corporation.

We had a duplicate file made for Warbucks. Toll, his usual immaculate self, came to brief me one last time on the funeral. He went over the incomprehensible formations for twenty minutes. "Everything clear now, Chief?" he asked.

"Absolutely, Captain. You'll be next to me, I assume?"

"Yes, sir. I'll be with you all the way."

"Anything else?" I asked when he just sat there.

"Nothing really important. But just to be super thorough I wanted to make sure you were aware that we always do a complete critique of SWAT operations. A funny thing, though, when I played back the recording of Petrie's call to the communications van, it was blank. A malfunction, I guess. Naylor was pretty upset when it turned out that Petrie was unarmed and all he had in his hand was his badge. Only you and Paul English were on the phone. There won't be any other record of what he said. I told Naylor not to worry about it. He did his duty like we all did."

"You're right. I told him the same thing. When he gets older, gets some more experience on the street, he'll understand that these things happen."

"See you tomorrow, Chief." Toll left, his uniform still as neat as it had been ten hours before.

The day of the funeral was clear, a temperate, Northern California eighty degrees. Three hours before the services were to begin, Warbucks called. "You either live right or you stepped in some dog shit for good luck, Fraleigh."

"I'll check my shoes."

"Yeah. Forget what I said about living right. I must have been thinking of someone else. But we hit the jackpot. Some hours ago agents of the FBI duly armed with a search warrant from the United Stated magistrate in Honolulu proceded to the dwelling place of Yoshomo Tanaka on Maui and seized documents identified as the property of Middleston Electronics Limited. It was quite a pile of stuff and several of the research papers were clearly marked as top secret. The incredible thing is that a guy who was leaving the house panicked and tried unsuccessfully to elude the viligant agents of the FBI. Fortunately, the creep didn't know how to drive or he would have outdistanced the piece of government crap the agents were driving. Instead, he wrapped himself around a telephone pole. This chap turned out to be a middle-level diplomat from the Polish mission in Toyko and he just happened to have copies of two of the top secret research papers."

"I'll be damned."

"Undoubtedly, but in the meantime I will be obtaining an arrest warrant and if you see me at the funeral you'll know that I will be loaded for bear. The Polish factor increases the chances for both a conviction and a maximum sentence."

The church service was mercifully short. Yet it took two hours before the motorcade followed the hearses out of the church parking lot. Four thousand uniformed police officers took a long time to form, march in and out of the church, and re-form so that the casket-carrying pallbearers could pass in front of them. The troops then retreated to the more than one thousand marked police cars and one hundred fifty escort motorcycles. The cops were from everywhere. California departments were represented from San Diego to Eureka. And large cities throughout the nation sent representatives. A major city police chief had been gunned down in the line of duty. NOBLE—the National Organization of Black Law Enforcement Officers—sent a delegation of ten men. Louis had been a founder. LPOA—the Latino Peace Officer's Association—sent an honor guard of twelve. Raoul was a past president.

When we got to the cemetery I saw the FBI helicopter sitting on a paved area. Warbucks waved to me and we had a short conversation before I walked to stand at parade rest next to Toll. Behind us police ranks were forming that would stretch thousands deep. Immediately in front were the raw, freshly dug graves, the dark holes only partially camouflaged with strewn flowers. Just beyond the graves, folding chairs had been set up for the families. In the distance, I could see the top of City Hall, the former corporate headquarters of Middleston Electronics Limited. The brass-ornamented roof flashed sunlight back into the eyes of those of us who dared to look at the edifice. To our left, twenty yards distant, the hearses and funeral limousines were parked in the cemetery roadway. The temperature had risen. I saw sweat appearing on many of the uniform shirts as officers walked from where they had parked to form up. But I was cold. I had been shivering all morning.

Finally the undertakers led the families to their seats. Sarah came first, walking erect. Her hands rested lightly on the shoulders of the twins, who were on each side of her. That was it. No other family. She wore high heels and a simple black dress that had cost money. There was no sign of grief on her face. She looked like a model. A beautiful enigma. I saw the eyes of the policemen following her.

Maria and her family came next. She was plump.

Sobbing hysterically, she practically had to be carried. Her brother and father supported her. The four children, ranging from four to sixteen, were dressed in their best. The two little ones didn't know what was going on. The oldest girl, Teresa, who was fifteen, was crying almost as hard as Maria. Enrique, sixteen, was trying unsuccessfully not to cry. The policemen looked away.

When the families were seated, two groups of police honor guard pallbearers slowly bore the flag-draped coffins toward the graves, where they would be placed in the harnesses suspended above the raw holes.

"TEN . . . SHUN!" Toll bellowed out the command immediately after the pallbearers began their walk. You could hear the crisp leather of thousands of cops creaking in the noon silence as they snapped to.

"PRE . . . SENT . . . ARMS!" We saluted en masse as the coffins were lowered into their holders. Far overhead a 747 was losing altitude in preparation for a landing at San Francisco Airport.

"ORDER . . . ARMS!" Thousands of right arms dropped to their sides. "PARADE . . . REST!" Again the creaking of stiff leather gun belts.

The chaplain moved forward when the coffins were in place. The honor guard stood at attention. He was a man in his mid-fifties, his face as gray and colorless as his hair. I wondered how many funerals he had presided over. His black suit and roman collar contrasted with all the blue uniforms. But his voice was deep and resonant. "I read from the Twenty-third Psalm. 'The Lord is my shepherd; I shall not want. He maketh me to lie down in green pastures. . . .' " My eyes slid from Sarah's composed face to the sobbing Chavez family to the mayor and Lorraine, who stood immediately to the left of the family seating area. Farther to the left out in the roadway I saw Paul English carrying a folding chair. He walked under a shade tree where . . . where Ken and Janice stood. Paul opened a chair and she sat. It was too far for me to see her face clearly.

The chaplain had finished. He blessed the coffins and

moved back. Toll shouted "TEN . . . SHUN!" To the left, I heard a hoarse command: "DETAIL . . . ORDER ARMS!" Twelve uniformed police officers raised their rifles to the sky. "FIRE!" The blank rifle shots resounded over our heads. The families and civilians winced. The rifle detail fired six volleys.

When they finished, the bugler raised his instrument to his lips. "PRESENT . . . ARMS!" Toll commanded. We saluted our fallen comrades as the mournful notes of "Taps" echoed across the cemetery grounds. I didn't see any dry eyes, except those of the mayor and his wife and Sarah's and . . . mine. Sarah and I were locked together in blank stares.

The bugler finished and after Toll gave order arms, the honor guard surrounding the coffins began to fold the American flags with military precision. When they were finished they pinned Louis's and Raoul's police badges on each of the respective flags. It was time for me to do the chief's job. I marched forward to the edge of the grave. One of the honor guard did a sharp about-face, handed me the flag, and saluted. I returned the salute and made a sharp right turn. I marched toward Sarah. Her eyes were steady on me, still without sign of emotion. For a moment I thought I saw a hint of sarcasm surface, but when I got closer she was expressionless. I handed her the flag and then, to Toll's horror, I'm sure, broke military protocol. I squatted down and hugged the twins. "I'm going to call in a couple of weeks to see if you guys can go fishing." They were somber, but a trace of a smile showed on their faces.

I stood, saluted Sarah, made an about-face, marched back to the grave, and repeated the process, taking the second flag to Maria. She never looked up. Sixteen-year-old Enrique stood up and squared his thin shoulders. I wanted to put my arms around him, but it would have been wrong. I presented him with his father's flag and detective badge and saluted. When I returned to my position Toll dismissed the formation and people began to move. They had gotten stiff.

I approached the mayor and Lorraine, who still stood near the family seating area. "Fraleigh. You look awfully cute in uniform." Lorraine flashed her usual dazzling smile.

"I'm sorry you're not going to make it to Washington, Lorraine," I said. "Unless it's to testify in your husband's trial if he gets a change of venue." Her eyes slid over to see how her husband was taking that remark, but her smile was undiminished.

"What was that you said?" Solly demanded.

I handed Warbucks's card to Solly. "Special Agent Warbucks is here with a federal arrest warrant for you, Mayor. I understand that they are quite willing to let defendants of your stature select which federal prison they will do their time in."

"Arrest! Are you insane? On what charge would he dare to arrest me?"

"You're being charged with espionage," I told him. "The selling of defense secrets to an agent of Poland, an Iron Curtain bloc country, through an intermediary by the name of Yoshomo Tanaka. The maximum penalty is life in prison."

"Poland," he whispered, his eyes turning to watch Warbucks's deliberate approach.

I turned and walked slowly across the roadway to where Janice sat. She stood and opened her arms to me. Only when I felt her against me did the tears come for Raoul and Louis.

ABOUT THE AUTHOR

Joseph D. McNamara, who is now the police chief of San Jose, California, was born in New York City and, like his father, walked a beat in Harlem for the New York City Police Department. He received his Ph.D. from Harvard and is the only police chief in America to hold such a distinction.

TOUGH. CLEVER. CYNICAL.

*An ex-cop, a deadly shot,
a man who plays by his own rules.......*

W. GLENN DUNCAN'S:

RAFFERTY